AFTER THE FIRE

a novel

MARIA RIGOU

AUTHOR'S NOTE

After the Fire is a story that takes place the fictional town of Tres Fuegos, in the province of Córdoba, Argentina. Although this town does not exist in real life, it was inspired by a real place. Many of the cultural and societal aspects depicted in this novel are unique to this country. For example, it's important to note that in Argentina, law school typically takes six years to complete, and students attend straight out of high school.

This novel includes elements that might not be suitable for some readers. Mentions of death of a parent, reference to alcohol abuse and cheating are present in the story. Although not explicit, please take note.

Additionally, there are instances of strong language and on-page sexual content throughout the book. Mature readers only.

Please read with care.

I hope this story inspires you to find the strength and courage to let go of your fears and the expectations of others, and to live a life that is truly yours.

Espero que esta historia te inspire a encontrar la fuerza y la valentía para dejar de lado tus miedos y las expectativas de los demás, y vivir una vida verdaderamente tuya.

1

THE PHOTO

MY FACE WAS ON FIRE—NOT literally, of course—but it felt like steam was coming out of my ears. My whole body was burning from the inside out, flames constricting my chest and making it hard to breathe. I looked at the phone screen in my hand and looked at it again, and I couldn't believe what my eyes were seeing. In every sense of the word, it was absolutely unbelievable. *Is it though?* Clearly, my brain was playing tricks on me because this couldn't be happening. Not to me. *Not to Victoria Aguirre Saenz on the morning of her wedding.*

"Cata, I..." I said, stuttering the words out. "Let me call you right back."

My coffee sat on the side table, still hot to the touch. My phone buzzed in anticipation of the day's activities, not to be minimized by whatever was going on in my head. From the corner of my eye, I could see my dress hanging from the door to the bathroom in what used to be my childhood bedroom. I could see my reflection in the bathroom mirror —my brown hair was down, and my eyes had an unusual shine, maybe from all the tears I was trying to withhold. My freckles were definitely out today, possibly as a result of all the sun I'd been getting in the previous days. The only thing I could hear was my heart pumping inside my head and my erratic breathing.

"What's going on?" my best friend asked. She was getting ready at her house and then would drive to mine later in the afternoon, but we were already talking on the phone to iron out some last-minute details. "Are you okay?"

"Yes." *No. Fuck.* "Um, jus—something came up. Give me a minute. I'll call you back," I muttered as I hung up the phone.

The house felt giant around me, always had, and we still had a few hours to go until it got swarmed with people— including but not limited to the photographers for the biggest society magazine in the country, very obviously arranged by my grandmother.

The last time I spent the night here I was probably in my mid-twenties—close to a decade ago now—but on my grandmother's insistence, I was getting ready for my "big day," as she called it, here. Secretly, I thought she wanted to control the situation, try to avoid anything that could go wrong and make it easier on her and on my unreliable father. She was making this event a spectacle, her house front and center in what had been deemed "the wedding of the year" by the local media.

"Victoria," Susana called from the bottom of the stairs. The woman had put her life on hold in her mid-fifties after my mother's tragic accident and had really raised my brother and me like her own children, although she'd never let us refer to her as anything but Susana. Not even a tender, kind, loving *abuela,* like my cousins did with their other grandmothers. "Come here, *por favor.*"

I groaned, my face still hot with embarrassment. "*Sí,* I'll be right there." I took a deep breath, trying to center myself to face her. The long and puffy garment bag was taunting me, the zipper half open. The top of the dress was peeking out, made of a sparkling white lace that my grandmother had purchased in Italy years before I was born. She bought it during one of the lavish trips she'd made with her husband, anticipating that maybe one day, one of her daughters would wear it at their own weddings.

My phone kept buzzing in my hand, but I didn't need to look at the screen again because the image I saw a few minutes earlier was permanently burned into my brain. A million thoughts ran through my brain in a microsecond. *Could it be a photo of Manuel?* I saw him in bed, with a woman on his lap, her long, blonde hair brushing her bare back. It was probably Manuel because that was very much the apartment we shared together. The lamp to the right was one of the few things he'd chosen when we decided to move in together, and I'd hated it since that first day we unloaded all our boxes. It was absolutely Manuel because I could clearly see that tattoo on his left thigh—another thing I hated.

The question was: why was my fiancé in bed with someone who was obviously not me? And who would send me this photo on the day of my wedding?

"You need to make sure we triple check with the florist the exact time they will deliver the bouquet and the boutonnieres, and if we need to refrigerate them, too, or if they should be good to go by the time we leave for the church," Susana said as soon as my left foot hit the landing. This was very much a normal Susana routine—she would drill us with orders and then we would obey them, everyone fearing the consequences of her disappointment.

She sat in the living room, lazily browsing through a society magazine, probably catching up with the latest gossip. She most likely knew everything before it even got to the media, but she always needed to be prepared, as to not be caught off guard if anything hadn't reached her ears.

"Victoria, are you listening? Did you call María to give her instructions on how to get here? We don't want her to run behind and then derail the whole schedule," she added. She always spoke in a calm and uniform tone, even when she was disparaging the behaviors of others. It was, at times, almost dull. Easy to tune out.

Susana was, by all accounts, intentional. She never, ever spoke to anyone before practicing her words. She never deviated from her speech. She knew what to say at all times, and people respected her for it.

The woman had been up since four o'clock in the morning—her usual time—and now, five hours later, she still looked as fresh as a baby. Her skin glowed; she looked twenty-some years younger than she was. She had a full face of makeup already and, if I were a betting woman, I would one hundred percent guarantee that she wouldn't need to redo anything but her lips by the time evening rolled around.

The house was quiet except for the soft humming of Lali, the cleaning lady, in the back. She was outside watering the plants, probably having run away from Susana. The orders kept on coming, one after the other without even a pause in the middle for me to stop her to tell her what I'd completed.

"Victoria? It's your wedding today." I did my best to contain my eye roll. It would be completely unacceptable to disrespect her in any way, so instead, I cocked my head and looked straight into her eyes. "Everything has to be absolutely perfect. Are you listening?"

"*Si*, Susana, I'm listening. I've taken mental note of all the things that need doing. I was going to drink my coffee while I called the planner to let her know of the small changes. A few friends called already to ask a few things, and I needed to get on that immediately. If you don't mind, I'll head upstairs." I started moving, but she closed the magazine enthusiastically and smiled at me.

"Have you spoken to Manuel yet?" she asked. "He must be excited, huh?"

I turned, swallowing my tears. "Uh-huh," I said noncommittally. I couldn't let her see me like this. Even if she saw me crying, I doubt she would ask what it was about. Because the way to Susana's heart was acknowledging and acting on what she told you, and if you did that, you'd stay on her good side. She couldn't argue with my logic, so I went up the stairs, my feet echoing into the darkness of the hallway.

Was it because my brain was moving at warp speed that I noticed that Susana hadn't even asked how I was feeling? I had to be more transparent than what I gave myself credit for. I knew I had a good poker face—years as a lawyer gave me enough practice, I thought—but I was sure that *some* of the things I was feeling had to be on display. Right? Manuel always said that he could tell when I was lying, and I took offense, because my professional career depended on *not* having such a trait.

The thirty-two years of my life had, so far, been a series of moments, one after the other, that aggregated, made a full picture. It just happened that the moments that made up my life up until this moment had been deliberate and thought-out ahead of time. All of my movements had always benefited my family, especially Susana.

That was how I ended up being a lawyer and working for my family's firm. It was an exciting career, and I was good at it. Very good. I'd taken planned steps to get where I was today: a well-respected corporate attorney at a top firm in Buenos Aires, successful professionally and with a growing group of clients, ready to take the next step towards a picture-perfect life. Worthy of those society magazines my grandmother obsessed over.

I scanned the room, buying some more time. Maybe I would be able to come up with a solution to this. Surely I wasn't getting married. That was clear to me—and apparently to Manuel and his lady friend too. But what was the best course of action? Calculated moves. Intentional steps.

I felt my phone buzz against my palm. I didn't even need to look at the screen to guess who was calling.

"Hey," I said, taking a deep breath. "Sorry abou—"

"What happened?" Catalina asked me, knowing exactly when to interrupt. On top of being my best friend for the past ten years, she was married to my brother. We met our first week of law school, forming a quick bond over how out of place we both felt. "Is it Susana?"

"No, actually," I replied. "Something bigger."

"Okay, what do you want me to do?" She immediately knew that something was wrong. "Do you want me to come over?"

"I'm supposed to meet Manuel for coffee in a few minutes but…" I sighed. "I'm sending you something."

I needed a moment to think, to step away from this and look at it from the outside, exactly like I would approach one of my cases. I didn't have the luxury of time because this needed to be remedied—and fast. The clock was ticking.

My suitcase—almost ready except for my toothbrush and other toiletries—sat closed by the door to my bedroom, ready for our honeymoon to Australia and New Zealand, a trip I'd been planning for months and months, the culmination of seven years of courtship. It, too, was taunting me, almost like it knew that my marriage was over before it even started. Incomplete even before I tried to complete it.

"Okay," I said once I texted her the photo I'd seen only minutes earlier.

"Fuck," she rasped.

"It's him, right?"

"Yeah, no doubt."

"Okay," I said as I scratched my forehead. "Okay, I'll call you later. Please don't worry about me. I'll call you."

"Victo—" she protested, but I hung up on her before she could stop me. Catalina was pregnant with her first child, and the last thing she needed right now was for me to be a burden on her and my brother. Could I figure this out? Yes. Did I have a plan? No. But I could improvise, right?

So I did something that I had never done before.

I grabbed the piece of luggage and started toward the stairs, trying to go as fast as I could, feeling the cold marble under the soles of my bare feet. I was wearing a white sundress, given to me by my grandmother when Manuel and I announced our engagement, although now it seemed foolish to be wearing such thing, given that I was suddenly single.

"Lali, I'm going out *un minuto!*" I yelled at the woman

who was now most likely making lunch for us. I could hear her say something to me as the door closed behind me. I took a moment to fasten my sandals right outside the front door and stepped out the gate.

"Hey, baby," Manuel said. I felt his presence even before I saw him in my periphery. He looked relaxed in his worn jeans and a wrinkled linen shirt. His hair was still damp, and he had one sleep wrinkle running from his temple to his jaw. I was already rolling my eyes so hard; I couldn't contain myself, because not even on his wedding day did he care to do things right, sleeping until the last minute as usual. *This,* this was my biggest tell. "Are you going to load the suitcase in the car? You won't need anything else for tonight?"

"How long?" I asked.

"Well, I think we can manage an hour before she catches us, but I guess we can ask for forgiveness," he said with a cocky smirk. He knew he was charming, and he had my grandmother wrapped very tightly around his finger. "She won't say no to me."

"How. Long."

"What are you talk—"

I never raised my voice; I was calm and collected. Calculating and intentional. But this was probably the straw that broke the camel's back. I grabbed my phone and flashed the screen.

"Who sen—what is that?"

"Manuel, you know I'm not stupid. How long has this been going on? Who sent this to me? I just—"

"Baby, that isn't me," he said. His tell was much more noticeable than mine. I had figured it out years earlier after our first big argument. It was stupid—he told me he'd only had a few beers with his friends, but I knew it had been more than that. He bit his thumb and shifted his weight from foot to foot. "Why would you even suggest that? We're getting married today. We shouldn't be fighting."

I released a sigh. No relief though. My gut told me, without a shadow of a doubt, that the man in the photo was him.

"You know what? I just need a minute to clear my head. I can't right now," I said.

"Where are you going? Did you tell Susana that you were going for a walk?"

"¡*Basta*! Stop. Stop talking. I'm not going for a walk, Manuel, please be smarter than this."

And I left. Without knowing where to or until when, but the fear of disappointing my family was stronger than my desire to fight for my relationship. And deep down, I knew that if I stayed, Susana would end up convincing me to marry this man.

2

THE FLIGHT

I OPENED my eyes as the bus slowed down and approached a little town on what looked like a small, yet stunningly luscious hillside. I had never even heard of it before, yet here I was. So, so far from my so-called perfect life.

Right across the aisle from me sat a couple who looked like they were in their early thirties and had heart eyes for each other. They were both ridiculously attractive, but she had this shine that made her particularly so. She was glowing. They looked to be in love, drunk on life and each other. I'd heard as they whispered sweet nothings into each other's ears all afternoon. As soon as the bus started to slow down, families and couples reaching their destination started to collect their belongings. The chatter increased; laughter was everywhere. These people were happy to be here. A total contrast to how I was feeling.

Instead of running through possible scenarios in my

mind like I had done for the whole nine hours of the bus ride, I started to find things to distract myself with. I looked around and made up stories of the families sitting in front of me. Maybe they weren't able to take a proper summer vacation, so they opted for an extended weekend somewhere closer to home. Or maybe some of these people were on their honeymoon.

Like you should be in about twenty-four hours. If you had chosen to fight instead of fleeing.

My phone had been off since I left my grandmother's house without even turning back to take one last look at Manuel. He hadn't even tried to stop me, not even uttering my name with a little regret.

I considered myself to be a smart woman, but Manuel was certainly my kryptonite. The first time I saw him, I was having lunch with my grandmother in the restaurant at the country club where she was a member. She used to get together with some of her oldest friends for lunch every Thursday, and it was a well-known fact among the families in our social circle that the "ladies" were there to see and be seen. And that day, I was there too. I was close to finishing my fourth year of law school and I had an exam a few days after that, so I'd taken the day off work to study. During one of my many breaks, I decided to visit with my grandmother.

Manuel came to our table to greet us. I'd never seen him before, and it was rare because Susana was *very* well connected. Anyone that was someone knew who she was, and vice versa. He'd just returned from a six-month trip to

South Africa with his buddies, a gift from his parents after he graduated college with a marketing degree. His skin was golden, almost pearlescent, his hair in a permanent state of tousled, probably because it was longer than it should have been. His eyes, deep brown like chocolate, were shining with mischief. He was handsome, with so much charm that it oozed from his pores. He was a few years older than me but looked boyish, with soft, full lips and an untroubled attitude. He emanated joy and happiness. Could that be contagious?

He was carefree, and it was blatantly obvious. Probably because he didn't care much about his career or what his family said. And he lived in a world of happily ever afters. I wanted that for myself.

Up until that point, I'd never really believed in how fairy tales or romance novels described love: those insta-connections and love-at-first-sight situations where the main character fell head over heels for a man instantly, even before anyone had spoken a single word.

I'd reserved all my giddy daydreaming abilities to the stories my grandmother told us about her husband, the grandfather I'd never gotten to meet but had heard so many things about, almost idolized in our family for his courage and his honor.

But in that instant, I knew. Right there, with my grandmother as witness, I knew and understood that my life was about to change from having almost everything to having it all. Even without uttering a single word.

Manuel and I dated for what seemed like an eternity. By the time we started our third year of dating, people were asking questions. My go-to answer had been that I wanted to be done with school and established in my career before we got married or took the next step, but the reality was that Manuel never seemed to be as committed to me as I was to him. I was ready to marry him the day I met him. Him, not so much. That had to have been my first red flag, I reckoned.

Once we moved in together—my idea, of course—and the rumormonger aunts were calming down, Susana took it as a good sign, although with some reticence (because why would her perfectly educated, upper class Catholic grand-daughter live in sin? "*¡Ay! ¡Que horror!*" she had said). And Manuel's parents understood it as a sign that maybe their son was choosing the right path and that I was guiding him in the right direction. It still took some convincing but finally, *finally* Manuel hinted that it was time we took the next step, and I held on to it like my life depended on that one single statement.

My perfectly, impossibly handsome boyfriend wanted to marry me. Finally.

That was almost two years ago, and now I was in a bus in front of a bus terminal in the middle of who knows where in Córdoba, without knowing a soul and with no plans whatsoever for the first time in my adult life. I couldn't remember when the last time was that I didn't have anything planned—probably when I was in my teens—and for a second, it almost felt as if life was playing me a bizarre prank and transporting me to easier times to soften the massive blow I had just been given.

The bus rolled to a stop at the corner of the town square, right in front of the community center. Dusk was finally descending on the rooftops, the last of the long summer nights upon them. The air felt strange, almost giving me a tingle all over my exposed arms. It somehow felt cleaner, lighter. It felt different than what I was used to, kind of like the feeling of relief after getting good news. Or maybe how you would feel right after a good night's sleep. I felt a rush of adrenaline out of nowhere—perhaps my body's way of telling me that I was making a mistake and I needed to run back to my grandmother and apologize for putting her through that.

I turned on my cell phone with the sole purpose of trying to find a hotel that could take me in for a few days until I could come up with a plan. I didn't know what I was doing there; my life was pure contradiction. The air was inviting, the town alive with movement and its people. But I felt angry and lonely, dragging all that I had with me.

Maybe if you closed your eyes, you could be transported back to your real life.

As my phone started up, I looked around me. It looked like a small town, laid out in a grid pattern as far as I could see. From my vantage point, I was able to glimpse a large house at the edge of town surrounded by smaller ones lining the street north of the square. No tall buildings in sight—the biggest contrast with the large city I was so used to.

To the south of the square, I could see rolling hills, lush with native landscape. The trees were slowly changing their leaves, with pockets of yellow and orange in between the different green hues. It was faint, but I could hear a creek nearby.

It felt like a pleasant, quiet mountain town.

My phone started buzzing with messages and voicemail notifications. They were relentless.

2:03 p.m.: "Victoria, *¿dónde estás?* Have you any idea what chaos you've created here? Do you realize what you've done? Manuel said that you were supposed to meet him for coffee, but you never showed up. What type of person does that? Don't you realize the importance of today?"

2:15 p.m.: "Victoria, answer the phone immediately. This is a scandal. Manuel is here trying to fix what you've done. What are we going to tell the gues—"

Susana's voice bounced around in my head. I didn't need this right now. My relationship—dare I say potential marriage—had just ended, and this woman had the nerve of putting this on me? And what was Manuel doing there with her?

I knew I was a smart woman. I was excellent at my career, very dedicated to my job. I could sniff out a lie from miles away. How did I not see the red flags? I mean, yes, seven years was a long time before getting married. Also, yes, pressuring your boyfriend to move in with you could be, maybe, who knows, part of why this was happening to me. *No proposal either, remember?* Our decision to get married was more of a conversation—a conversation and an arrangement and a transaction between two adults, no less—about taking the next step.

Had I had it wrong the whole time?

"Hi," Catalina answered on the first ring. "I've been waiting for hours, you know?"

I rolled my eyes and smiled for the first time since my morning started. "I'm fine, how are you?"

"Victoria, what the hell!" she screamed into the phone. Her breath was short nowadays, that baby in her belly doing a number on her. "You know I can't breathe well with this freaking baby in here. You're going to give me a heart attack."

"Oh, don't be dramatic," I replied. Catalina had a flair for drama. She loved telling wild stories, embellishing everything that came out of her mouth. In the years since I'd known her, she had told hundreds of stories, each one more preposterous than the previous one. It was incredible. "You sound like my grandmother."

"Speaking of, she called me about eleven million times," she said. I could hear concern in her voice. "And came to my house."

"Why would she go to your house?" I asked. I would have never expected Susana to leave her home, even during such an important day like that. Her *modus operandi* was for people to meet *her*, even Catalina, a thousand months pregnant with Susana's first great grandchild.

"I don't know, but I'm glad I actually don't know where you are because her fucking death glare gave me shivers." She was probably one of the only people I knew who wasn't terrified of my grandmother, who, granted, had a gaze that could melt a grown man. Catalina and Susana never got along, and my brother never really cared. It definitely created some strain in the relationship and the family dynamics, Susana choosing to exclude Catalina at times. "She should be a professional interrogator. Wouldn't even have to lift a finger to get the truth out of someone."

"Oh, believe me, I know," I said. It was impossible to lie to her growing up. Like me, she could sniff a lie a mile away. The first time I got drunk, I was in my mid-twenties, when I already lived alone and there were at least ten miles of distance between us, just enough space to make sure she wouldn't call me to question me about my actions. "I'm okay. Sorry I left so suddenly."

"You could have called me, and I would have gone to pick you up," she said. Her voice was soft, almost apologetic, as if she could have done anything for me to make it better. "Where are you?"

"Um…" I looked around me. Right above the bus stop there was a sign—Tres Fuegos—which I assumed was the name of the town. "In Córdoba. Tres Fuegos is the town?"

"How'd you end up there?" she replied, a tinge of confusion in her voice. I could almost picture her, already looking up where this small town was. Catalina was the go-to-person when you needed any sort of information. It was her job as a prosecutor, of course, but also, she was passionate about it. Her phone was always close to her, and she would look anything up during a conversation. "Hmm, okay, looks picturesque!"

"Is that your way of saying it's ugly?" I laughed. "Maybe rustic?"

"No, really, I'm being honest. Looks cute." She sighed. "When are you coming back?"

I shrugged like she could see me, as if we were in front of each other. "I need a few days to clear the air. Some space from them would be nice."

I tucked my phone between my shoulder and ear and grabbed my suitcase. I dragged it across the town square where some kids were playing hide-and-seek. It reminded me so much of the long summer evenings with my brother when we were young. We used to stay playing out on the street until well past dusk, coming back home sweaty and filthy and running up the stairs directly to the bathroom so Susana wouldn't yell at us for not being presentable. The memory made me smile; it reminded me of a simpler, happier time.

"Okay, well, if you need me, let me know and I'll come get you."

There were still a few people at the bus stop, waiting for their friends or family to come pick them up. How lonely of my existence that I not only had no one to pick me up, but also, I had almost no one to talk to about what was happening. Catalina was my best friend, but her life path was drifting from mine—in a great way—and there were moments where I couldn't fully relate. I was happy, ecstatic even, that my best friend was also going to be the mother of my first niece, but at that moment, she felt miles away.

"I'll call you tomorrow," I said. "*Beso.*" Kiss.

I switched off my phone and headed towards what looked to be a restaurant. I could hear the laughter and see the lights twinkling from my location. Like I told Cata, I needed some space, time to think about my next step, and this town seemed sleepy and quiet. Just what I needed.

The restaurant had a few tables set up outside on the sidewalk adorned with little candles in the middle and a centerpiece of a few flowers and some greenery. The table was set informally, with a paper place setting with the menu written on the side. It reminded me of the many times Manuel and I had gone to breweries, where I felt completely out of place. Manuel had so many friends. I think that was what attracted me to him in the first place—the way he lived life, like nothing or no one depended on him, his ability to start up a conversation out of nowhere about anything at all with anyone who crossed his path. In contrast, I was a person with few friends—by choice, of course—because my career always came first. That was what mattered to me and to my family.

But you are lonely.

"Are we waiting for someone else to join you?" the waitress asked while setting down a basket of bread and a plate with butter. She filled the glass with ice water from a pitcher. "Maybe I can get started on some drinks for you while your friend gets here."

"Um... It's just me today, thank you," I said with a small voice. I knew if I tried to speak louder, I would start crying. "Just the water for me, please."

"Great. I'll be right back to take your food order," she said as she cleared the second place setting across from me.

And that was what did it. That was the straw that broke the camel's back. The tears welled in my eyes and fell in big blobs as soon as I blinked because my life was over, and I was the only one to blame for this.

"Victoria?" a voice said behind me, and I immediately knew who it belonged to. I could recognize that voice even underwater.

Standing right behind me, in the most unlikely place in the country, was Santiago Williams, my nemesis.

3

THE ENCOUNTER

I wasn't sure how he recognized me. The last time we'd seen each other had been probably close to a decade ago in college. We did the first few years of law school together, but by the third or fourth year, our paths widened, mostly because I went into corporate law and he chose family law.

"What are you doing here?" he asked, stopping right by my side and slightly leaning his strong body on the table, making my glass of water shake in its place. His hair looked almost the same as when we were in our twenties, except that maybe it had a little white peppered in now. He wore faded jeans and a tight-fitting white shirt, his long sleeves rolled up to his elbows. Time had served him well.

I blinked my eyes at him, unsure if this was a trick my mind was playing on me—not the first one that day. He hadn't been top of mind for years, and in that moment, he was probably the last person I wanted to see, right behind

Manuel and Susana. I'd heard about him in passing, some people mentioning his name here or there because he had represented a few celebrities in their divorces. He was notorious, recognized, and always far enough away from me that I only had to hear or read about him, never see him in person.

"Um, what are *you* doing here?" I replied a little childishly. This man had the ability to turn me into the heartless bitch I was sure many of my colleagues said I was behind my back. He was so easygoing, his limbs were so free, that it made me envious. Jealous of his ability to be and live serenely. No expectations of him.

Santiago and I met on our first day of law school. We were both enrolled in the same history class our first year, and we sat close to each other on that gloomy Tuesday morning. He had just moved to the city after growing up in a different part of the country and didn't know many people. Like me, Santiago came from a long line of lawyers, and in a way, we were both fulfilling our legacies. Except that he was (and I would never admit this in public) much smarter than me and had a passion that I couldn't even begin to put into words. What I had in determination and responsibility, he made up for in talent.

I felt like a fish out of water; he moved like a shark amongst a school of fish. In a good sense. He was a natural at what we did and had an uncanny ability to remember small details. It almost felt like the man had eyes in the back of his head because he could recall everything, including things I had witnessed but had no memory of whatsoever.

"Cat got your tongue?" I said after what seemed like the world's longest and most uncomfortable silence. He had always been so smug and cocky, winking at me when he passed me by in the hallways, or smiling his stupidly big smile when he saw me in class. He oozed charm from every single cell of his being, and he never had to work too hard in order to be liked by people. It was annoying to no end, because the only reason I had an in most of the time with anyone was because of my last name and what that meant. I doubted people *liked* me for me. And people *liked* him. A lot. No doubt this man made me see red. He was absolutely and irrevocably infuriating; his long pauses were the death of me.

But then.

Then he smiled a slow smile that reached his eyes. And he expelled the loudest, most exasperatingly pleasing laughter I'd heard in years, probably since the last time I saw him.

"Well, considering you're in my hometown, maybe you should be answering first? What brings you to our lovely neck of the woods?"

He didn't know?

I cocked my head. "I didn't know you were from here," I said. I vaguely remembered talking to him about where he was from but never paying close attention. Those types of details were never too interesting to me, especially since I went to college with a plan—make it in, excel, get out—and mostly stuck to it, except for Cata. I never had a lot of time for friends or acquaintances. Or any interests, really. Susana always said that I needed to focus on my studies and the rest would come later, naturally.

He narrowed his eyes.

I sat up straight, lifting my chin in defiance. "It's none of your business," I said with my most saccharine smile, despite the obvious puffiness of my eyes and the tears still lingering around my eyelashes. I shook my head and cleared my throat. "I'm on vacation."

He stiffened, his spine straightening. I could see it in his look. The pity. And I immediately felt all the color drain from my face because his expression made it evident that he knew I hadn't gotten married. All it took was probably a text message from one of our former classmates. Or not even that. I was sure my name was trending on social media.

The thought made me cringe. My family was socially notorious. Some of my cousins were occasionally followed by cameras and appeared in magazines when they went to large events. We were recognized. It was fine; we learned to live with it. But it wasn't fine when your life turned upside down so much that you had to flee on your wedding day.

"Who told you?" I asked him, avoiding his gentle eyes. "Actually, please don't tell me."

He took a step back and cleared his throat, then did a once-over and looked both ways. He was holding a paper bag in his hand, his long fingers clutching the handles tightly. He tilted his head and looked into my eyes, holding his gaze there for a minute. I swallowed at the intimacy and looked away, running my hands on my thighs.

The waitress came back to take my order and stopped short at the sight of Santiago.

"Hey, Santi," she said with a bright smile. "I didn't know you were coming over for dinner tonight." She turned to look at me and narrowed her eyes, possibly trying to understand what this man was doing talking to the human wreck that I was. Maybe also trying to place me—this outsider that showed up to the small, sleepy town with a large suitcase and makeup running down her cheeks.

"No, I'm just saying hello to my friend here," he said, without taking his eyes off me. "I'm headed to the inn tonight."

"Ah, gotcha," the waitress said, her smile softening. She then turned to me. "You ready to order?"

"I'll have the house salad with grilled chicken," I said as I handed her the specials menu. Santiago's gaze was still parked on my face, and I could feel his eyes searching for answers. "Thanks."

"You got it."

As soon as the waitress walked away, I turned to face Santiago. He was still stiff, his hand clutching on the paper bag like his life depended on it. I took a moment to study him and assessed how he had changed since we last saw each other. The wrinkles around his eyes were more pronounced, and he had bulked up. His shoulders were broad, his shirt tight across his chest. He looked happy, but probably anyone would look happy in comparison to me.

"What's this about an inn?" I raised one eyebrow at him. His jaw clenched, but then he relaxed his shoulders. He looked behind him to the next block over, and I followed his eyes. I could see a wooden sign hanging from a metal bracket with the words *The Inn* carved into it. The building occupied the whole block, and the large front door was right in the middle, flanked by symmetrical windows on either side.

"An inn," he said, a small smile on his lips. From my seated position, I had to crane my neck to be able to look at his face. His profile was breathtaking—a sharp jawline with a perfectly proportioned nose. The streetlights were shining on part of his face, creating large shadows under his dark, long eyelashes. He pointed with his thumb to the big structure and then turned to look at me. "Over there."

I rolled my eyes at him, trying with everything I had to avoid laughing at the absurdity of it all. "Ah, a hidden gem, clearly," I said flatly.

"I'll let you eat," he said suddenly, just as the waitress approached the table with my food. "See you around?" He rapped his knuckles on the table once, twice, then dropped his hand to his side.

I nodded, and he turned around and walked in the direction of the inn, his paper bag still clutched tightly in his other hand. I took a deep breath and turned to my meal, sighing at the first sight of food I'd had all day.

While eating, I looked around. Catalina was right: the town was picturesque. It looked almost like the English countryside, except that all of the houses were painted in different shades of white and only a few of the larger homes had stone exteriors. The town square seemed to be at the center, and the streets were laid in a grid pattern around it. Across the street from the restaurant was a small, inconspicuous trailhead in between two medium-sized bushes. The night was getting darker, but I could barely make out some hills on the horizon.

Once I'd settled the bill, I grabbed my things and headed towards the inn. It was the next logical step in this highly improvised plan I was slowly devising. Maybe if I kept enough distance, I would be able to figure out what my next step would be.

As soon as I walked in the door at the inn, I felt the strangest feeling of being home. The lobby was small and welcoming, and the large reception desk floated on the right side of the room. I could hear chatter coming from the left, most likely from a restaurant, judging by the sounds of silverware against plates. There was a loud, booming laugh, followed by a few people cackling at whatever joke was said. It was familiar, intimate. Like this town was one big family, and this was where they got together on the weekends.

I approached the receptionist, an older woman wearing a tight bun and standing in front of a computer, her eyes moving fast across the screen. As soon as she heard me stop in front of her, she lifted her face and smiled.

"Oh, hello," she said, beaming. "You made it!"

"Uh, sure?" It came out more like a question, my voice shrill with surprise. I widened my eyes and looked around, but I couldn't see anyone in the small entryway. Could it have been that Catalina called ahead to make a reservation or to make sure there were rooms available? My phone had been off since I spoke to her, so I had no way to quickly check. "I... I made it?"

"Oh!" The woman laughed. "Santi mentioned that a friend of his would stop by."

Ah, my friend. It was the second time he'd referred to me as his friend. The silence stretched between us, and I used the reprieve to look further into the hotel. I could see a large sitting room towards the back. It reminded me so much of Susana's house—the large sofas around an unlit fireplace. Large chandeliers hung from the tall ceilings, and the far wall was scattered with French doors that opened to a back patio. There were a few cafe tables out there, but it was void of people.

"Here we go," she said, interrupting my browsing. "This is your key. My name is Julia, by the way. If you need anything, just let me know."

"Thank you," I said, smiling softly to this warm stranger. "Have a good night."

I pulled my suitcase behind me and headed towards the elevators, admiring the carved stairs right behind the lobby. The whole inn was a vibe. There were multiple seating areas distributed around the large room. Wood paneling covered the walls, and there were almost no spaces left empty. Despite being cluttered, it felt homey, cozy. Like a breath of fresh air during a particularly nasty season.

My room was on the top floor of the building, and it had a small seating and dining area and a separate bedroom to the side. The large windows overlooked the front of the hotel, and from the foot of the bed I could clearly see the town square and beyond. It was already dark by the time I made it up there, so I quickly unpacked and got ready for bed. My brain was still moving at lightning speed, trying to go over the events that had changed my life not even twelve hours prior.

As soon as I got into bed, I noticed that there was a flashing light on the room phone.

"Hey," his voice said. "Julia told me you checked in. Just wanted to make sure you were okay. Please let me know if you need anything." He sounded thoughtful, caring. Santiago had always been a patient man, using his words wisely and always paying attention to his surroundings and to the context. "Sounds like maybe you need some space to think, so I'll let you be, but know that I'm around if you need to talk." Pause. "Okay, good night."

It was almost like he had read my mind, knowing exactly what I needed when I needed it. It was, for sure, the complete opposite to my family's reaction. Whereas Susana's messages were almost menacing, Santiago's were comforting. And despite the fact that we couldn't stand each other, he was being nice? It was confusing. I was confused and exhausted.

And as soon as my head hit the pillow, I fell asleep, but my dreams were more than nightmares, because my life was slowly burning down, consumed by a roaring fire that started the moment I left the comfort of my family.

4

SUSANA (1988)

I HEARD THE DOOR OPEN, the clear creaking that had been bothering me for months, alerting me of his arrival. He walked in and with a thud, he dropped his briefcase on the entryway floor. Roberto had been doing this for over twenty years now, every single Wednesday evening without fail. I was sitting in the living room, a drink to my left, while the staff in the kitchen finalized the last details of what we would have for dinner that cold fall night. Josefina had called earlier that evening to tell me something about her neighbor, and I was still sitting by the phone when he entered the house.

"Are you home?" I asked, turning my head towards the foyer. I expected him to poke his head through the doorway and nod in acknowledgment, like he'd done thousands of times before. "Don't forget that tomorrow evening we are having dinner with Teresa and Carlos at the club. Also, did you remember to call Juan to confirm?"

I didn't receive—or expect—an answer. I knew it was him. I knew the cadence of his steps by heart. They were etched in my brain. I knew he would answer in due time. I was merely planting the seed of these questions into his head, and he would give me an answer later. We had operated this way for years.

He was never too interested in our social activity; I was the one who handled our agenda, filling it up with dinners and cocktail parties and charity events. We were frequently seen at our church fundraisers, as well as at the weddings of those who most mattered in our social group. To say that we were influential was an understatement. And it was a combination of his hard work and my buzzing that gave us notoriety.

From where I sat in the sitting room, I could hear our home. Not quite literally, of course, but there were still those sounds in the background that narrated our lives. We'd had seven children in almost a decade, the oldest now well into adulthood. We were in a new moment in our lives: our youngest was to be married soon, and we would *finally* be empty nesters. I was looking forward to the next phase, excited for the chance to travel the world.

Doors were opening and closing, and I could hear quiet chatter. I could clearly differentiate his fast steps to our daughter's. The heaviness meant that the ceiling in this old, classic home vibrated with the movement.

We had a perfectly acceptable routine: he would drop his briefcase in the entryway and make his way to the kitchen. He would kiss my temple on his way to the refrigerator to search for the club soda, then proceed to grab a tall glass from the cabinet and fill it with the fizzy liquid. While this was happening, I would drop off his briefcase in his home office and then go back to the kitchen to hear about his day. He didn't talk much, only the bare details, but enough to be able to communicate the important things.

But today, today was no such a day.

In the time it took me to stop what I was doing and get back to the front of the house, he had walked up the stairs, grabbed one of our old suitcases, and descended the stairs, holding a few stray documents in his hands. I had no idea what those were or where they had come from. Maybe they were from his home office, or maybe he had gotten them from the drawer where we kept all our important documentation in our shared dressing room.

He stood at the bottom of the stairs, his gaze empty and devoid of any feeling. He was a serious man, always had been. Responsible and absurdly loyal to his family.

It had been almost forty years to the day since we'd met. I remember it as if it were today. I was standing outside my house with my younger sisters, who were playing hopscotch with a piece of an old brick they'd found lying around. We lived in a middle-class neighborhood close to the railroad tracks. All the neighborhood children went to the same schools—the girls went to the one up the hill, the boys to the one ten blocks down our street.

Roberto got out of his small, moss-green car, the sleeves of his shirt rolled up to his elbows, his forearms visible. His hair—so thick and dark—was styled to perfection. I remember thinking that his hairstyle was modern for the times, although now, four decades later, he was still wearing it the same way. Without looking ahead of him, he walked directly to my neighbor Pedro's door. Pedro was waiting for him, leaning on the door frame with a naughty smirk on his face, looking right at me. Roberto was impeccably dressed. His slacks looked freshly pressed despite the fact that he had just been driving, his shirt stiff and starched.

I felt myself flush with embarrassment, like I'd been caught doing something forbidden. That was probably the first time I ever looked at a man with any sort of desire. I was just shy of sixteen years old and didn't interact much with men outside of my immediate family and some of the neighborhood boys. Perhaps it was because I wasn't supposed to be looking at that mysterious man. It had long been assumed that Pedro and I would end up together. Our families were friends. We were neighbors and had a good, friendly relationship. It was easy with Pedro. He was older than me, but we understood each other in a way that I was never able to replicate with anyone else, not even my sisters or my mother. But this boy, this man, exuded stability and power. Even without knowing his name, I knew that if I tried hard, I could end up with him.

Roberto and I were formally introduced to each other a few months later at an acquaintance's wedding, and despite what it meant for Pedro, he encouraged my relationship with his friend. Three years later, we were married, and soon after, our first daughter was born. Ten years after that, we had a house full of children, we traveled yearly to Europe, and we were very active in our community—both at the church and at the country club. I dared to say we were living an idyllic life.

As I patiently waited for him to speak, I could feel how his hands were unsteady. Why was his gaze so empty? Why was he standing in front of me like words escaped him? He was relentless, unyielding in his professional life and tough and firm on our children at home. He always had a thing to say. He was a man of few words, but those words had the potential to cut like a knife. After a long beat, he clutched the documents harder, turned, and exited through the door.

Stunned in place, I could only look at what was happening from my place by the kitchen door. I followed him, quickening my pace to try to catch up with him, but he averted my gaze.

"*¿Adónde vas?* Are you going out of town for work?" I asked. I heard my voice, trembling and shrill, a combination of astonishment and emotional collapse.

Without a single word, he opened the trunk and put the suitcase inside. Still clutching the documents, he walked around the vehicle and sat in the driver's seat. He started the car and drove off without telling me where he was going or how long he'd be gone.

I felt my heart racing. I was frozen, holding a cloth napkin I had dragged with me from the house in my hand. Tiny and vulnerable: that was how I felt in front of such a structure behind me, slowly crumbling to the ground.

I was speechless.

5

THE HELP

I told you so, said that voice in my head. *This is uncommon for you, and you should be back in the city, trying to fix this.* I had tossed and turned all night in the hotel bed. I was so used to sleeping in my own bed with my fiancé next to me that the slightest unfamiliar sound made me perk up. The late afternoon was so quiet and warm, and the windows were open so that the constant sound of the cicadas outside would help drown my thoughts.

My phone buzzed on the desk by the TV, probably a message from Susana. I didn't need to guess at this point. The voicemail notification had haunted me for almost two days now, gnawing at me every second of my day. I hadn't been a rebellious teenager—Susana had had enough with my brother in his teens, who followed it up with a massive *f-you* when he married Catalina. I was the complete opposite: quiet and reserved and didn't have many friends. At one point in my life, I considered my grandmother my best friend, until Cata came into the picture. Not answering the phone was probably the biggest act of rebellion, I would say.

"Victoria, where are you? Do you realize what you've done?"

"Victoria, answer the phone immediately. This is a scandal. Manuel is here trying to fix what you've done…"

"Victoria, for the love of god. I can't believe you would do this to me. Do you have any idea the humil—"

The messages kept playing on a loop in my head. Nothing I did was helping me shut them down. The voices of disappointment and humiliation. That was the worst of it all. She had never been disappointed in me; I had given her no reasons to be.

I grew up in a strict household under her watchful eye. My mother's passing revealed that my father was wildly unprepared to raise two toddlers, sinking his pain in alcohol to try to make sense of his loss. So he moved us to his childhood home, where Susana helped. And she took on the role very seriously. I would say that of all of the cousins, I was probably the one that was closest to Susana, acting more as a confidant than a grandchild. And I liked it. It gave me a sense of purpose, to be able to make her proud and to share many different things with her.

Ever since we were old enough to recognize the consequences of our actions, Susana taught us to be intentional in everything we did. She believed that if we made a plan with very clear steps, then we would accomplish everything we needed to have the perfect life. "We make a plan and stick to it," she said. "Calculated and intentional."

Except that "calculated and intentional" was suddenly foreign to me. Because "calculated and intentional" had brought me here, to a place that felt so strange and unfamiliar but gave me peace at the same time. It was like my own existence was a contradiction. Whatever was going on was a sick joke, and my brain was in on it. Maybe I should consider listening to that voice in my head and go back to the city. Call them back. Get married. Forgive him.

I needed to get out of my head, but I was dragging my feet because I didn't want to risk running into Santiago. I had been out of my room a few times in the three days since I'd arrived in town, and the times I did, I saw him. Either from a distance or close by, at the hotel's restaurant or behind the desk in the lobby. It was almost as if he was a larger-than-life character—he was everywhere. His laughter welcomed me as I walked into the hotel's restaurant, finally hungry enough to brave it out of my room. He was sitting comfortably at a table off to the side, his arm draped casually on the back of a chair right next to him. He was surrounded by older men looking at him in awe, everyone smiling and laughing together.

I glanced around the room, the place full of locals immersed in their conversations and their stories. It looked like it belonged to perfection in this quaint town. The walls were clad with wood wainscoting, and just like the sitting room right outside the doors, vintage sports memorabilia adorned the space. From the ceiling, discolored bunting hung in a zig-zag pattern, reminding me of a medieval castle or maybe a fancy circus. It definitely had an English pub vibe to it—no surprise there since the original settlers of this town were wealthy British families.

I took a seat at the bar and placed the book I brought right next to me. I knew from my previous nights there that the service at the bar was great, and the conversation was even better. The night before, Julia, the hotel manager, told me about the origins of the town, how it was now mostly dependent on tourism and the residents were getting ready for the off-season. She said that during the summer, the town was a very popular hiking destination because the trails led to many different parts of the mountain, from creek beds to the tallest peaks.

"Hey," the bartender said as he approached me.

"Oh, hi. Wha-what are you doing here?" I almost couldn't believe my eyes. Santiago was standing in front of me with a rag on his shoulder, looking like the quin-tessential bartender. He smiled one of his smiles, the one that made the corners of his eyes crinkle. "Why are you behind the bar?"

I narrowed my eyes, trying to understand why this man was standing where he was. The last I knew, he was still doing family law back in the city and had been part of a team in a very high-profile case.

"Julia had an emergency, so I took over," he said calmly. "I used to work here during my summers, and I think I remember a thing or two."

"Ah, is she alright?" Julia had been extremely welcoming to me in the past few days. She sent breakfast up to my room every morning and immediately called me to let me know that there was a tray waiting for me outside my room. "I was looking forward to more of her stories tonight."

He smiled, grabbed the rag on his shoulder, and proceeded to wipe the counter right in front of me. His hands were big and tanned, working in slow motion like they were taunting me. His movements were natural, confirming that he had indeed done this many times before. The back wall of the bar was full of liquor bottles, many I'd never seen before, in all different shapes and sizes.

"Is that common?" I cocked my head, trying to understand the town dynamics. He looked surprised at my question but smiled. "Do people around town just cover for others when they need help?"

"I mean," he said with a soft smile, "Julia is my aunt, and she owns the inn. And also, I'm on vacation, and I don't have much to do so…" He shrugged, not finishing his sentence and letting me use my deduction skills.

"Interesting," I replied, looking around the room. "Well, I guess I could read my book then."

I motioned to my right where I had set my book down. This was probably my most well-kept secret: I was a bookworm. I loved reading romance and mystery novels, the latter something that I had apparently inherited from the grandfather I never met. But not only did I read because it gave me a connection to him, but also because it was an escape from my reality, and right now I needed all the escape I could get. Susana hated it. She said multiple times that it took away from my time to socialize, to see and be seen.

"You like to read?" he asked, lifting one of those perfect eyebrows of his. *Focus, Victoria.* "I didn't know that. What do you like to read?"

"Oh, a little bit of everything. Except self-help. Yep, not for me," I said, looking over at him. His serene expression and carefree demeanor were so calming. "My grandfather was an avid reader, and they keep telling me that I inherited this trait. Although in the past few years, my reading time has been significantly reduced. I'm sure you can relate."

He huffed in agreement. "What can I get you?" he asked with a big smile, his eyes twinkling with something I couldn't quite place. He was so calm and collected—a trait I envied a lot and one thing I had to constantly work on. He had always been this way, ever since I met him. I remembered his easy smiles and how he paid attention to everyone. Like he was mesmerized by everything.

The laughter in the restaurant got louder and when I scanned the room, it looked packed. It almost felt like everyone was eating together, although at separate tables. People stopped by to chat with others, dragging chairs and their drinks for moments just to catch up. It had a familiar atmosphere, even if these people were only acquaintances to each other.

The only other comparison I could think of was the club, but that was more of a place to see and be seen than to actually enjoy other people's company. All of the smiles were pasted on. The scene today was genuine.

"I'll have the pasta, thanks." In the time it took me to scan the room, Santiago had poured me a glass of wine and laid silverware and a place setting on the tabletop. He had arranged my book neatly right next to my glass, placing it over a napkin to avoid getting it wet. "Oh, thank you," I said, blinking a few times at the thoughtfulness.

Santiago lingered at the bar until my food arrived, then disappeared behind the doors to the kitchen. I opened my book and started reading, but I was derailed as soon as he sat right next to me with his own plate, almost like he intended to share this moment with me.

"What are you doing?" I asked, and I felt my face bunch up in a scowl I couldn't hide. This man brought out the worst in me for sure, and every fiber of my being knew it.

He responded with one of his easy smiles, all teeth and crinkled eyes.

"Well, I needed to take a break anyway, so I ordered some food and I'm sitting here. Do you mind the company?"

"You are free to sit wherever you want, but I told you already that I'm reading my book tonight."

He stared at me, unfazed by what I had just said. "Did Julia tell you the story of those two lover kids that ran away from their families and came here?" he asked with an amused smirk on his face. How did he know that I was a sucker for a good love story? It made me a little nostalgic, knowing that could have been me. That I had, once upon a time, the chance to my happily ever after.

"What's the face for? You look like a fool smiling like that. Don't your cheeks hurt from all that muscle contraction there?"

He let go of a deep, roaring laugh, making me jump with surprise. It had been a long time since I'd heard anyone laugh like this, like he actually meant it. He was pure sunshine, this man, and I didn't understand why or how people like this lived, just happy with their mere existence.

I scowled just so that I could hide the smile that was forming on my lips. It was like my brain knew that I shouldn't be enjoying this man's company, but my body had other plans.

"Oh, come on, don't be such a grump," he said. "Live a little, Victoria! It's okay to laugh, you know?"

He could also read minds, apparently.

I buried my face in what was left of my food, trying to avoid looking at him. My hands itched for my book, and despite my dislike for him, I still had some manners. It had always been this way, ever since college—he was so... gleeful. It was almost like he sparked joy, and then used his perfect smile to rub his happiness in my face.

Just as we were both finishing our meal, a blonde woman approached us.

"Hi, baby," she said. "There you are. I couldn't find you." She kissed his cheek and wrapped her long arm around his shoulders. She was tall, dressed impeccably. She was stunning. "I went looking for you at your grandparents' house, but you weren't there, and you weren't answering your phone." His girlfriend, maybe? Yuck.

Santiago tensed up. It lasted all of one microsecond, and if I wasn't looking so closely, I wouldn't have caught it. But he turned and smiled that easy smile of his, and he looked up to her from his seat while she squeezed his shoulder a little possessively for my taste.

"Ah, sorry, I've been here all afternoon. Julia had an emergency, and I volunteered to take over for her shift," he said to her, even though I could tell he was uneasy. She was looking straight at me, almost staring daggers in my direction.

"How rude of me, apologies. Victoria, this is Clara. Clara, this is Victoria," he said, almost like he had done this thousands of times. Was she his girlfriend?

I raised my hand and gave her a small wave and my best

formal smile—the one I knew was one hundred percent fake and used for my business associates only. "Nice to meet you."

"Nice to meet you too. I've heard so much about you," she said. The corners of her mouth inched up a little, and her eyes thinned. Santiago stiffened at her side as soon as she uttered those words. "Santiago has told me all about you."

Santiago laughed an uncomfortable laugh, like he was caught red-handed doing something he shouldn't have been. "Victoria and I went to law school together," he added quickly.

"Are you from around here?" I asked her, regretting those words as soon as they left my mouth. I didn't want to make small talk with anyone, let alone this stunning woman beside me. She looked happy, just like Santiago. Like they were both living their best lives together.

"Actually, we're here for Santiago's grandmother's birthday party this weekend. I just came a few days early to spend some time with Santi since he's been here since the beginning of the year," she responded and looked at him with stars in her eyes. Yes, she was the girlfriend, I could confirm.

"Well, I'm going to take off. I hope you enjoy your night. Sorry if you had plans, Santiago. Didn't mean to interrupt," I said, feeling more and more awkward in this situation. "Can you charge this to my room?" I asked as I grabbed my book and stood up from the bar.

Santiago, who hadn't said more than a few words yet, looked at me intensely. "Sure, no problem," he said. No easy smile for me now.

I turned to leave and as I was reaching the staircase to go up to my room, I heard his steps behind me.

"Hey, are you alright?"

"Yes." No. "Yes, I'm fine. Just tired."

But I wasn't alright, and at that moment, I realized I was in trouble.

6

SUSANA (1988)

For the entirety of our marriage, my husband had taken Saturdays off to play golf at the club with his business associate and best friend, Pedro. And that day, like every other Saturday, Pedro was at our door.

"He's not here, Pedro," I said to the man who had once been my childhood best friend. I could immediately notice that my tone of voice wavered. His eyebrows shot up; I assumed because I was never an anxious mess. "I've been calling you nonstop for three days, and you haven't had the decency to return my calls."

Desperate.

Three full days had passed since he had gotten in his car and driven away, without having the decorum of telling me where he was going. Pedro remained silent, his expression unreadable, but I could almost hear him thinking.

"I saw him leave a few days ago. He didn't utter a single

word—not that that is uncommon for him. But he hasn't even called me to tell me what is going on. I thought maybe you were with him, out of town for work."

He moved inside the entryway, taking a seat in one of the small chairs by the large painting of an old family home in Europe—one of the few family heirlooms we actually kept and the only thing that was actually worth anything— which made him look like a giant. Even at sixty years old, Pedro still looked like he was at his prime. He had a large back and wide shoulders, and his hair was full, albeit peppered with white strands. He had some expression lines, the most notable ones being the ones around his gray eyes that really tattled on his joyful demeanor. He was very attractive still, and dare I say was even more attractive now than in our youth. He had never married; no one ever under-stood why.

"Susana, why don't you take a seat? Let's talk this through," he said, his voice extremely calm for the situation. Maybe he knew what was happening and had waited to see me in person to tell me. My face remained blank although my patience was being tried. I worked very hard to avoid showing my emotions on my face—in part because I knew that it wouldn't help with my appearance, and in part because this way, I could remain in control longer.

"No. I know you know, so might as well tell me right now," I added sharply. "Tell me right now."

"Do you remember that young girl we hired back a few years ago to man the phones? I can't confirm this with certainty, but I have a suspicion that they left together to start a new life. I've seen them looking at each other adoringly throughout the years. Maybe those looks meant nothing or maybe they meant a lot."

"Wh-what? He would *never,*" I said. "He might be many things, but he is loyal to me and our family."

"Susana, don't be naïve! No one can keep up with you or your lifestyle. Do you think that he's married to you because he is *in love?*"

His comment was supposed to be a punch in my gut; it was anything but. I knew he wasn't in love with me. I wasn't in love with him either. But it was convenient, and it gave me everything I wanted and more. Specifically, it gave me notoriety, a society push. And it was probably why, since the day I saw him, I altered all my plans to be married to him. Back then he was a rising star, and I was a nobody, and today we were considered to be members of one of the best families in San Isidro. We had an idyllic life. We had a gorgeous, large family, we were active socially and recognized by everyone in the area, and we had everything we needed and more. I was definitely being taken care of— exactly my intention when I married him.

"*Ay,* Pedro. Who is being naïve now? Of course he's not in love with me. People with money don't marry for love, they marry for convenience. It's transactional. But that doesn't mean that he could afford to be disloyal. We have a reputation to maintain, and it goes both ways between him and me."

In any case, this needed fixing, and Pedro was a fixer.

"What are you going to do about this?" I asked him, planting myself firmly in front of him, showing him that this was serious. "We need to fix this. Even *if* he ran away with another woman, that can't be what we say. Do you have any idea how that will make me look? No one cheats on me. No one."

Pedro sucked in a breath and scanned the room. I looked around, confirming that the only daughter that still lived in our home wasn't close by and that the help was out of earshot. He was clearly avoiding my gaze, an indication that he knew something else I didn't.

"Pedro, don't lie to me. What else do you know?"

"*Dios mío,* woman, you are relentless," he said, a small smile etched on his lips. "You could have been an excellent lawyer if you had wanted to."

Yes, I knew that.

I turned and walked to the kitchen, and he followed in my footsteps. Pedro and I had been close, once upon a time. His family had moved to the house next to mine when we were in our teens, and we had attended many events together. In a way, it was like we had been in an arranged relationship—the friendship felt easy, the families got along well, and we shared many similar views. But then Roberto came along, and I instantly knew it had to be him. The man who would later become my husband showed promise. Where Pedro was joyful and carefree, Roberto was serious and focused. He had finished his law degree in record time and by the time he was in his early twenties, he was employed at a large firm in the city, working on some very notorious cases with his team. He was named in the front page of all the newspapers, mentioned in the society magazines, and had a long list of women waiting to dance with him at events.

The maid was in the kitchen, preparing our dinner for that evening. "Leave," I said as I moved towards the stove to heat up some water for tea. This was something I used to do with my girlfriends on the regular. We would sit at the kitchen table, having dismissed the help, and catch up on the recent developments in society. Gossip, some people would call it. But it was far from it because it really was beneficial to us to know what happened and to whom.

"Would you like some tea?" I asked Pedro, not expecting an answer.

He sat at the table and rested his hands on his lap. Ever since he walked in, he couldn't look me in the eye. This had only happened a few times early on in my marriage. He'd been hurt because I chose Roberto over him. Occasionally, I would catch him watching my children with a look that could only be explained as longing. Longing for what we could have had together, maybe even some anger because I didn't end up marrying him.

"*¡Mírame,* Pedro! What is this nonsense? We are not in our twenties anymore," I said, almost a little out of control. I needed to get a handle on the situation. "What do you know about this woman? Do you know where they are? Are they coming back?"

"Well, I think she's from Córdoba, although I can't confirm because I never had the inkling to check. I think the affair has been going on for a few months now. I've caught a few looks here and there and some smiles coming from him."

"Do you think I'm stupid? He doesn't smile; he's a serious man. Please give me some credit and don't treat me like a child. Where is he?"

The seconds extended, and after what felt like minutes of him looking everywhere but at me, he sighed, almost like he was giving up. Was he making this up on the go? Pedro had always been quick to provide solutions to problems, but it seemed that this time he was stuck and couldn't form words.

"So? What is it?"

"Do you really want to know the truth, Susana? Are you sure you're prepared to face whatever comes after you hear this? I know you, and you will not like any of this."

"Out with it! It can't be that bad, can it? I mean, what if he left with that woman? We can pretend nothing happened; I can forgive him." *As long as no one knew the truth, I could.* "*Por favor*, please, just tell me what the hell is going on."

He knew, *oh*, he absolutely knew, and I was certain he was in on it.

"He's being investigated because he made some questionable deals. So he left because they were close to charging him with embezzlement and corruption, and he *spared* you the humiliation. You are right. He *is* loyal."

"When is he coming back?" I asked a little too quickly. "Where did he go?"

"I don't know, Susana. He has to lie low for a while, get these people off his back and wait for it to die down. Maybe a few weeks."

"*A few weeks*? What am I supposed to do for *weeks*? Stay in my house and pretend like nothing happened? I have functions to attend, people to see, things to do!"

"It could be months, to be honest. And, well, you have to know that you can't touch your accounts or make any cash flow movements. You also have to lie low."

"I don't understand." I blinked a few times. I was desperate at this point. My hands were shaking, and I had to fist them to my sides to avoid throwing things around and destroying my perfect kitchen. "So let me see if I have this right: he made a few murky movements, he disappears to *spare* me, and now I can't continue to live my life because of *his* mistakes? What kind of man does this? I can't believe this is happening to me."

Pedro stood up from his chair and walked over to me. The water was boiling, and the kettle was making that obnoxious sound that irritated my husband so much. He wrapped an arm around my shoulders and pulled me to him, which immediately made my head rest on his chest.

"What am I supposed to do, Pedro? This is terrible."

"We will figure something out together. I can assure you I won't let anything happen to you, and I will cover your expenses for the time being. We don't have to tell anyone where he is, maybe just that he's on an extended work trip."

"No one will believe that. He always travels with you and never more than a few days at a time. His business is here in the city. There's no reason for him to disappear for that long."

"Whatever you choose to do, Susi, I will follow your lead. You know that. You've known that for years."

He looked hopeful, like maybe this could bring us together again. And he used my childhood nickname, one that was reserved for only a select few, never to be used in public.

At this point, I'd had more than enough time to plan possible scenarios in my head. We had been constantly hearing of these people disappearing off the streets, being held hostage for ransom. There had been a case recently involving the eldest son of a very wealthy businessman in the area. He was kidnapped and later released after a large amount of money was paid to the perpetrators. Was there any way we could concoct this story without anyone catching on? Lies had a tendency to spiral out of control, but if we kept it close to home, I was sure we could get away with it. After all, I had my reputation and my family to protect.

I sighed, feeling some relief for the first time in three days. Three days in which my grown children had asked nonstop about their father, three days in which I had to cancel more than one social outing, claiming illness, three days in which this new narrative made more and more sense in my head. I needed to protect myself.

"Remember how you were telling me about that man who was kidnapped a few months ago?" I asked Pedro, with a face that I could only think had the intention to plead with him.

"What are you getting at?" he replied. That longing again, followed immediately by a sigh. "I don't think anyone is going to buy it. There's no reason for him to be taken hostage, Susana. No way. He has no enemies."

"I think we can sell it. He's a wealthy man, notorious. His name has been on the news recently, for sure attracting unwanted attention, we could argue. That recent case was notorious, Pedro. Or perhaps we only say that he hasn't shown back up to the house after work and let people make their own assumptions?" I sighed. "Pedro, I am *not* willing to subject myself to the humiliation of either being called a cheater's wife or even worse, a thief's wife! *Dios mío,* how will people react to this?"

It was settled then; this was our course of action. Pedro would undoubtedly back me up, just like he had done every single time for the decades since we'd met. He was on my side, and he would remain on my side.

"Susana, this sounds a little too drastic. We can lie low for a while, figure something else out. I can support you financially. You and your daughter can move in with m—"

"And what? Even worse. I will be called an adulterer! Pedro, use your brain for once. This is the only way out. Either you are in or you are out of my life."

Pedro let me go, and at the same time, I felt my body relax. This was what I had to do to protect myself, my reputation, and my family. From this day on. Now I needed to make my next calculated move.

"Alright, if that's what you want," he said, a sad look on his face.

I grabbed the kettle and made two cups of hot tea, then placed each one on the table. Pedro remained standing in place, frozen in thought. I sat down in silence and began to drink my beverage, looking at him and waiting for his reaction. A few minutes went by and finally, he sat next to me. He extended his hand, searching for mine, then placed it on top of mine and squeezed.

"I guess that's the plan then," he said and smiled.

Yes, that was the plan.

7

THE CLEARING

Because of course this kept happening to me. Santiago was everywhere. At this point in time, I was convinced I was hallucinating. I went from thinking that a disgusting prank was being played on me, to maybe my brain tricking me, to actually thinking this was my personal hell. He was *larger*, and I mean ginormously larger, than life.

For the first time in years, I felt like I didn't fit in. Like I stood out like a sore thumb in a place that didn't belong to me because it belonged entirely to Santiago and his giant soul. I left my hotel room with the sole purpose of eating, and then I returned to grieve my pathetic existence and everything I should have by now. I was supposed to be on my honeymoon, but instead I was stuck in time in a town where everywhere I looked, there was a reminder of my previous life, and where there were no happy couples, there was Santiago.

His practiced laughter reverberated through the halls of the hotel. I could hear his voice out my window calling out to the locals taking their daily strolls in the town square. I didn't know what his deal was. Maybe he was doing it on purpose. Did he know that I was here in this very room, using every single second of my time to grovel with life itself?

Denial, check. Anger, check—or so I thought. And I moved on to bargaining. So desperate and sad that I was willing to do almost anything to minimize the pain. Even staying in this town with that man who only made me angrier at myself. He reminded me of all the things I could have, and he reminded me of the actions I wasn't taking. I had yet to speak to Susana, hadn't even thought of calling Manuel and letting him hear my thoughts.

"Hey," Cata answered the video call. She looked tired, the circles under her eyes a deep purple, like she hadn't slept in weeks. "You look good."

"I haven't left my room except for meals in three days, and I haven't showered either. Not sure what you mean." I smiled, trying to pry a smile off of her. "You look tired."

"I can't find a comfortable position to sleep at this point, and the heartburn is killing me. I'm going to start my maternity leave early because I can't function."

"Do you want something to do in the meantime?" I knew she was going to take the bait. I hadn't told her about Santiago yet. "Guess who I ran into the other night?"

Her eyes widened, and she grinned. "Oh, I love this

already!" She sat up and rested her back on the headboard, shuffling her body under the covers a few times to get comfortable.

"Santiago Will—"

"Oh my god!" she screeched. "Ugh, I'm so jealous."

"Jealous? Of what?" I laughed at her comment.

"He was so handsome. Does he still look the same?"

"He looks exactly the same and acts exactly the same. It's so annoying."

If there was one thing I remembered from our time in law school, it was the competition. It was expected of me to be at the top, so that was what I did. And Santiago was right there with me. He was passionate about criminal justice, and the way he spoke about the justice system was so eloquent and informed. He used to take really long pauses when he was speaking, and it annoyed me to the point where sometimes I sighed or grunted so hard that the people sitting next to me had to elbow me in the ribs so I would keep it down. I could say that it was because he was calculated and intentional but not malicious at all. More like stopping to analyze his thoughts, putting them in order, forming an opinion, and then sharing that. Compared to me, he was the polar opposite.

"You've been hanging out with him?" She sounded incredulous. "You hate him."

"Hate is a strong word, Catalina. I think I prefer to say that I strongly dislike him." I pursed my lips, trying to suppress a smile. "And he's been hanging out with me. It's like he's everywhere."

"What is he doing there?" She furrowed her brows and tilted her head. "I heard he took a leave of absence from work after a particularly difficult case last year."

"How do you even know that?" *Huh.* Was that the reason why he'd been in this town for a few months, like his girl-friend mentioned? Catalina had always been very well connected. Her job demanded it, but she also made it a point to keep in touch with a lot of the people we graduated with, something I never cared to do.

"Oh, you know, I heard it through the grapevine." She wiggled her eyebrows and smiled. "Anyway..."

"He's from here, apparently," I replied quickly, trying to avoid whatever would be coming out of her mouth next. "And he's here because it's his grandmother's birthday party this weekend."

"Interesting," she said. She rested her head on her hand and looked into the screen. "Anyway. Susana is going insane, by the way." She grinned at me, her eyes shining with something mischievous. "Your brother is furious because Manuel is playing the victim so hard."

"No one told her where I am, right?" I needed to avoid them as much as I could. I needed a plan, and then I could start taking action to figure out what my next move would be. "I need a little more space."

"Your brother is the one who answers the phone every time she calls me. She won't get a peep from me."

I sighed with relief, but my mind went into overdrive.

"Thank you," I said. "I'll let you rest, and I'll go get coffee. I'll call you soon."

I needed to get out of my head, because turning over my thoughts every which way would do me in. The sun was shining, and the sky was a blue I'd never seen before, almost blinding. I could see a lone gray cloud in the distance.

As soon as I stepped outside the hotel in search of some food, I could feel his presence. The hairs on the back of my neck stood to attention. I hadn't seen him in almost a decade before our encounters here, but my body was trained, and the muscle memory was alive and well.

I walked the opposite way than I intended with the sole purpose of avoiding him and his stupid, blinding smile. He was so annoying, always had been.

"Victoria! Hey! Wait up!" he shouted as he ran to me. Even though I was ignoring him and didn't stop walking, I could hear his steps grow closer and closer. "Where are you going?"

"What have I ever done to deserve this, Santiago? Stop following me." I rolled my eyes. I felt like a rebellious teenager when talking to him. Attitude for days. "I'm just getting some food."

"You do realize that the only restaurants that are open right now in town are in the opposite direction?" he said, his mouth lifting a millimeter on one side, almost like he was trying to hold in his smile. "I can walk with you if you want."

"I'm sorry, did I not make myself clear? I don't need a babysitter." He let out a deep laugh that made every single one of my cells vibrate. "I have enough to deal with, and I don't want any more annoyance, thank you very much."

"Always so grumpy, Victoria." He added while turning around, "Well, I need to grab some lunch so I'll go ahead and walk in the correct direction, and you are free to join me if you want to. But only if it's not *too* annoying for you."

"I just..." This man. "Fine. Whatever. Separate tables. I brought my book with me."

"Are you reading the same book as the other night?" He waited for me to catch up and matched my stride as we walked in the direction of the little corner café across from the community center.

"None of your business." Maybe I was being a little rude. *Tone it down, Victoria. He's been nothing but nice to you since you've arrived. Might as well agree to some small talk on your way to lunch.* I sighed. "It's a new novel that I was saving for my trip. It's a fictionalized version of a real story that happened in a small town many years ago, detectives and crime and whatever." I cringed a little at my word vomit. "Anyway, nice day today."

Yes, change the topic to the weather. Smart.

"Do you have any plans today? Have you been doing some exploring? There's a really nice hiking trail that starts over at that corner of the town square and makes a loop around town and brings you right back," he added, pointing in the direction of the trailhead. It felt almost like this was a practiced speech for the guests at his family's hotel. I didn't know how to take the recommendation, so I nodded, focusing my gaze ahead. "Or the creek bed is also nice this time of year because the water is still a little warm from the summer and the tide is low."

"Hmm, that sounds nice." There, I could do this. I could be cordial. He was just being nice to me, like he would any hotel guest, right? "Perhaps later."

We kept walking in companionable silence towards the café. The same one where he found me bawling my eyes out after my immense failure. If I were him, I would be embarrassed of being seen walking with the likes of me.

He walked ahead a step or two and opened the door to the restaurant, and that stopped me in my tracks. Manuel was a nice guy, so, so charming that he even had Susana enamored, who looked over at him with heart eyes every time he spoke. But one thing he wasn't was attentive. He never opened doors for me, and he couldn't even recall minor details like how I took my coffee, despite the fact that he would see me prepare it every single morning, including weekends.

"Care to join me for lunch?" Santiago asked, immediately bringing me back to the real world. "No pressure though. I can already see a few people I know that I could join."

"Please join them. Don't miss out on catching up with your friends on my account. Like I said, I have my book," I responded, tapping lightly on the hardcover of the mystery novel I was reading. "I'm fine."

Santiago shrugged and waited for me to walk in. The place was really charming—it reminded me of the little corner cafés I'd frequented on my trips to Europe with Susana. There was a small marble table by the window, with direct visibility to the trailhead Santiago had mentioned earlier. I walked over and gave Santiago a small wave that he didn't even notice because he was already absorbed in conversation with someone sitting by the door. His laughter was everywhere, and his eyes gleamed with mirth. And he was *radiant.* I didn't think I would ever use such an expression to describe anyone, let alone this man who I *thought* I hated with all my might.

Ugh.

In the few moments it had taken me to walk over to my table, pick up the menu, and gather my thoughts, Santiago had sat down and was already eating a salad. When I said this man was everywhere, I meant it. He was—literally—everywhere.

———

"I see that you've decided to listen to me. That's a first," he said as he took a seat next to me on the bench.

"For the love of god, don't you have better things to do?" I looked at the sky—which had slowly started to fill up with white and gray clouds—trying to see if maybe this would help me get rid of him.

"As a matter of fact, I do. This is it," he replied, waggling his eyebrows.

We were at a small clearing called Eagle's Nest. After lunch and going over every word of the exchange I'd had with Santiago earlier for what seemed an unhealthy amount of time, I decided to accept his tour guide recommendation and head to the trail. I walked for about forty-five minutes and at that point, the trail split in two and a sign pointed towards this place, which dead-ended on a bench that overlooked the creek below. The clearing was small, fitting maybe a handful of people at a time, and the bench was old and worn. The initials *RAS* were carved on the back, and the spot was overgrown with native plants. At a distance, I could see the neighboring town, with houses built on the mountain slope, surrounded by lush trees that were slowly changing their leaves.

"When I'm in town, I come and sit here to gather my thoughts," he said casually, like we were the best of friends. "I made a habit out of it when I was a teenager, and it stuck. It's my favorite place in all of Tres Fuegos, and it brings back so many memories. I can't quit it," he added with a small laugh.

"It's so quiet here," I said without looking at him. I opened my mouth to say something else but decided against it. We weren't friends. Santiago didn't need to hear about my problems at all. I creased my forehead and looked down.

A worn trail could be seen carved on the side of the hill, leading to the riverbed below.

"You can say it, you know. I won't judge."

"It's nothing. I just... I see why you like it here."

There was a silence that followed the conversation, but it didn't feel uncomfortable. I could hear insects buzzing around us. The wind picked up speed, and my hair blew in every direction.

"My grandmother used to tell me about the man who put this bench here. He had moved to Tres Fuegos with basically the clothes off his back and always kept to himself. He was a serious man, apparently. And just as fast as he showed up, he was gone. He died in a fire in the home he was renting right next to my grandparents."

He squinted, trying to interpret my blank expression.

"And so you like it here because it reminds you of what, exactly?" I said as I glanced over at him. It took a moment, but he let out one of his big, happy laughs that had me biting my cheek to avoid smiling.

"You said it: it's quiet and peaceful and not many people visit because this man's story is so tragic, so I almost always have it for myself," he said quickly. "I come here because it reminds me that life as we know it can end in an instant; it's a good exercise to stop and think and focus when things are bad."

"Yes, life does have a tendency to screw you over when you least expect it." My eyes widened, and I closed my mouth as quickly as possible. I averted his eyes. *Don't go around telling him your problems, Victoria.* "Hmm, I'm actually on my way back to town. I have some things I want to do before dinner tonight, so I'll head out."

As I stood to leave, I saw how Santiago was looking at me. He gave me a once-over and then looked away, with a half-smile on his lips. One that I had never seen on him before.

This, how he was looking at me, was the complete opposite of how Manuel used to see me. Almost like I was invisible to him. Santiago's gaze was intentional, deliberate, and it made me wonder if he was up to something.

"Bye, Santiago."

8

THE PARTY

MANUEL WAS UNFAIRLY HANDSOME, but his mouth was out of this world. His smile was incredible, and his full lips looked soft and enticing. And his attitude was so attractive, I wondered many times if maybe it was contagious. He never cared about what people said or thought of him; he lived a carefree life. Maybe if I associated with him, I could start thinking the same thing, managing expectations and doing my best for myself.

That was what drew me to him at first. That and the mischief in his eyes. It was almost like he promised a good time while always respecting my boundaries and those of Susana. I clearly remember thinking that no man who looked like him and acted like that had a bad bone in their body.

But I was wrong. So, so wrong.

And what was also wrong? Me standing in front of

Santiago's family home, waiting for someone to come to the door. I was out of my depth, wearing a dress that might have been too formal for the occasion, or maybe not formal enough. I styled my hair in loose waves, something that I had almost never done because I could never get comfortable with the many tools and products needed to tame my locks. But the way he had looked at me earlier confused me. And then he had the nerve to call me and invite me to this get-together. I wasn't sure what I was feeling, but I *was* feeling.

I had gone back to the hotel in a huff. Angry at myself for letting him get under my skin while I was supposed to be grieving my nonexistent marriage that ended way too soon. As soon as I walked in the door, I noticed that I had a voice-mail on the room phone, the light flashing an angry red and matching my mood exactly.

"Hey, it's me," he said, assuming—*freaking correctly*—that I would recognize his voice. "Um, you left too quickly this afternoon, before I could mention that a few of my cousins are getting together tonight at my parents' house for a game night."

What? Is he inviting me over to his house?

"Um, anyways, I thought that maybe you might need a break from all your moping around. Just fair warning: it gets wild, but it's fun and a good distraction. Ask Julia at the front for directions to my house. It's almost a straight shot from the hotel. See you at nine."

So there I was, admiring what was possibly the largest

house in town. I couldn't see much, but it was clear to me that the property ended where the hills started. The landscape was crisp and impeccably maintained. The house was large, covered in brick and stone, a big contrast between this home and the other buildings in town. The circular driveway could fit multiple cars, way more than were parked there already.

I shifted my weight from foot to foot, nervously biting my lower lip. *What are you doing here? This is self-destruction, Victoria.* To add to my life's contradiction, I was officially "hanging out" with Santiago, like Cata had called it. On the one hand, my logic was screaming at me because I didn't have a good relationship with this man. On the other hand, my heart and my emotions were confused. Was it because I was a jumbled mess of feelings? So maybe I was grasping at anything I could hold on to.

Two stone steps led to the covered entryway, and the door was painted a very dark green—almost black and barely noticeable in the dark of the night. I could see a large entryway inside the house through a window immediately to the right of the door, and I could hear the laughter and the chaos coming from the back.

I rang the doorbell once more and waited. In a matter of seconds, I heard a series of quick steps, followed by a sharp and deep roar of laughter.

The door opened, and whoever was behind the door froze for a fraction of a second and then smiled such a familiar smile. His sister, I assumed. Her coloring was wrong

—she was blonde, and her skin was covered in freckles, but the eyes were the same.

"Hi, sorry, have you been waiting long? We couldn't hear the doorbell over the ruckus inside."

"Ah, no, just a few minutes. That's fine. I'm Victoria."

"Oh, I *know* who you are." She winked. "I'm Lucía, Santiago's sister. Come in, we're back in the sunroom."

Were they expecting *me?*

The inside was as magnificent as the outside. I was used to this—Susana's home was large and opulent—but this house looked lived in. It looked like people were happy here.

I followed Lucía as we made our way to the back of the house—assuming she was taking me to the sunroom. To the right of the entryway were a series of doors. Maybe a closet, a powder room, or an office? And immediately across from that, a large staircase that curved to the right and led to the upstairs. The banisters were painted white, and I could see the years of wear and tear already visible. This house looked *loved.*

"What are you doing in our small town? Santiago never mentioned you were planning to visit."

Does that man actively talk about me to people? I haven't seen him in years, yet it seems like everyone knows who I am.

"Um, it was a little unexpected, actually." I tried to smile, but I knew it looked stiff. Lucía turned to look at me, confusion in her face. "But I'm really enjoying myself. Santiago never told me it was so charming and picturesque."

She smiled and stopped at a double door, opening it and standing to the side to let me through. Immediately, all my senses were flooded. I could see and hear people laughing. I could smell the delicious food, probably coming from the kitchen to the left of this large family room. As soon as I stepped in the sunroom, Santiago turned, his megawatt smile hitting me right in the chest. If it weren't for the noisy room, everyone would have heard me gasp.

"Hey," he said, lifting one side of his mouth. "Glad you could make it. Would you like a drink?"

I could feel all eyes on me. The room suddenly went silent. The only sounds were the insects in the night outside and my heartbeat in my ears. I felt myself blush. *Get a freaking grip, Victoria. What in the actual fuck.*

"Hi. Yeah, thanks for having me," I answered in a rush. "I'll take that drink. Who are all these people?" I asked, just for him.

"Oh, um… just some cousins and whatever. Beer? Wine? I don't remember what your drink of choice is, actually," he said as he guided me to the kitchen, his hand on the small of my back.

"Wine is fine, thank you," I replied. "I'm actually not that much of a drinker."

Shut it down, immediately. Do not talk about yourself. Don't let him touch you.

"So is this where you grew up? It's a beautiful house," I asked, curiosity getting the best of me.

"This is my parents' house, yep. My grandparents live

right next door. My family owns the whole block, actually, so I grew up with all my cousins. It was like a permanent summer camp around here," he said, smiling wide, his eyes crinkling at the memory.

A few people walked in the kitchen through what looked to be a butler's pantry that led to a large dining room. The lights were dimmed in that room, but I could see a few shapes sitting around a huge table, and I could hear multiple conversations happening at the same time. The couple, who was probably in their late fifties, approached us, the woman smiling wide. The man to her side looked wildly familiar, his arm around her shoulders in a possessive yet loving grip.

"Hello. I'm Gabriela," the woman said, taking a step towards me. "I'm Santi's mom."

I *frowned.*

"Mom, Dad, this is Victoria," Santiago said at the same time as his mother kissed me in the cheek. I turned to Santiago, wide-eyed, and he *grinned*, like this was the funniest joke someone ever uttered.

"Hi," I said shyly. "You have a lovely home."

Get it fucking together.

"Thank you so much for coming, Victoria. We are glad you were able to join us after all," she added, her smile reaching her eyes. Her husband was moving behind her, reaching up to a tall cabinet above the refrigerator where they had a few bottles lying on their sides. "We're just going to grab a few bottles of wine to bring over to the table and get a drink for Granny."

As quickly as they came over, they left, taking three bottles of wine with them and heading back to where they came from. Santiago's father didn't say anything, just smiled at the interaction, going along with whatever his wife was doing.

I turned to face Santiago, who was busy opening a bottle of wine. I cleared my throat to call his attention, and a small smile formed on his lips.

"What the hell, Santiago! You said a few friends. Is this a family get-together?"

He had the nerve to laugh, tilting his head back and closing his eyes. "It's my grandmother's birthday party today. She turned eighty last week."

Puta madre. Shit. My eyes were locked on his, and I scowled. *But also, where is Clara?*

"If I had said it was my grandmother's birthday, you would have never shown up, so I regret nothing," he added, almost like he was reading my mind, and handed me a very full glass. He turned to face me completely, smiling wide. "*Vamos.* Let's go play some board games. But again, fair warning, this gets *wild*. They are complete savages."

It *was* wild, for sure. But most of all, it was such a welcoming atmosphere. Santiago didn't introduce me to anyone in particular, he just said "this is Victoria" to everyone, and that was about it. He sat by me the whole time, talking directly to me at times but also engaging with others in conversation. After a very violent round of *Uno*, the food was served in the dining room, buffet style. We all joined the "grown-ups" for the meal, the older people eating at the long table while the cousins held their plates on their hands and ate casually standing up.

The room was spectacular. In the middle, a long table that looked like it could easily fit twenty diners, surrounded by ornate chairs with embroidered seats. It most definitely looked like a family home where multiple generations still enjoyed its comforts. The walls were painted a bright orange and decorated with elaborate paintings of fruits and vegetables and some flowers here and there.

Santiago's grandmother sat at the head of the table, surrounded by her family. There wasn't a moment of silence all evening. Laughter floated in the air and was conjured up without a moment's notice.

It was so different to what I was used to, how I grew up. Our family home was remarkable, too, but our get-togethers were rigid, formal. Susana would sit at the head of the table, drink her tea, and ask pointed questions to everyone in attendance. It was almost like a panel interview, everyone silent until it was their turn, listening to what Susana had to ask and say. There was no laughter—we had learned how to tame that down early on. I had many cousins on my father's side, but nothing like the scene I witnessed now.

There was teasing and poking, a lot of banter and joking around. All these people had easy smiles for each other. It was mesmerizing to see. Santiago's grandmother was magnetic, exuding a calm presence while also commanding the room. She was the center of attention—it was her birthday, after all—but she also made everyone around her shine their own light. Lucía sat on the arm of her chair, her whole body leaning against the older woman's and a soft smile on her lips. Her grandmother rubbed her hand up and down her arm while engaged in conversation with a man sitting across from her. I could see, from where I stood at the back right by the kitchen, that everyone loved her, and she loved everyone back in the same way. *Is this what unconditional love looks like?*

This family, this home, was everything I thought I had but nothing like it. I had a big family—my father was one of seven children—so that meant I had my fair share of cousins. But this felt different. This felt like a place where no one had to bite their tongues to protect anyone's ego, where respect was a two-way street. No one had to choose honesty over loyalty; no one had to make decisions thinking about Susana's reaction.

"Do you like it?" Lucía said, moving her head left and right, showing a few women her hair. I slowed down my pace, surprised by the levity of it all. Her grandmother was smiling up at her, and one other woman ran her fingers through her long locks. "It was getting too long, so I got a haircut today. It makes it easier for work."

The women were looking at her with respect. There were no pointed comments, no criticism. Just a series of *oohs* and *ahhs* to convey support. It felt so natural, so honest and organic. So *different*.

"Can you guide me in the direction of the restroom, please?" I asked a man standing to my left.

"If you go out to the main hallway through that door," he said as he pointed to a hidden door at the other end of the dining room, "it's the second door on your right."

"Thank you," I replied and quickly made my exit from the dining area, emerging right at the entrance to the home through a hidden door that I hadn't seen on my way in.

I felt agitated, out of place. Once in the restroom, I tried to calm down. Because nothing of what I had seen resonated with my experience. It was night and day.

I needed to get out of there, fast. This wasn't a place for me. Santiago wasn't for me. I needed to shut this down, quick. My brain was getting confused because being kind and caring didn't equal love, right? Being kind was a basic human response, and just because Santiago and his family were being kind, didn't mean anything else.

As I walked out and headed towards the front door, my eyes caught something that was peeking out from a partially open door. I pushed my way in and found myself in a massive library, filled to the brim with books. The far wall had floor-to-ceiling shelves and a rolling library ladder to reach the highest of heights. The walls were covered in striped, burgundy-and-green wallpaper, with wood wainscoting on the bottom half. On the left was a gallery wall of photographs and what looked like newspaper clippings, identically framed and neatly arranged.

I made my way to the first frame: a photo of Santiago and his siblings as children, probably in the backyard of this home. He looked tiny compared to the man he was today, much more similar to his sister than now. That easy smile was plastered on his face though. I stopped and looked at a few more. A photo of what seemed to be Santiago's grandfather by a golf cart, club in hand, stopped me in my tracks. Right next to him, standing tall and looking as handsome as ever, was *my* grandfather. The man I'd never met. The man I would recognize from a mile away. His gaze was fixed on the photographer, and his eyes were sharp and dangerous. I would recognize that gaze anywhere because those same eyes looked back at me every morning. Those were my eyes too.

"There you are. You escaped me," Santiago said as he made his way to me with a glass of red wine in his hand. "I've been looking for you. Granny is about to blow out her candles," he added, with a small smile on his face.

"I just needed to use the restroom, and then I got side-tracked," I retorted, fixing my gaze on the door.

"Are you okay?" he asked as his forehead creased and a line appeared between his brows. He looked genuinely concerned for me. He lifted his free hand and after a second, pulled it back to his side, tucking it in one of his jean pockets. His eyes drifted to my lips and quickly returned back to my eyes.

"Where's Clara, by the way? I haven't seen her at all today, and I thought she was attending this party," I asked, quickly changing the subject and trying to contain the tears that were starting to form, a knot on my throat that I couldn't get rid of.

"Eh... She went back to the city. I'm glad you decided to come. You look beautiful," he added, a little surprised.

My nose crinkled. *What?* Goosebumps ran through my whole body, my spine stiffening in response.

"You know what? I'm just going to go. I'm out of place here. Please thank your parents for me, and thank you for inviting me."

I took one last quick look at that photo on the wall, like it was taunting me. My vision started to get blurry as tears filled my eyes. I blinked, and a few made their way out, running down my cheeks. I squeezed my eyes shut, willing everything to go away. *Maybe if you close your eyes this will all disappear?*

I felt Santiago's expression before I saw it. He studied me closely, almost like he was memorizing the scene. "What's happening to you? You can talk to me, Vee."

In a matter of days, my life had changed once already because of a photo, and now everything that I thought I ever knew about my family and my legacy was possibly a lie? How did I explain something like this to this man who had proven to be more attentive than everyone else in my family so far? Who seemed to really care about me—about everyone—but who I needed to keep at an arm's length because he didn't know me? *Why do these things keep happening to me?*

"I'm fine, just overwhelmed," I said. "I'm leaving." And I turned on my heels and ran through the door to the library, up the hallway, and out the front door, letting it slam behind me. I ran all the way to the hotel, climbed in bed, and sobbed like I'd never done in my life.

9

THE CONFESSION

I BLINKED. My eyes refused to focus, but I could see the red light from the hotel's phone flashing to my right. My body ached for no reason at all, except that my life had been consistently crumbling down. *When is this going to end?*

This seven-year ordeal started with a smile and a few stolen glances. Maybe an incorrect assumption on my part that what I was feeling was love and not just a new, flashy influx of attention.

I. Couldn't. Stop. Thinking. About. Him.

Santiago, not Manuel. *Why Santiago and not Manuel?*

Although I *should* be thinking about Manuel, definitely. I was careful and calculated and organized. I was intentional. Cool and collected, I guessed. Nothing really ruffled my feathers anymore. I planned every single step I had taken in the past decade.

And look where that got me. My relationship was over, finished in a second. Seven years, seven years of planning and wishing and dreaming and waiting—for what? For it to be over in one flash of a screen? I would never be able to get that time back. He took this time from me, and I'd never get it back. I screamed into the pillow until my throat was hoarse.

I was paralyzed. I didn't remember walking back to the hotel after leaving Santiago standing in the middle of that massive library. I couldn't remember if he followed me or yelled after me, but that flashing light on the room's phone told me something. He was the only one who could contact me this way, although I was sure he still had my cell phone number and could easily text.

What just happened?

My hands shook. My heart beat so hard it felt almost like I could hear it from outside my body. The image of my grandfather was burned in my brain, those stern, stoic eyes looking back at me as if he'd been physically in front of me. *Maybe it's your brain playing tricks on you again?*

I grabbed my phone and did the only thing I could think of at that time. I texted Catalina, hoping she would be awake to answer my call. My phone buzzed immediately with an incoming video call.

"Are you hiding in the bathroom?" I asked. Her hair was up in a messy bun, and she was wearing her pajama top.

"Agustín is sleeping. I'm glad you texted because I'm getting more and more pissed at him when he sleeps." She sat on the toilet and rubbed her belly absentmindedly. "I'm this close to waking him up and keeping him up. This pregnancy is making me unhinged."

I laughed. Catalina and my brother met at one of my birthday parties. I was already dating Manuel by that time, so my parties ended up being a bunch of his friends and my brother and Cata. They hit it off immediately, and within the year they were living together, much to my grandmother's chagrin. My brother was also an attorney but wasn't as committed as I was, which was fine. He lived life differently, and clearly it was working out for him.

"What happened?" She interrupted my thoughts. "Do you need me to come get you?"

"The weirdest thing," I said, trying to put my thoughts into words. I needed to speak to Susana, figure this out. Figure out the reasons why my grandfather was ever in this town. I didn't remember my grandmother ever talking about this town or even having any ties to the province. But in order to speak to Susana, I would have to answer questions that I didn't want to answer, questions I didn't have an answer to. "Santiag—"

"I knew it!" She grinned. "I knew you were hanging out. God, I love this for you."

"What are you talking about? There's nothing to love." I was lonely, and he was being kind. End of story. "He was just being nice, and he invited me over to his parents' house and... That's not the point."

"To his parents' house?" She scrunched up her nose. "You met his parents already?" She smiled playfully.

"Cata, stop." I laughed. "Anyway, I was snooping around and found an amazing library filled to the brim with books. Ugh, it made me so jealous. So I was looking around, and then I saw, hanging on a wall, a framed photograph of someone who could be Santiago's grandfather and guess who? Fucking Roberto. I swear to god, it was him. He looked almost identical to the photo of him that Susana has framed in the entryway."

"What?" She furrowed her eyebrows. "Your grandfather?"

I nodded. "Yes, standing right next to Santiago's grandfather. Like, what are the fucking odds?"

"Okay, I need a second to think," she said. She knew all the details of my grandfather's disappearance in the eighties. He was taken hostage for ransom; the hefty sum was paid, but he never came back. Thirty-some years later, it was obvious he wouldn't return, but he was still desperately loved and honored in our home. "I'll call you tomorrow." Catalina hung up the phone, probably to start investigating things immediately. She was obsessed with knowing everything, and my grandfather's story always piqued her interest. She was never able to find any information—it was like he just vanished off the face of the earth. Maybe I needed to approach this new information in steps, just like I had approached my life for the past fifteen years.

Yes, a plan.

First, sleep. Then, figure out what the hell was going on.

———

I tossed and turned all night, getting short periods of deep sleep that were interrupted by my brain running through all possible scenarios. As soon as I got off the phone with Cata, I checked my messages and was not pleasantly surprised to see that my grandmother was still calling me, leaving voice-mails, and texting me. Manuel was still missing in action, not a peep or sound from him.

Susana kept using the same accusatory tone—and she was partly right. I *did* walk away from the biggest step I was ever going to take, both for me and for my family. A union of two powerful people that represented more than just the illusion of a happy ending, but also the joining of two fami-lies that would have a lot of power. I knew this. Susana knew this.

But I had walked away without saying a word and found refuge in this small, charming town that was slowly teaching me how to let go.

Her latest voicemail kept repeating in my head: "If you don't come back immediately, you will deal with the consequences of my wrath. This is not a warning, *estás avisada.*"

You've been warned.

It was a threat. Definitely. And it angered me to no end that I never saw the red flags. Of anything. Not in my relationship with Manuel or in my relationship with Susana and the rest of my family.

I was resolved that I needed a plan. I needed to take steps to figure out what was happening to me, but being inside these walls was probably not helping me.

I went down the stairs to the hotel restaurant, asked the woman at the front for a coffee to go, and within fifteen minutes, I was making the short trek to Eagle's Nest to sit down and think. The morning was clear, the sun was shining, and there was a sole cloud in the sky, drifting slowly away from the town and into the mountains. I could see, very far in the horizon, a set of dark gray clouds.

So for the second time in as many days, I found myself at Santiago's clearing, *his* space, where he used to go to clear his head when things were bad. *Think about next steps and think about figuring things out. Don't think about him.*

A few things were clear by this point: my relationship with Manuel was over, no doubt. He hadn't contacted me at all, but Cata mentioned that he was playing the worried part back at home. This couldn't be saved, and maybe I was okay with that. But I still needed some peace of mind, knowing that leaving was the right thing to do.

Smart women don't believe the words people say. They believe the actions they see.

And the actions I saw were none. No actions at all. It was like he wanted to get out of our marriage and ran at the first chance he got. Maybe I wanted that, too, since I ran at the first chance I got?

And then there was Susana. And my grandfather. And my family. How would I deal with that? Because I couldn't just walk away from my family. Susana sacrificed her life after her children were out of the house to raise my brother and me. Dedicated her life to us. And she never had it easy.

After my grandfather was taken in the eighties, she had to figure out how to live without him. They were wealthy, well-off, so she was taken care of. Her group of friends supported her. It was such a tragic situation that everyone came out to help her. She had been—still was—respected by society and had Pedro walking with her every step of the way. He was like a grandfather—the one we never had.

And Susana really sacrificed it all. She loved my grandfather; his disappearance was hard on her in more ways than one. She was never able to replace him. I always thought that deep in her heart, she believed he was alive somewhere. Sometime in the nineties, there was a rumor going around that he was seen in Mexico, but that was only a case of mistaken identity. That had the whole family hoping, something they hadn't done since his disappearance.

And then there was the photo. In Santiago's family home, of all places. Why was life trying to bring him close to me when I wanted to be miles away—maybe even in a different world than him?

"Victoria?" *Oh my god. Why?* I rolled my eyes as I turned around and saw him standing there with his arms on either side of his body, smiling. That easy, slow smile that gave the butterflies in my stomach an invitation to take flight. "Good morning," he added, his smile finally reaching his eyes.

"Seriously, I can't get away from you. It's like you have spies in this town that tell you where I am."

He hummed softly, a sparkle in his blue eyes.

"You know that I *am* from here, right?" he said as he scanned my face. "It's also a *very* small town. There are not many places you can go without running into people. *Pueblo chico, infierno grande.*" *Small town, big hell.* I wholeheartedly agreed.

I sighed, turning back to admire the view. The dark clouds were moving into town faster than what it looked like earlier that day. The wind picked up speed, and the trees across the way danced with urgency.

"You left quickly last night."

"Uh-huh." I looked down at my hands, my fingers moving nervously on my lap. I couldn't look him in the eye because I knew, without a shadow of a doubt, that I would tell him everything that was going on with me the minute his eyes were on mine.

Santiago was so different than what I was used to. He was happy. I had seen it all over town. I *thought* I was happy, but it was becoming clearer to me that the things I had—my relationship, my family, my memories—were superficial. A house of cards.

"Look at me. Stop avoiding me."

Goosebumps covered my back at his commanding attitude.

"I can't. It's too much, I think. I made a mistake, and I don't know how to fix it, and I'm humiliated and embarrassed and scared. Buried deep in a hole that I can't get myself out of. And now, apparently, I'm babbling to the last person that wants to hear about my mishaps."

"Why do you keep saying that, Vee? Isn't it obvious that I enjoy your company?"

Vee. He called me Vee again. No one ever called me that. A few people called me Vicky growing up, but Susana shut them down immediately, saying that nicknames were beneath us and that Vicky was such a *common* nickname. And we were anything but.

I couldn't look at him still, but I could hear him moving, his body heat occupying the space to my right.

"Why are you here, really? What happened to you?"

"Well... um..." I licked my lips. My throat was completely dry, and I could feel a knot forming. I swallowed, hard, but the knot didn't budge. If I said this out loud, it would automatically make it real. Could I maybe hold it in a little longer? Live in denial for maybe just a few more moments, making it real only in my head, only for me and my little universe of one.

My heart started beating fast. My pulse galloped, and sweat began collecting at the base of my neck. The hairs on the back of my head stood to attention. Santiago's eyes swept my body, top to bottom, stopping for a fraction of a second on my eyes, lingering there almost like he was pleading with me to tell him.

"Manuel cheated on me, I think. No, actually, I'm almost one hundred percent certain he did. So I ran away instead of facing that head-on." I buried my face in my hands, taking a deep breath, and kept going. "The morning of my wedding, I woke up to a text message from an unknown number. I thought it was a vendor that was most likely asking for last minute details and as soon as I opened it, I saw a photo of Manuel with a woman in bed—*my bed*. And, like, whatever, it could be anyone. Like, maybe it was doctored. But in the days I've been here, he's not contacted me once. Not a single call, no voicemail. I'm sorry, but *what?* What the fuck, Santiago, who does that? If he wanted an out, he could've talked to me. We are in our thirties; we're not kids anymore. We've been together for seven fucking years. Seven years of my life he just took from me, and I'm never getting them back. And honestly, I just want to laugh at this point. It sounds so ridiculous..." I breathed, realizing only then that I had just uttered the words without pause. "Sorry, I ju—I feel like an idiot. No, I *am* an idiot because I let this happen to me. How did I let this happen? How did I even—"

"Stop." He turned, bending his left leg and setting it on the seat. His whole body was now facing me. He moved his hands a millimeter, almost like he was trying to reach out for mine, but then placed his left hand on the back of the bench, his right one playing with his shoelaces. "Stop it, immediately. You are no idiot, you know that. Everybody that knows you, even for a minute, knows that, so stop. You calling yourself names changes nothing. So let's move on from there." He expelled a breath and looked to the left. "Who sent you that photo? Do you have any idea?"

All I could do was shake my head. My face was still buried in my hands because I was embarrassed, so deeply embarrassed.

"What do you want? Look at me," he said as I turned my head to look into those eyes. His expression was serious. "What do you need from me? I'll make it happen."

Honestly, I didn't even know because this was only, like, half of my problems right now. I hadn't even told him about what I saw in his family's home. I wasn't sure I wanted to know what was going on there.

"Tell me about your cases right now. I need a distraction. I think I need to figure this out on my own."

He sighed a loud sigh. "Not something that I want to talk about right now, actually," he added as he looked up at the sky, like he was trying to figure out where the clouds were coming from. "Do you want to know something that I've never told anyone?"

My ears perked up, not because of this strange admission and immediate intimacy, but because he had, so far, seemed so transparent, like he had never kept a secret. My eyes went wide, and I immediately scrunched my face.

"Uh... sure? I mean, do you trust me with such an important secret?" I winced as soon as those words left my mouth, and I tried to hide it with an awkward smile. Maybe he was only telling me this because I had been vulnerable with him? Like a secret for a secret.

He turned to look at me and cleared his throat.

"Well, believe it or not, I don't like being a lawyer," he said, like he was spilling this deep, dark secret that would change the world. "I guess I just got swept into my family's legacy. I don't know if I'm able to name a person in my family that hasn't been a lawyer, except for maybe my sister, but my dad and his dad and *his* dad before them... every single one of them has been a lawyer. And I... I just do it because I'm good at it, but it doesn't mean I enjoy it. Remember when we started college? The plan had always been to graduate and then move back here and start working at my family's firm—it's small and only handles a few things like divorces and estate management and whatever. But I couldn't envision myself here. So I told my dad and grandfather that I would stay in the city for a few years to get more experience and then come back, and I've been stuck. And then I look at you, and you make it look effortless and I..." He sighed. *What?* "I'm too far in to tell my family that I want out, but not only that, I have no idea what I want to do. Like, what does a former lawyer do if they are tired of the professional path *they* chose?"

Stunned. That was what I was. My mouth was open, gawking at him like, in fact, this deep, dark secret would change the world.

"I'm sorry, what?" I shrieked, my voice pitchier than what I was trying to go for. "But you're *good*. Like, good, good. Great even. Your name pops up everywhere I go. I'm so confused."

He laughed. One of those deep, throaty laughs that made everything inside me vibrate with energy.

"Yeah, but being good is not enough sometimes. Being selfless is not enough. Sometimes we also have to think about what we actually want and put that above all else."

Huh.

10

SUSANA (1988)

"Aʏ, Susana, *que terrible noticia*. How are you handling this?"

Such terrible news.

Of course it was terrible news. But rumors in this town ran fast, and many of the people in our social circles had shown up in support. Exactly like planned.

It was rare that I opened the door to our house—the staff usually took care of that—but in this case, it seemed fitting. I welcomed these ladies into my home and invited them to mourn with me. We grieved together.

"Thank you very much for coming, Josefina," I said as I closed the door behind her. She was wearing all black, almost as if she were attending a funeral. Her expression was grim, and she scanned the room as she moved further into the home. "It's been difficult, certainly, but our friends and family have really been here to support me."

We walked in silence toward the sitting area. There was a group of approximately twenty wives of our friends already in our living and dining rooms, sipping tea and eating little treats the maid put out. Groups had been coming and going for the past weeks, concerned for the well-being of my husband and obviously there to support me. The air felt tense—I wanted to treat the impromptu get-togethers like our normal gossip time, but I had been restraining myself to save face, of course. Staying in character proved to be hard, even when I'd done it in some way or another throughout my life.

"Have you heard anything?" Josefina said. She sat furthest away from me and set her purse on the floor. She then placed a cloth napkin on her lap and looked at me with pity in her eyes. "I can't imagine what you are going through."

"Nothing since that first time, but we are still hopeful, as you can imagine," I replied. It had been four weeks since my husband willingly walked away, but these women were still convinced he had been kidnapped. "It feels like I haven't slept in weeks. So much waiting."

On this day, the group of ladies organized a prayer circle, led by Marta, who spent a significant amount of her free time volunteering at the church and went to mass every day. I couldn't really imagine what praying could do to help me, but it was serving well to keep up with appearances, and it was definitely in line with the narrative I was trying to sell.

"They said not to contact the police, and we haven't yet,

but I'm sure Pedro will connect with his contact if we don't hear soon." They all knew Pedro to be a fixer, finding solutions to problems everywhere. Whether it be additional funds needed to reach a fundraising goal or even if an event was running low on food, he was the first one to take action. "Although I'm terrified, it could affect our chances of getting him back."

Pedro was not convinced of what we were doing. He agreed, yes, during our intimate moment the days after my husband left, but since then he took some distance; he was sure the lie would come back to bite us. So far, there had been no signs of Roberto.

"*¿Mamá?*" I heard my son scream from the entry, followed by a sharp slam to the door. "*¿Dónde estás?*"

"Ah, Robertito," I replied, my most saccharine smile pasted on my face. He deadpanned at the nickname; we hadn't called him that in years. "What a pleasant surprise," I added, standing up and expecting him to bend down to kiss my cheek. He looked so much like his father. The stern, stoic look was uncanny. His eyes were brown, after me, but everything else seemed to be his father's. Including his name.

"You're not canceling the party?" he said, his voice raising with every word he uttered. "What is wrong with you?"

"Roberto." I widened my eyes, looking around at the women in my home. They were frozen in place. "*Por favor,* keep it down," I said with a smile plastered on my face and for his ears only. "Of course we are not canceling the party. Your poor sister."

My youngest daughter was engaged to be married, and we had been planning her engagement party for months. Her father's disappearance was a surprise, of course, so I had decided to move on with the plan despite his absence. My husband very well knew what he would be missing out on when he walked away from me. "We've all been through so much recently, and we need a little happiness. There is nothing better than to celebrate love, don't you think?"

My son turned around and walked out of the dining room where I was sitting. My friends were still silent, looking stunned and speechless at the scene in front of them.

"*Discúlpenme. Ya vengo*," I said to them with a small smile on my face.

I followed him as he went up the stairs, straight to Cristina's bedroom. She was lying on the bed reading one of the many magazines I received on a weekly basis. Her name had been in the media recently, the announcement of her wedding a big deal.

"Cristina, tell her," he said without looking at me. Cristina sat up and sighed, then looked at me. She was beautiful, probably the prettiest of all my daughters. She had her father's eyes, a light blue that looked almost translucent in certain lights. Her pupils were rimmed with silver threads that made her eyes look gray when it was overcast. Her skin was white with a rosy undertone and when she blushed, she looked like a doll. Her hair was long and blonde after years of perfecting her color at the salon.

"Roberto, I already told her, but she's not listening," she said. Cristina was the most distraught of all my children. She had taken her father's disappearance badly and had been adamant we cancel the party.

"You are both being ungrateful, spoiled children," I said. My temper rose with every word uttered, and I ran the risk of losing control any second. "Why would you not want to celebrate in a moment like this? It's the least we can do."

"Mom, what are people going to say?" she said as she rested her back on the headboard. "This is ridiculous. It's not the time for this."

"Cristina, *por favor, no digas estupideces.*" Don't say stupid things. "It is exactly because I think about what people will say that we're having the party. This is the end of this discussion."

"*Mamá,*" Roberto yelled. "What is wrong with you? Papá, *your husband*, is missing, and you are pretending to live life as if he were still here. I don't understand."

"Keep your voices down," I said as I turned to leave. I walked out of my daughter's room and took a deep breath, trying to control my emotions. It was a bold move, I was aware of that, but life had to move on, and we couldn't look weak. This had already been dubbed the wedding of the year by one of the magazines, and the title was too coveted to let it go so easily.

I went back down the stairs, and Pedro was waiting in

the entryway. He had been distant, but as soon as he saw me, his eyes lit up. I knew Pedro was in love with me the first time we had a dance at his school. Pedro was handsome, with broad shoulders and a full head of hair that was constantly untamed. He went to the all-boys school close to our homes, so he walked us to our school every morning and then back in the afternoon until he went to university. Our relationship was easy, playful even. For the longest time, I even believed I would marry him.

It was easy.

Growing up, I'd known I wasn't the most attractive girl, but I thought I made up for that with my wit and my charm. I knew that I was smart because I was able to really get what I wanted. Every. Single. Time. Some would say I was manipulative. I said I was smart. I had always been able to read into situations and use them to my advantage, to my benefit. To this day, that was most likely one of the only traits that remained from my teenage years: the determination to grow and climb up. Develop, if you will.

"What's going on?" he said, looking concerned. "What are they going on about?"

"They are ganging up on me," I said, walking straight to him. I stood on my toes and stretched up to him, kissing his cheek. He grabbed my waist and pulled me to him, taking a deep breath and inhaling my scent. We stood there for a minute, neither of us willing to move.

"*Ya se les va a pasar,*" he said. They'll get over it. I didn't think it would be as easy as that, but I always managed to get what I wanted. I took a step back, then looked at him. He looked tired; his hair was a mess. I couldn't remember ever seeing him like this, so affected. He always kept his composure, even during the most trying times. "Be patient."

He smiled at me, a sweet, shy smile, then kissed the top of my head. If I were a weaker woman, I would melt. But I needed to take care of things, so I took a step back and turned, heading to the dining room.

"The ladies are here," I said over my shoulder and left him standing there, looking at me with that longing in his eyes that I'd only seen a handful of times before.

11

THE OTHER ONE

Santiago's overwhelming presence was aggravating me, but at the same time, it was so calming and peaceful that my brain was jumbled. I had never, ever been jumbled.

My goals had always been clear to me. Calculated and intentional, in every single thing I did. It was taught in our home, and it was what was expected of me, always.

But suddenly, the circumstances that were trailing me exceeded me.

"Cata," I answered, my phone propped up against a vase on the small dining table in my room. I had been mindlessly scrolling on my phone for hours, not paying close attention to anything in particular. In that period of time, I found out that two girls from college were having babies and another one was getting married. "What's up?"

"Okay, so I have to tell you something, but I need you to

promise me to stay calm." She looked straight into my eyes, and even through the phone screen, I could see her concern.

"Cata, what could be worse than everything that's happened to me in the past ten days?" My shoulders sagged, and I tilted my head, waiting for her to say whatever was on her mind. I could hear rain pelting down against the bedroom window. The morning had been gloomy, perfect reading weather, and as the afternoon progressed, so did the storm.

"Manuel is in Australia," she said quickly. "Your brother confirmed it today."

"What?" I blinked. "On my trip?"

"Yes," she said. "He's not alone."

"Who is she?" It was the first thing that came out of my mouth, but I didn't want to know. I shook my head and lifted my hand to stop her. "No, I don't want to know."

Manuel and I had courted under the watchful eye of Susana. From the beginning, we were complete opposites: he was a man of many, many friends, and I was a loner who preferred to spend time with her family and had, quite literally, one friend. He was well connected—both of us were—both because of his family name and because of his profession at a creative agency, where he bumped elbows with the city's elite.

He loved going to a brewery close to our shared apartment, even after I repeatedly told him that I didn't like beer. That was where he took me for our first date.

"I don't think we know her," she said, knowing that I

would still want more information. "I think it might be someone from work or work adjacent."

"What does that mean?"

"Like, acquaintances with someone from work, maybe a sister or best friend of someone from work?" It didn't matter. "It doesn't matter really."

"So I guess I'm not the only one who runs away when the situation doesn't suit her," I said, scrunching my nose at the thought of comparing myself to Manuel. "What a fucking coward."

"Who, him or you?" She stuck her tongue out and laughed.

"Where did I go wrong?" I was defeated at this point. My life was on fire, burning rapidly from the inside out. Catalina was impulsive, passionate. And she never had a plan, but always had something to do. Was that why everything was working out for her? "Was I so blind that I didn't see the red flags?"

"Victoria." She sighed. "This isn't on you, you know?"

"Yeah, okay, let's pretend that for a minute," I said. "How did I let this happen?"

"You didn't let anything happen, Victoria, it just did," she replied. "And I don't think there's a right answer here. You know I love you with all that I have because you gave me the things I love the most in my life, but also it takes two to tango, you know? I think we take many things for granted, in general, and it's easy for things not to work out in the long run. I mean, seven years is a long time."

She smiled a small smile, her eyes soft.

"I don't need your pity too," I said, knowing well there was no pity in her eyes, only concern. "I get plenty here."

"Bitch, please," she said, and I laughed in response. "Pity? Fuck you. How's Santiago doing?"

I pursed my lips. "I don't know, I haven't seen him in a while," I replied. And it was true, for the most part. I felt his presence everywhere, but I was purposely avoiding him. "Do you think I should call Manuel? Get some closure?"

"Oh, for sure, but also you need to fucking rip him a new one, pardon my French." I laughed so hard that I snorted. I could hear thunder rumbling in the skies beyond the town. The evening was getting darker and darker, and the streets were empty. The life that had been so characteristic of this town was nowhere to be seen. "I don't know where he gets off going on that honeymoon without you *and* with another woman. I don't think Susana knows."

"Ugh, don't even go there." But I did wonder how Susana would react when she found out that her precious golden child had cheated and then fled the country. "She'll take his side for sure. Tell me I did something wrong, that I'm to blame because I can't hold on to a man or something."

Cata laughed and then stood up. "Would you forgive him?" she asked on her way to the kitchen. She dropped the phone on a flat surface, the camera looking up into the ceiling of the room.

"That's a no from me," I replied. "I stop at cheating."

"Oh, speaking of cheating..." She was back in front of the camera and looking as giddy as ever. "Guess what?"

"What now? I mean what el—"

"Santiago broke up with his girlfriend." She grinned and closed her eyes in slow motion, giving me time for that to sink in.

"Why are you so happy?"

"I just think it's awfully convenient, don't you?" Her eyes were shining. "You show up back into his life after ten years and suddenly—what?"

"Suddenly what?" I cocked my head. "There's nothing going on."

"Yeah, okay." She sighed dramatically. "He's always had a thing for you."

"Whose side are you on, traitor?" I smiled at her.

"Yours! Always yours! But that boy used to be so handsome, and if he's looking the same after ten years, then he must be delicious now."

"He looks better," I blurted and immediately regretted it. But there was nothing I could hide from my best friend. A few weeks after we met, we were inseparable. Catalina was a first-generation college student, and her parents weren't able to help her navigate the new experience. For me, college was a chance to reinvent myself away from Susana. Up until that point, my life had been controlled. My friends and acquaintances were the same people that I saw on the weekend and at events, the children of our family friends, well within an established and approved social circle. Cata was a breath of fresh air, impulsive and out of control but extremely caring and loyal.

"I'm so jealous."

"Does my brother know you're ogling other men?" I grinned.

"Absolutely not, and you won't tell him."

"*Te quiero*," I said.

"I love you too. Talk soon." And with that, she was gone.

The phone in my room rang a few times. I rushed to pick it up, expecting Santiago on the other end. "Hello?" I answered with caution. He was probably going to ask me to lunch or something like that.

"Victoria? It's Lucía, Santi's sister."

"Oh, hey," I said, confusion in my voice.

"Do you want to have dinner with me downstairs?" she flat out asked me. Maybe it was a family thing. Maybe they were the official town ambassadors, and they were supposed to welcome everyone like this.

"Uh, sure? Now?"

She laughed. Her laughter was so similar to Santiago's. I could almost picture her, her head tossed back and her eyes closed. "Yes, now."

"Okay, I'll be down in a minute."

Lucía waited for me at the bottom of the stairs. Her hair was down, a little wet from the rain. She frowned at her phone, but the moment she saw me, she put it away and smiled at me.

"I didn't know you were still here," she said. "Julia told me earlier today. I just got off work, so excuse the way I look."

I smiled at her, but I had a feeling it looked stiffer than what I was intending. The people in this town were too friendly, and I was out of practice with my smiles. I didn't grow up with tons of friends, but I did have my cousins. It was easy—I would see them at school during the week, and we played well together at recess and then again on the weekends. Thinking back, I would say they were more like playmates rather than friends, but they were built into our family dynamics, and it worked. I had Susana—I could consider her my friend, my best friend, even at some points —my family, my cousins. Manuel. Cata. That was it. So this friendliness was weird. Uncomfortable? *Unexpected.*

We walked straight to the back of the restaurant and sat in a booth by the kitchen door. I noticed in the few weeks I'd been here that the regular customers sat towards the far wall, leaving open space at the front for tourists. It was the off-season by now, but the locals still did it.

Lucía dropped her things on the bench right next to her and scooted inside. I sat across from her, copying her movements.

"Are you having fun?" She grabbed the menu and started looking at it absentmindedly. She scanned the room, probably looking for the waitress, and then put the menu back on the table. "Our town is small and there's not much to do in the off-season, but I bet Santiago's been showing you some of our prime hangouts." She laughed. "When do you leave?"

"I don't know yet," I said honestly. Because I still had to make a plan. So far, I floated in a cloud of numbness, trying to get my thoughts in order. But I was working towards making a plan—taking baby steps to figure out what was going on with my life. Certainly, trying to figure out what was happening with my grandfather would inch me closer towards closure—of at least one thing. Would that open a can of worms? Absolutely. And I was ill-prepared to clean it up.

"Still trying to figure some things out. I took two months off of work, so I still have some time," I added, without going into any detail. I wasn't sure how much Santiago had shared with her, and this wasn't the appropriate time to tell her my little sob story. "I heard you're the town's pediatrician?"

Her face lit up with pride, and she smiled. Those siblings all had the same smile, and I could definitely see the resemblance now. She took after her mom, her skin white and her eyes a light blue. "Yep, only one in the family who deviated from the plan. Although, you know, it's not like I chose to do something 'easy' compared to law. I just paved my own way." She smiled. "I think the only reason I got away with it is because I'm the only girl, and as my brothers love to say, I have our dad wrapped around my finger." She laughed, a deep, comfortable laugh. It made me smile, how it seemed she didn't take anything too seriously.

"She's great at what she does," said the waitress, who was standing right next to us, ready to take our order. "Everyone loves her. She even has some grown-up patients because they refuse to see another doctor."

"Nonsense," she said and then looked at me. "Really, it's either me or Dr. Martin, and we all know he's past due for retirement, so some of the younger patients are more comfortable with me."

The waitress took our orders and left, going through the kitchen doors to the back of the house. I ordered the pasta; I had been ordering the same three things since my arrival and wasn't ready to try something new. Too many new things in the past few weeks left me craving routine.

We engaged in some small talk, Lucía telling me how she went to med school in the city but came back to town as soon as she'd finished her residency because she couldn't stay away for too long. It made it seem like this town had everyone hooked, like they were all addicted to it, and no one could stay away for long.

"He was the broodiest, grumpiest teenager," she said, rolling her eyes with a huge smile on her face. "He was always going to that bench in the clearing. I assume he's taken you there?"

I nodded, not knowing where this was going.

"He doesn't know this," she said, looking at me with mischievous eyes, "but I caught him sneaking out of the house so many times the summer before he left for the city. We had a really strict curfew, and he broke it every single night that summer."

"Did he party a lot? I can see that for sure."

She laughed. "No, he hated parties. He just went to that bench and sulked."

I smiled. I couldn't contain it this time. Just the idea of Santiago sneaking out of his house to clear his head made my stomach flutter. Lucía narrowed her eyes at me, searching my face for something.

"What's going on there?" she said. The corner of her lips ticked up, but she relaxed her face immediately. I pursed my lips—I knew exactly what she meant but wanted to play coy. I wasn't even clear on what I felt; I couldn't tell a virtual stranger what was happening.

"I don't know what you mean," I said after a moment. She didn't buy it at all. Instead, she smiled and planted her hands on the tabletop.

"Did you know that he broke up with Clara?"

Shit.

"What? She was here last week. I saw her," I answered too quickly.

"She was supposed to stay for Granny's birthday, but she didn't show up. Instead, he invited you. Weird, huh?" She smiled, then hid her lips, like she was trying to stop herself.

"So weird," I said, avoiding her gaze.

"He was also supposed to leave yesterday. This is the

first time in *years* that he's stayed more than what was necessary. Usually, he leaves the day after whatever function we have going on," she added. "Oh! Maybe he's avoiding Clara? I mean, they did live together, so he's giving her time to move out or whatever? Yeah, that makes sense."

She was talking to herself now, going through all these scenarios out loud. My head was clouded with thoughts of Santiago, the way he treated me, my reaction to him.

"Actually, it's getting late, and I have to finish up some things in my room. Do you mind if I take a rain check on dessert?" I said.

Lucía stood up at the same time as me and hugged me. A comfortable, cozy hug. A hug that felt like we had been friends for years.

12

THE OTHER CONFESSION

As soon as I heard the knock, I immediately knew who it was. Life had a stupid tendency to take me back to a place I never wanted to be, like it was making fun of me for the choices I'd made.

"Hey," he said, his arms crossed over his chest. He was leaning on the wall across the hall from my door, his hair still damp from a shower. Santiago's mouth turned up in a smile, a smile so genuine that it crinkled his eyes. His eyes, normally a deep blue, looked lighter today, like they were lit from within. "I just wanted to make sure you were okay. I haven't seen you in a while and the last time we actually spoke, you ran away."

This infuriatingly considerate man. Why couldn't he just ignore me and pretend like I didn't exist? I knew I had been doing that for the better part of a decade—not just to him, but basically to anyone that wasn't my family or Manuel or Cata.

"Why are you here, Santiago? I want to think I've made it pretty clear that I'm doing alright with my book and my own self. You don't need to follow me like a puppy," I said, immediately regretting my tone. For the past few days, he had shown me that he was, indeed, concerned for me. "I don't need your pity, thank you very much."

He sighed, the longest sigh I'd heard from him, his brow creasing in confusion. "Vee?" he asked. "Are you okay?"

And that was all it took for me to break down, for the tears to start running down my cheeks, giant blobs of water that wouldn't stop. I furiously swiped them with the back of my hands, embarrassed at how vulnerable I was around him. I nodded, then hid my face behind my hair and covered my eyes with the back of my hand. I felt so uncomfortable, the thoughts running in my head, all while trying to keep my composure in front of this man who was decidedly not my friend.

I felt his large arms wrap around me before I could even hear him move. His right hand went straight to the back of my head, pushing down ever so gently so that my head rested on his broad chest. His left hand trailed up and down my back in a move so intimate and tender that my heart fluttered. "You can tell me, you know? You don't need to hold it in. Can I help with anything?"

The tears eventually stopped. Maybe it had been ten minutes, maybe two hours, but he held me the whole time, in silence and swaying slowly to the beat of a silent song. I took a deep breath and a step back. "I'm sorry, I don't know what's wrong with me. I'm not normally like this," I said apologetically.

Santiago's face contorted with what I could only assume was anger mixed with confusion.

"What? I'm sorry, I don't want to trouble you with whatever is weighing me down. You've been really nice, and this is how I repay you." I huffed a sad laugh, and the corners of my mouth lifted in a pathetic attempt at a smile. "Thank you, I'm okay."

"What can I do? Put me to work, anything. Even getting you food, going for a walk? Let's go for a walk."

"No, I'm good. I'm just going to stay here and fight with my thoughts. I'll probably go back to the city soon. I've created enough of a mess as it is, and I need to go clean it up."

"Seriously, Victoria? What mess did you create? Manuel cheated on you. I think that's enough to want to get away from, don't you?"

But it wasn't just that. It was much more than that that had me paralyzed in this hell of a town. It wasn't that simple; it wasn't simple at all.

"It's not that simple, Santiago. And you're just saying that because you have everything you want and need." I looked at his face, his features softening as the words kept coming out of my mouth. *What is wrong with you? Stop talking.* "A really great career, an amazing family to rely on, a gorgeous girlfriend. I'm just a sad, pathetic nothing that ended up in a town in the middle of nowhere because she's not strong enough to stand up to her grandmother and tell her she's not marrying her cheating fiancé. How is that for pathetic?"

"Self-deprecating looks ugly on you," he said, taking a step back and sitting on the bed. "Why do you care what everyone else thinks of you? You should be doing what *you* love, not whatever anyone else—your grandmother or your friends or your fiancé or whoever—thinks you should be doing. I understand mandate, believe me, I do, but that doesn't mean you have to follow the path that's been presented to you."

"It's not really like that. Remember how I talked about my grandfather? I told you he was a reader and I kind of inherited that. Well, he's been this larger-than-life presence in my life. He disappeared, was kidnapped in the eighties, and never returned. And our lives, our collective lives, were never the same. He was a lawyer, so naturally I was encouraged to follow that path. He was a reader, I'm a reader. He was a serious man, focused on his family and his career, and I want to think I'm similar, but everything that is happening around me is like... I don't know. It's like my life is a house of cards and suddenly the wind is blowing a little bit harder, and the whole house is swaying dangerously." I took a giant breath, almost relieved to be letting go of this. "And then this whole thing with Manuel exploded in my face, and then I see that picture in your family's home, and it's too much.

My life is burning around me, and I don't know how to put the fire out."

"What picture? What are you talking about?" he asked curiously. I sat right next to him on the bed, his eyes searching for answers on my face. The sounds of the night could be heard even through the closed windows. People on the street laughing and enjoying themselves, having fun. Carefree. Like the weight of the world was solely on me.

"That's the reason I ran away the other night... Seems like it's a pattern with me," I said, looking out the window and wishing that life were different. "You know, your family was so nice the other night, and I was having a really good time. And then when I went to the library, I just wanted to take a peek at all those shelves and the many books your parents have there, maybe even borrow one to keep me company. Anyway... I walked in, and there were a bunch of photos hanging on the wall, and in one of them, your grandfather is standing right next to mine. Which is, like, the strangest thing because my grandfather disappeared, and why would he have ties to this town, but also *what*? I'm sure, almost one hundred percent certain, that man is my grandfather. I have his eyes, you know? And the house of cards rocked a little harder and the wind blew a little stronger and I just don't know what to do. It's too much."

"Wow" was his only response. He kept searching my face in complete silence. Like he was thinking thoroughly about what he would say next. "Okay, let's go."

"Where?"

"C'mon." He held out his hand and as soon as I stretched mine towards him, he locked our fingers together and dragged me out the door.

———

Of course we were at his clearing. It was dark out, the night warm. I wondered how many times this man had been here because he guided me through the dark and knew every single dip and turn of the way.

"There was one summer I came here almost every night," he said, like he was reading my mind. *Did I say that out loud?* "You did say that out loud."

I felt myself blush, something that hadn't happened to me since my early teens. This man was confusing me, making me *feel.* I was suddenly thankful for the darkness.

"I had a lot on my mind right after finishing high school and before I moved to the city, and I couldn't sleep. So I just sat on this bench for hours until my eyelids felt heavy."

"What was on your mind?" It was only fair he share his mind with me, given that I had really blabbed—a lot —earlier.

"I just… I wasn't sure that moving was the right choice for me. As you can see, our family is really close-knit. And, you know, at eighteen, I thought I had the world at my fingertips, but really it was just so much." He sighed. "It worked out, I guess."

I couldn't read his expression in the dark, but his voice

sounded rough, heavy. Like something was really weighing on him. He had a smile on his face, but it was sad, almost pained.

"Did I ever tell you that I almost didn't show up for our first day? I think it was, like, History 101 or something like that in that giant lecture room at the end of the hallway, and it was raining, and I just wanted to go home so bad. I never felt more defeated or like a child that day. I hated, hated college."

I turned to face him, confusion all over my face. "What are you talking about? You were born for this."

"Exactly," he huffed. "You're not the only one that's weighed by their choices, I guess. I don't enjoy it, but I do it anyway. I feel useful being a lawyer, helping others. Although I'm not sure if this is what I would have chosen for myself."

Back in college, Santiago moved comfortably, like a fish in water. He was always so thoughtful about anything and everything. I would have never guessed his chosen career was something he wasn't passionate about.

"Why do you do it then?" I asked. "It seems to me that your family would support you no matter what, right?" And that was the biggest contrast with my family—Susana would shun me, I guessed, if I ever went against her wishes. Or maybe not explicit wishes but *suggestions*. Becoming a lawyer, getting married, working for my family's firm. That was my given path, and I was supposed to take it.

"I don't know. It's not that easy. I guess I just got

dragged into it, and now it might be too late to switch careers."

"Santiago, I—"

"Vee, what do you want to do about this picture you mentioned? We can go to my grandparents and ask them about it. I know some people in the municipality that maybe can help us with some of the town records. See if we can figure this out."

"You know, I'm just so confused about this whole thing. Because I'm sure it's my grandfather, but what does that mean? I think eventually my grandmother gave up looking for him, but should I get my hopes up that he's still alive? I wouldn't even know where to start. If he *is* alive, where? And what happened? And how do I even approach it? I'm terrified of calling Susana and asking her, of even mentioning this to her. From what I know, it was such a painful time for her and my father and his sisters. Like, is it even worth it to try to find some answers?"

"In the time that I've known you, I've never seen you shy away from a challenge. Why now?"

The night was getting colder, but the silence was a welcome sound. Santiago sat there, with his head tilted up to the sky, giving me the space I needed to think. So far, he had shown so much respect to me, something that I wasn't used to. This was a new Santiago—friendly and warm and welcoming. His embrace lingered on my skin, my arms still tingling from the moment we'd shared at my hotel room hours earlier.

The sky was littered with sparkling stars. The dark blue, almost black background made the white lights shine. I couldn't remember the last time I saw such a bright sky, even in the dead of night. Maybe this town was, in fact, heaven on earth, instead of my personal hell. And I just needed to change my outlook.

"Okay, let's go to your grandparents'."

13

THE BACKGROUND

THE NEXT FEW days went by in a blur. My phone was still off, but my brain wasn't. Santiago had called me a few times directly to my room phone to tell me that he made an appointment with the clerk at the records office, so we were set to go see them that afternoon. I had tried (but failed) to find any information relating to my grandfather on the internet. He disappeared in the eighties, so of course there wasn't any information online, but it was surprising to me that there weren't even mentions of him in articles anywhere.

The son of a well-known businessman in the country had also been kidnapped, and even thirty years later, there were articles about that online. If my grandfather was the man Susana told me he was, why wasn't there any information about him?

I was still lounging in my pajamas when there was a

knock at the door. I knew it was him because he was the only person I had any contact with here, with the exception of his sister and those at the hotel that served my meals or cleaned my room.

So I made my way to the door and opened it. His permanent smile was plastered on, and his hair was tousled, like he had nervously run his fingers through it all morning long.

"Oh, wait, it's noon already?" I asked nonchalantly.

"No, sorry, I just couldn't wait. Want to get an early lunch?"

"Um, alright, give me a minute."

I closed the door on him and made my way to the dresser, thinking about the way Santiago's smile made me feel. The way he had been looking at me the last few days made me feel *alive*. I should be mourning the end of my relationship with Manuel, but instead I was thinking about how fast my heart beat when I was with Santiago, how his gaze tortured my dreams, how his mouth lifted at the corners every time he looked at me.

I put on a pair of old jeans and a white t-shirt, then grabbed a sweater out of the closet. I opened the door and Santiago was standing across the hall, his arms crossed over his chest. His eyes lifted and sparkled as soon as they reached my face.

He cleared his throat. "You look good," he said and then frowned and turned towards the stairs.

I closed the door and followed him out of the hotel.

"I thought you said we were going to get an early lunch. What are we doing here?" We stood by the front door of his parents' house. The one I'd been in and where I saw that image of my grandfather. "No, no, no. Let's go back. I can't go back there."

"Nope, we're going in there and asking questions. We need to figure this out, one step at a time. I can't help you figure out your shit with your grandmother, but I can for damn sure help you with this. Besides, I already texted my grandmother, and she's expecting us for lunch."

"Santiago, please." What if it was a dead end? What if I was holding on to hope, and there was nothing to hold on to?

"Victoria." He looked at me, completely serious. "In you go."

He opened the door to the massive house like he owned it, then let me go through first, his hand finding the small of my back and guiding me to the end of the hallway right into the dining room.

The room was massive, something I'd noticed when I had been here before, but now that it was empty, it was much more evident.

"We never eat in the dining room. Usually we hang out in the eat-in kitchen with them unless we're having a large gathering like the other night," he said, reading my mind. "But I guess my mom wants to impress you or something because she really decked it out today." His smile turned up, a little mischief in his eye.

"I hope you're not tricking me into yet another family gathering. I really can't handle it," I said, almost without thinking. But I could feel myself trying to smile a shy smile, remembering how much love and happiness and laughter was in the air in this house. Santiago looked at me, grinning from ear to ear.

"I'm home!" he yelled, loud enough so that there was movement immediately. I heard a few murmurs coming from the kitchen and some footsteps descending down the stairs.

My stomach churned. *You are not ready for this. Tell him.*

"Hey," Santiago said, his voice close to me. I could feel his breath right by my ear. "I'll ask some questions and as soon as we have at least a little bit of detail—a name, maybe an address—we can go to the records office and poke around. Deal?"

His grandmother, Adelaida, emerged through the butler's pantry door, walking directly to me, completely ignoring her grandson.

"Victoria, thank you so much for coming. I didn't have much chance to chat with you on my birthday. These grand-kids of mine really hogged you up." I frowned. I wasn't under the impression she was looking to chat with me—an outsider—but this wasn't surprising. It was like Santiago had prepared everyone for my visit. "I'm glad Santiago dragged you here today to have lunch with us. Please, sit."

"Oh my goodness, thank you for having me again. It was such a fun time. I'm sorry I left so soon, but I needed to take care of some things back at the hotel." I smiled, imagining this could easily be one of my grandmother's friends. Santiago kept looking at me, his smile plastered on his face.

"Where's Grandpa?" he asked as he pulled a chair out for me to sit. "Is he joining us for lunch?"

She smiled fondly as she took her seat at the head of the table and nodded at someone by the door to the kitchen. "He's at Julia's hotel with your parents. She needed help with the water heater or something, so off they went."

Huh, so I guess this is a family thing? Considerate and helpful and nice. Nice *people.*

"Oh, okay, well, maybe we can come back? I don't want to intrude," I said directly to her. Santiago's hand landed on my knee, and he squeezed a little, sending shivers down my back. He looked at me, but I shook my head and widened my eyes.

"Nonsense! They'll join us for dessert later," she added, waving her hand and dismissing my comment. The woman acted like she *wanted* to have me here for lunch. "Santi tells me you are a lawyer too. What do you do?"

"Oh, um... I focus on mergers and acquisitions. I work for my family's firm in the city. It's run by my older brother now, but it used to be run by my grandfather. He founded it with his best friend," I said, feeling Santiago's heated gaze on my face.

"Interesting. You also come from a line of lawyers,

then?" she asked, a gentle smile on her lips. "My husband and all of our sons are lawyers too. The only one who chose a different path is Santiago's sister. She's the town's pediatrician."

I looked at Santiago, who had a stiff, uncomfortable smile on his face. If anything, he looked worried, like I would betray his trust and tell his grandmother that he in fact did not like being a lawyer.

"We are so proud of all our grandchildren, really. I'm surprised all of them chose to become lawyers," she said in between giggles. "What are the odds, right?"

My father was one of seven children, and he was the only one who followed in my grandfather's footsteps, but both my brother and I were lawyers, so I understood. Maybe it was different. Maybe for us, it was a mandatory suggestion. It didn't seem like Santiago's family would make him become a lawyer.

I looked at Santiago, who was silent sitting right next to me. He turned slowly, smiling softly up at me in reassurance, and the moment was broken when a woman—the housekeeper?—walked in, carrying a tray with hot food, and set the different serving bowls right in front of us.

Santiago's grandmother was *excellent* at small talk. She asked me about my family, about my hobbies, asked Santiago about work and details of his recent cases. She even filled us in on some new town gossip—although nothing like what my grandmother would do. It seemed like Susana would gossip with malice—like knowing things about other people and sharing them with others would make her feel superior.

As soon as the dishes were taken back to the kitchen, Santiago stood up and walked out of the dining room and into the hallway. The silence was awkward, but he was back moments later with the exact picture I told him about, the picture that had been hanging in the library all this time.

"Granny, can you tell us who this is?" he asked her, straight to the point. I didn't want to look at her, scared that whatever she had to say would shatter my very existence. "He looks familiar, but I don't think I ever knew his name."

She took a moment to gather herself, dabbing at her lips with her cloth napkin and then resetting it back on her lap. She grabbed the picture and looked at it, slowly focusing on my grandfather's face. Her eyes softened and her lips parted a little, like her thoughts were taking her by surprise. My heart started beating faster than I'd ever felt it beat. The only sound I could hear was my hard breathing.

Santiago's hand found mine and he squeezed, not letting go. He inched a little closer to me, showing me that he was there for me.

"Oh," she said, a small, sad smile on her lips. "This is Enrique, your grandfather's friend from law school." Her voice was small and weak, longing for something I couldn't pinpoint.

I cleared my throat and blinked, trying to contain the tears that were right at the edge, about to spill over.

"He lived in town for a while in the eighties," she added,

much more firmly. "He actually worked at the firm for a few months. Moved here from the city."

So far everything added up. Enrique was his middle name. He was a lawyer. He moved from the city. Without a shadow of a doubt, this was my grandfather. But what was he doing here? *He was kidnapped!* My thoughts moved quickly. The tension was palpable. I opened my mouth to ask a question, but I was interrupted by Santiago's grandfather, who walked right in.

"Oh, hello! Victoria, so nice to see you." He walked over to me and bent at the waist to give me a small kiss on the cheek. "I didn't know you were coming; I would have joined you sooner if I'd known you were coming for lunch."

He made his way across from me to the other side of the table and took a seat right next to his wife. I could tell he had been handsome. Santiago had his eyes and his smile. He looked at his wife and reached over, giving her a chaste kiss on the lips.

My eyes filled with tears again. Knowing I'd never see my grandparents interact like this. Not even my own parents. It was such a happy image, stirring all these feelings inside me.

"The kids were just asking me about Enrique," Adelaida interrupted. "You can probably tell them more since you knew him the longest."

Turns out, the man in the photo was indeed my grandfather. Santiago's grandfather told us how they'd met the first day of college, sat together in one of the introductory lectures their first year, and then had been inseparable for the rest of their schooling. In third or fourth year of law school, they went their separate ways—my grandfather focusing on corporate law and Santiago's grandfather, Carlos, focusing on family law, mostly divorce and estate planning since that was what their family firm catered to in town.

"Honey, do you remember the wild games of Scrabble we used to play?" he said, almost like he was peeking right to the past. He laughed one of those giant laughs, so similar to Santiago's. "He was the most serious man, a man of very few words, but he came alive when he was doing anything related to language. He used to school us at Scrabble. The man had the dictionary memorized."

I took a deep breath. That was something that Susana had repeated ad nauseam growing up. *He had the dictionary memorized.* He knew obscure words, and he *always* won at Scrabble. Carlos also said that he was an avid reader, preferring crime and mystery novels because he liked the challenge of solving the mystery before it was revealed by the author. *It's him. They're talking about the same man.*

"Did he move back to the city?" I asked, seeing if this could take me somewhere in my search. Maybe if he had left a forwarding address, I could reach out to him. Santiago's gaze was planted firmly on me, his hand still holding mine tightly. I'd never been one for physical touch, but his warmth was a welcome gesture.

Carlos turned to look at his wife and both their faces

went blank, the smiles immediately erased from their mouths. Adelaida cleared her throat and shifted in her seat; Santiago tensed and squeezed my hand a little tighter.

"Um..." Carlos started to say.

"Would anyone want coffee?" the housekeeper interrupted. "I'll bring out dessert soon too."

He's dead. He has to be, right? Otherwise, they would have said something.

"Thank you so much for the invitation. I actually have to run back to the hotel and finish off some work," I said quickly, letting go of Santiago's hand and standing. "The food was delicious, and I had a great time. *Muchas gracias.*"

I shuffled quickly over to both of them and gave them a quick hug, not being able to linger for a second longer, even though my body kept wondering what it would feel like to be hugged by such lovely people.

"*Si,* I have to run too," Santiago added, walking quickly to my side. "I'll see you tonight at dinner?"

I walked out of the dining room and into the hallway, directing my shaking body to the front door. The world was vibrating from under me, walls closing in.

"Hey, I got you, okay?" he said as he rubbed soothing circles on my back. "Sit down for a minute?"

I didn't remember how, but we were suddenly outside, down the driveway and on the sidewalk. I could hear myself trying to get air into my lungs, my breathing heavy and erratic as I tried to stop myself from hyperventilating. I sat, putting my head in between my knees and shutting my eyes, letting my thoughts run rampant.

He's dead. I knew as much, although never confirmed. That was what we were told growing up. He was kidnapped, the ransom was paid, but then he was never returned to us, so it was assumed he was killed. But had he not been kidnapped? Should I have asked them directly if this was the case? About the whole kidnapping specifically? Susana would hate that because there was no point in doing it. He was dead, and that was that.

"I don't understand," I told Santiago in between breaths. "He was kidnapped. I mean your grandparents didn't mention any details, but I would know if he had *moved* here in the eighties, right? Like, the numbers don't add up."

Santiago kept running his hand up and down my back and held me tight to him with his other arm. He kept making soothing sounds, trying to calm me down, avoiding pushing me off the ledge.

"I need to call Susana," I finally said, putting my head in my hands.

14

THE TALK

My whole life, I strived to be perfect. Or as close to perfect as I could get for Susana. My mother had a terrible accident when I was a child. My memories of her were very limited, and the only things I *thought* I remembered were possibly images I constructed myself from pictures. My father was unable to cope with what happened, so we moved into Susana's home, the home she had shared with her husband and her children as she was raising them, and she helped my father raise us.

My brother was probably five or six when we moved, and he remembered a little bit more, although this was nothing we discussed openly. *Nothing* was discussed openly in our family, I had come to notice. What I did remember were those early years in that big home, getting off the school bus and running right into the door, dropping our bags in the entryway, and heading directly to the kitchen to have an afternoon snack.

The house was huge—it seemed that way practically well into my twenties—with a large entryway that was heavily decorated with wood furniture, paintings, and gold-leaf frames lining the walls, almost no space in between them. At the center of the far wall, leaning against it, was a large oil painting, one of the only things my grandfather kept of his family—the rest was inherited or selected by Susana.

This was how she operated—she would suggest something, and then it would get done. Either by my grandfather or her children or her children's children.

I started noticing her influence when I was in my early teens. We wore uniforms to school, but I noticed that I started paying more attention to *how* I wore it. The shirt neatly tucked in, my hair always up in a tidy bun, my shoes always shined and buffed. I would walk into the house, walk up the stairs, and drop my bag on my desk chair, which was waiting for me to open it to tackle my homework.

I wanted to say that my life choices and the path I took to get where I was were really honed in on by her. I saw first-hand how much she sacrificed to raise my brother and me, even after she'd done it seven times with her own children. She welcomed us to her home and gave us everything we ever needed. Her social life was active, but I could count on one hand the number of times she was not home after we got back from school, even as my brother and I became more independent in our teen years.

All this to say—when something crossed Susana's mind, it would get done. And I was not surprised now to have realized that everything I ever thought I'd chosen was guided and decided entirely by Susana. The biggest of these things was my professional career, one hundred percent influenced by her to honor her husband and follow in his brave steps.

Santiago walked me back to my hotel room and hovered by the door after the little episode at his grandparents' house. Neither one of us had said a thing during the few blocks it took us to get back, but I could feel his tension, the realization that the man that his grandparents knew was the same man *I* never knew.

"Vee?" he said, lingering by the door, one of my hands holding it so that I wouldn't close it on him. "I jus—"

"It's okay, you don't have to say anything. I don't want your pity really." But maybe I did want his pity, and maybe I did want his hugs and his warmth and his whispered words in my ear, calming me down. "I think I'm going to call Susana and see if I can figure this out. I definitely owe her a conversation. Thank you for walking me back. We'll talk later."

His shoulders relaxed, and his face looked almost defeated. Like he wanted to come in and hold me and whisper those words into my ear. Maybe he wanted to hold me and never let me go.

"Bye, Santiago."

I closed the door and immediately headed for the dresser. I picked up my phone and turned it on, expecting the buzzing to be nonstop. But to my surprise, there were no new messages since I had last turned it on. There were a few emails in my inbox, but nothing urgent or even remotely relevant since I'd outlined specific actions to take on any pending work. Because I was going away on my honeymoon and on an extended break for more than a few days at a time, and I had wanted to *enjoy* myself. I huffed at the thought. How naïve.

If I was going to call Susana to ask her all the questions I had relating to my grandfather, I would probably have to plan out my argument, just like if I were preparing for a case. I needed to present her my hypothesis, the facts that backed that up, and then the conclusion. But she most likely would want to talk about me fleeing, humiliating her in front of all her friends and acquaintances, tainting the family name.

So I did what I always did when I needed to talk through something, and I called my best friend.

"You look like shit," she said with a small smile on her lips. She was lying down on her side. "What happened?"

"Do you remember that photo I saw of my grandfather?" She nodded and waited for me to continue. "I got confirmation today that it is, in fact, my grandfather."

She nodded her head and bit her lower lip. "Okay," she said with a little reluctance. She scratched under one of her eyes and took a deep breath. "How did you confirm that?"

"Santiago's grandparents."

"What do they have to do with this whole thing?" she asked, not quite understanding what I was saying. "I mean, how are they related?"

"So apparently, Santiago's grandfather and my grandfather went to law school together. And then he suddenly showed up here in the eighties. That's about as much as they told me," I added. "Oh, and he went by Enrique Aguirre here. Plain enough so that people wouldn't recognize him, I guess."

"Interesting," she said, grabbing her phone and tapping furiously at the screen. "Enrique Aguirre, okay, got it."

"What are you doing?"

"I reached out to a prosecutor in Córdoba, and he was looking into things for me, but they have all been dead ends. I'm assuming this changes things."

"Yeah, I guess so." I stared at my friend for a while, and we sat in silence, each of us behind a screen. "I think I need to talk to Susana."

"Yeah, but can you wait until I can find more information? We should go in knowing everything." This was a team effort, for sure. Even if she wasn't with me, she was on my side.

"That makes sense."

"Did you talk to Manuel?" she asked like she was reading my mind. I needed closure. Maybe this was the first step I needed to take to start to understand what was happening. "What are you going to say to him?"

"No, but I think I might call him right now actually."

"Okay, I'm going to go back to sleep. Call me later. *Beso.*"

In my resolve, I dialed Manuel's phone number. And to my surprise, he answered on the first ring.

"Hey," he said, his voice groggy with sleep. "I miss you."

Confusion went through my brain. *Why is this man missing you? He practically called off your wedding!*

"Where are you? What time is it?" he continued, and I could hear sheets ruffling in the background and strong and even footsteps, followed by a door closing.

"We need to talk," I said, clearing my throat so that I sounded strong and brave, although I was anything but. There was silence on the other end of the line, so I assumed that was my cue to continue talking. "What the fuck, Manuel?"

Anger. It was just coming out. I was confused and angry. I wasn't hurt at all, because I had been slowly realizing that maybe this had been a good thing.

"I'm angry, but also, I don't understand it," I continued.

He let out a long breath, almost relieved. Manuel was transparent. He wore his emotions on his face and had many tells, and this was one thing he did when he was nervous. He would hold in his breath, not realizing he was doing it until someone spoke or delivered news or whatever it was that was plaguing him.

"I think that we both know by now that we wouldn't have survived a marriage. That's pretty obvious to me now. You would have been miserable, I would have been miserable, and I don't see us ever getting a divorce because that would have been an outright disaster and Susana would have made our lives a living hell if we had even attempted that. What I don't get is why you never talked to me. I didn't think it was that bad, was it?"

In hindsight, maybe it *was* bad. Maybe we were both stuck to this idea that marriage was the next step, and it made logical sense, since we had been together for a long time. I mean, Susana seemed to think so, so it made sense to me. But was I really in love with this man? Or was I in love with the idea of this man, and a wedding and a family and a house in the suburbs, just like what my grandmother had?

"Victoria, of course it was bad. The only thing you did for the past two years was go to work and then get home and curl up with a book. You've been disconnected from *us*."

"*I* was disconnected? The moments we shared together were always with others around. When I dared suggest we go on a trip together, you invited your cousin and his wife! It's like everything was more exciting than me." Early on in our relationship, I suggested we go on vacation together. I guess I was still in the honeymoon period or whatever that was called, and I booked a week-long vacation at a fancy estate upstate, with a spa and some outdoor activities we could do together. Manuel suggested to his cousin and his wife they join us, and our "romantic" vacation turned into a group trip that involved zero spa time and too much hanging out with others. "And I get it, maybe I was *too* domestic for your taste? You have so many friends, and I'm more of a loner, and I'm not embarrassed by that at all."

I could feel myself getting agitated and needed to rein it in. Calm and collected all the way. I was happy being with myself. Happy to sit by a fire and sit in companionable silence with whoever. But with Manuel, it always felt like we had to be doing something, anything. Attending events or visiting with friends and family or watching a movie. Together.

"Victoria." A sigh. "You wouldn't have listened either way. You are so obsessed with what Susana thinks of you that you would have gone through with the wedd—"

"Stop." Was he suggesting I didn't see the signs? "Do you love me? Or you know what, better yet, did you ever love me?"

Silence.

More silence.

Even more silence.

Too much silence.

It felt like five or six minutes went by in total silence. I could hear the noises coming from outside. The town was coming back to life now that everyone was heading home from work. From his end, I could hear the bathroom fan running, his foot tapping on the floor. Another one of his nervous tells.

"Okay, well, that says it all. I don't know who you're with now on the trip that was supposed to be our fucking honeymoon, but I hope she makes you happy. I'm moving on from you, just so you know. Might not be tomorrow or even the day after, but I will move on, and I will be happy."

"Victoria, can you ple—"

"No, Manuel, I'm over this. You were a shitty boyfriend. I was a shitty girlfriend. We were not meant to be, and I get it." Did he ever stop to think that he could have been leading me on? Letting me believe he wanted me, he loved me? "But cheating on me? That's way below your standards. We could have walked away from all of this, been spared the humiliation. Instead, you turned me into the villain. And I don't fucking deserve it. Call Susana and your parents and tell them we're over and why, or I will."

"Or you will what? God, you are just like your grand-mother, you know that?"

"You fucking cheated on me with who even knows and then played coy with everyone, suggesting I left you at the altar. Really? I'm like my grandmother?"

"Victoria, you need to calm down. It's not that big of a deal. So what? Our relationship ended. You'll move on, you just said it. It's not the end of the world, and maybe you need to start looking at life that way."

"*¿Me estás jodiendo?* Are you fucking kidding me right now? I wasted so much time on you, on nurturing some-thing that you knew wouldn't go anywhere. And you fucking led me on, Manuel, you led me to believe you loved me and you wanted the same thing." I took a deep breath. "You know what? I was angry before, but now I'm fucking fuming, and I hope you get what you deserve." He could rot in hell for all I cared. "Goodbye."

What is happening? I called him to make peace, to get some closure, and instead I was reminded that I was alone and that the only thing I'd managed to do with my life was to turn myself into my grandmother.

I started pacing around the room because after this conversation, I couldn't call my grandmother and apologize. I didn't deserve any of it.

My breathing was heavy, my heart pounding fast in my chest, trying to make an escape. The only thing I could hear was my heartbeat inside my head. Adrenaline rushed through my veins.

"Oh my god," I mumbled. "Calm down, crazy. Get it together."

It was fine. I simply needed some time and space to sort everything out, but damn if this conversation hadn't riled me up.

"Think," I muttered to myself. "Calm down and think."

I stood by the window, watching activity right outside the hotel starting to pick up. The streetlamps would soon be casting a golden glow on the diners walking to their destination, completely unaware of how my world was crumbling down.

The long silence brought up all of those feelings of inadequacy, feelings that I'd buried so deep I didn't even know where to start looking. Clearly, I wasn't good enough for Manuel, and obviously I wasn't good for him. I had always had to work hard to be good enough for Susana, but should that be how I lived my life? Always trying to be better rather than being enough?

The knock on the door jolted me from my thoughts.

"Hey," I said with an attempt of a smile on my face as I opened the door. "Did you forget something?"

He had the saddest smile on his face, his eyes lined with caution and pity.

"What happened? You're looking at me with your pity eyes," I said. "Just tell me, please. I'm not in the mood for anything else today."

"Vee. Sit down." He grabbed my hand as he made his way into my room and sat down on the small loveseat in the living area, tugging me to his side. "I went to the records office; I have some answers."

15

THE TRUTH

He's dead. Confirmed dead.

The expression on Santiago's face mirrored the one that his grandparents had back in the house earlier that day.

For the past week, the only thing I had been able to do was add on more questions to my already confusing life. At least I had something that resembled closure in my relationship. Now the questions as they related to my grandfather's disappearance kept adding up, and the answers we were able to start getting weren't even scratching the surface.

"*Dios.*" Oh, my god. "I mean, I—"

"I know," he replied, his eyes wide. "It's *literally* unbelievable. Like, I can't believe it."

Turned out, this man, who everyone referred to as Enrique, showed up in town with essentially the clothes off his back and knocked on Santiago's grandfather's door. They knew each other from law school and had kept in contact, so he assumed—correctly—that Carlos would help him out. He set him up with a job at his firm. Although my grandfather was a corporate lawyer, he was able to help out in the small family firm. He lived right next door to him in a small house that was owned by one of their family members and only used during the summers, so they came to an agreement and rented it out to him for the remainder of the year.

He worked hard, apparently. Kept mostly to himself, choosing to live a private life in the town where everyone knew who he was. No one asked questions, but everyone knew who he was—Carlos's friend from law school who was going through a rough patch with his family and needed time and space to sort things out.

Apparently, the town *loved* him. Like, adored the man. Even though he kept to himself, he was a generous citizen, donating his time to some of the local initiatives. Sometime in July or August of the year he moved to town, he was appointed to the board of the newly reopened community center, where he helped with some of the legal affairs and helped them set up their nonprofit status.

"Vee, on paper, he was an amazing man," Santiago said. "I don't get it."

"Welcome to my life!" I said, a little too loudly for my taste. I had been pacing the floor of the room as Santiago told me all these things. I tried to find a spot to sit but couldn't get comfortable. My skin itched, my heart hammering inside my chest. Essentially, everything I ever knew about this man had been a lie. A fabrication, but I wasn't ready to point fingers just yet. Had he staged his own kidnapping? Is that what my grandmother still thought to this day? That he had been kidnapped? "So what happened to him?"

"He died in a fire. Apparently, his house caught fire in December of the year he moved here. It was ruled accidental, and the case was closed."

"That doesn't make any sense to me at all." Why would he run away from his family with basically the clothes off his back and come to this town? Susana spoke so well of him, of how dedicated to her and their children he was. And he suddenly disappeared? I mean, the kidnapping story did make sense, right? He was a high-profile corporate lawyer, excelling in his career. With a dedicated wife and seven children, a very active social life, involved in the community.

It seemed almost like he plucked himself out of the city and moved here and continued living almost the same life, except without his family.

"Growing up, I felt like he was this larger-than-life figure in our family. I already told you this," I said, standing by the window and looking out to see the stars starting to pop against the dusk sky. I was repeating myself now. I had told him this already, but it kept coming out the same way. "Susana always— and I mean always—speaks so highly of him. Everyone, really. I don't understand."

"Do you think there could be a reason why the stories

are different? Maybe he faked his own kidnapping, and that's the only thing that Susana knows?"

"I mean, maybe? I know that the ransom was paid. Well, at least I was *told* the ransom had been paid. And then they never heard back so after a few years, they just assumed he was dead." I grew up adoring this man, hearing all about how my eyes were identical to his, how I took after him with all my reading. I became a lawyer *because* of him. To honor him. To honor his memory. "Do you think that if we go to the police, maybe someone can help us out?"

It was a stretch. It had been decades since the incident. What were the odds that anyone was still working there? But Santiago knew half of this town, his grandparents the other half, so maybe his connections would pan out.

"It's a stretch, for sure," he said, reading right into my thoughts. "But it doesn't hurt to ask. I also think we should stop by the community center and see if they have anything there. The woman that runs it has been there for over thirty years, so I'm sure she must have known him."

Santiago had always been a step ahead of everyone. Even in college, during our first year, he knew exactly what the professor would say ahead of time. He was always prepared. When he looked at you, he *saw*. He paid attention to details and knew where to look. It was probably the most annoying thing about him because it seemed effortless, like it was completely natural for him to be so consumed by whoever or whatever was in front of him.

"I'm going to call Cata," I mumbled as I turned to find my phone. "She told me she was looking into it."

"Catalina Sánchez from law school?" he said with a smile on his face. "I haven't seen her in years." His smile was genuine.

"She's a prosecutor in San Isidro now," I said. "Also married my brother three years ago, so I can't get rid of her."

"Really?"

I lifted my brows and widened my eyes in response, a smile on my lips. At least he could make me smile, despite the shitty situation. I propped my phone on a used glass that was on the coffee table and clicked on her name. She answered immediately.

"*¿Qué pasó?*" she blurted. "Oh." Her eyes went wide. "Santiago Williams?" I could see her eyes shining. She was enjoying this a little too much. She grinned and looked at me, then turned back to face him. We were sitting side by side, Santiago's hand resting casually on my knee. "How are you? I haven't seen you in years," she screeched.

"I'm good, how are you? Heard you're a prosecutor now?" he asked, paying close attention to her. "You're pregnant too? Congratulations." He turned to look at me, studying my face. I neglected to tell him that small fact, but we hadn't had time to really go into details.

"Due in a few weeks, actually. I'm on bed rest and bored to death." She scrunched her face. "Victoria's been keeping me busy though." She turned to look at me and mouthed "wow" and wiggled her eyebrows.

I could feel my face blush, Santiago's gaze fixed on my face. "You would have found something to do either way," I said, trying to manage the conversation. "Cata, have you heard back from your guy in Córdoba?" Catalina was still looking at Santiago, studying his face, a small smile on her lips. I bit my lower lip; the whole thing was very amusing. "We have some more information."

Santiago squeezed my knee and then moved a little closer to me. Our thighs were already flush against each other's, but the movement made my body tingle. He nodded and then smiled at me. "Okay, so this man, this Enrique Aguirre, he died in a fire in December of 1988."

"It was ruled accidental," Santiago interjected. "The official cause was smoke inhalation, but essentially his house caught fire and he was the only casualty."

Catalina took notes. She had a notebook propped on her belly and nodded her head as we spoke. "I haven't heard back from my contact in Córdoba, but I've been doing some research about the kidnapping, and I haven't been able to find it anywhere. It's not necessarily something to be concerned about, but maybe I'm not looking in the right places. I have a call with someone with the police tomorrow, so I'll dig deeper then. Vicky, check your email because I'm going to send you a few notes. And I expect more stuff to come in shortly, so we can look at it together."

"This is so weird," I said. "I can't understand this. It's just fishy."

"Yes, I agree," Catalina said. "Your brother said he would talk to your dad, but he hasn't been able to contact him."

"Oh my god." I closed my eyes and lifted my head towards the ceiling. "Do you want me to call him?"

Catalina sighed. "Honestly, I think Agustín is just going to go and find him tomorrow. He's probably hiding in his house. Maybe he feels guilty? Who knows," she added.

My father had been an alcoholic for the majority of our lives. It was the main reason why we moved into Susana's home: so that she could take over. I always thought that the trauma of suddenly being a widower, topped with his father's disappearance and the stress of running the law firm, broke him. He was unreliable, to say the least. We all worked around him to prop him up. It was no secret, of course, his addiction. But Susana worked hard to victimize him, to make sure no one spoke ill of him in our circle.

"Fuck," I said. "I didn't even think of that."

Santiago furrowed his brow and looked at me, searching for answers in my face. I smiled, but I was sure my expression betrayed me. He kissed my temple and then stared at me for an instant. Someone—Catalina—cleared her throat, and the moment was interrupted. I turned to look at the screen and saw she was biting her lip, trying to contain a smile. "Oh, your brother is on the other line. I'll call you later," she said. A lie, of course. "Bye, Santiago, nice catching up." She winked. "Hope to see you soon."

I sat there in absolute silence until Santiago interrupted my thoughts. "What are you thinking?" His hand was still draped on my leg, and his thumb was moving slowly back and forth across my inner thigh. It was hard to breathe, hard to think. My whole body was afire with his touch.

"Uh," I replied clumsily and shook my head. "Um..."

"What's wrong with your dad?" He was either trying to change the subject on purpose, or he hadn't noticed the effect he had on me. It was probably the former because this man paid close attention to everything.

"He's an alcoholic," I blurted. "It's honestly fine most of the time, and we don't really do anything about it except occasionally my brother will go kick his ass for a minute, and then he's fine."

"I'm sorry," he said. "That sucks."

"I guess." I shrugged. "It's not a big deal anymore."

It wasn't; it was the truth. My brother and I learned to rely on other people. My brother relied heavily on Pedro, and I relied heavily on Susana. It was how things were, and I never questioned them. But I wondered if the entire thing had been too much, that I had been too focused on what Susana said to me, what she said I should do, and I followed that blindly without ever wondering if it was the right thing to do.

"Do you ever wonder if the choices you made were the right ones?" I turned my body to face him, which meant that his hand shifted, and it was no longer on my leg. I felt its absence immediately.

"Yeah," he huffed. "All the time."

We sat on the loveseat for what felt like hours, lost in thought. Eventually, the room was dark, and the only lights I could see were coming in from the window.

"It's a weird feeling, like I'm frozen and the world around me is on fire, you know?" I said after a while. Even if I was frozen in place, I saw it move, evolve, change. "It sounds a little bit selfish, saying that my life is on fire so the world has to stop." I shook my head. "I sound delirious." I smiled in the dark. I could hear Santiago's breathing right next to me. Our bodies were next to each other, touching from shoulder to knee.

"What's your favorite color?" The question interrupted our long silence.

I laughed. "What? Why?"

He shrugged in the dark, then turned to look at me. I could feel the heat of his gaze on my face. "Just... cause."

"Publicly? Blue. That's what I'm supposed to say." It was weird to be trained on having a favorite color, but our family was so visible that I had to have answers to these ridiculous questions at the ready. "But it's really pink, although Susana absolutely hates it. She says it's too childish, and a woman my age shouldn't be saying things like that." I shrugged but couldn't contain my cackle, and he laughed in return, a laughter so deep that my whole being vibrated with want.

"Seriously?" He sounded surprised. I couldn't quite see his face; it was covered in the shadows that my own body cast. "That's, um..."

"She's fucking ridiculous," I agreed.

"Why do you put up with it?" He was curious now. We were getting into more intimate territory. So far, we had both shared things with each other. I knew I had been vulnerable, and I felt the same from him. Raw vulnerability as he shared his gripes and concerns.

"That's a great question." I rested my head on the back of the couch and closed my eyes. "I never really thought about it. When my grandfather disappeared, she really had a hard time, and then my mother died and she took over, so I guess I always knew she was looking out for what was best for me, you know? Like, she sacrificed so much for her family that I guess I never really doubted her. I mean, she's always looking out for me, so..." I shrugged. "What is *your* favorite color?" Never in a million years did I imagine I would be sitting here with him, asking him these questions. Getting to know him.

"Dark red," he said immediately. He didn't give it a second thought. "Like the dark, deep red of the leaves when they start to change in the fall."

"Why?"

"Why? Because there's nothing we can do about change except admire it, flow with it. It's necessary. Because the dark red leaves mean the promise of new things to come."

16

THE SUSPICION

THE NEXT MORNING WAS ROUGH. Santiago and I had stayed up late, chatting about everything and anything. When he left, he kissed my cheek so softly, it made me gasp in surprise. I wanted to ask about Clara, ask him what happened. Because our proximity had taken a turn, and suddenly there were touches and intimate looks and kisses. Hand holding. It wasn't much, but it wasn't not much.

I wanted to think I wasn't delirious. I hadn't been imagining all those glances and smiles, the way he touched me and wanted to be close to me. How he held me like there was no one else he'd rather be holding. Because there wasn't.

Oh my god.

And to top that off, I barely slept. So many thoughts running through my mind, so little time to figure them all out. The proximity to Santiago—albeit helpful—was confusing me even more.

There was a knock on the door. Of fucking course. The universe was playing a trick on me, so every time I thought about Santiago, the energies that were summoned him to my rescue.

"Santiago, how are you not tired? I nee—Oh."

"Hi, Victoria. I hope you don't mind me dropping by without notice," Carlos, Santiago's grandfather, said with a big smile on his face. "Were you waiting for my grandson, or can I come in for a minute or so?"

"Um, yes, sure, come in." I shook my head at the image of Santiago's grandfather walking into my room. The man was dressed to the nines, wearing dark charcoal slacks and a white shirt that was impeccably pressed. His cufflinks caught in the sunlight seeping through the blinds, his initials clear as day. He walked to the end of the room and sat on the loveseat. I moved my laptop to the coffee table and closed it shut. He smiled at me and nodded to the seat next to him, and I sat. Carlos interlaced his fingers and set them on his lap.

"You have his eyes." He sighed. "I saw it that first night you came to the house, but it was too much of a coincidence. I didn't believe it at first. I mean, what are the odds? But those eyes are so unique. It's not only the color, but the way they narrow and your forehead creases when you are unsure about something."

My hands were shaking on my lap so uncontrollably I

had to sit on them to calm myself down. The man talked to me like he knew me.

"And then Santiago comes around asking questions about him, and it clicked. It's been years since I last saw him, but I wouldn't ever forget his eyes."

I looked at him, his eyes soft and patient. I shook my head at him once more, trying to process what this man was telling me.

"What happened to him?" I said, my voice barely above a whisper. He sat up and straightened his spine. He draped one of his arms casually on the back of the couch, a move so similar to what Santiago had done a number of times when he was around me.

"He died as a consequence of a fire in his home, the same year he moved into town. It was unexpected, obviously, but accidental nonetheless." He pressed his lips together and frowned. "The official manner of death was smoke inhalation—the house was in a little disrepair since it was a summer home, and the gas fireplace leaked occasionally. I can't recall the details of what started the fire but, you know, it is what it is."

"Yes, Santiago mentioned something along those lines," I said, my tone flat. "I meant to say: why did he move here?"

"You know, I think I was the only person that knew the full truth. He got in over his head with some creditors, used some money he wasn't supposed to touch. He deeply regretted it; I can ascertain that."

"But that doesn't make any sense to me. We've always

known he was kidnapped and despite the ransom being paid, he was never released. We assumed he died, obviously, because we never heard anything else." I locked eyes with him, and he nodded, trying to understand what I was telling him. "At least, that's the story I've been told. It happened before I was even born, so it's not like I have any recollection of that."

"Victoria, honey, I don't think that is the full story," he said. His voice was soft and calm. He moved closer to me, his hand reaching for mine and squeezing lightly. "I think that what you know, at least the narrative you've been told, is bent. It's not the truth. But I'm not here to tell you what to think."

I looked at him, bewildered. This man was confirming some of my suspicions. The story about his kidnapping was fabricated. Now I had to figure out who did it. And why.

"Why would my family lie about that? It just seems a little extreme, if I'm being honest."

"I don't know, but maybe you should talk to your grand-mother about it. It was a difficult time for him, there's no doubt in my mind about that." I blinked at him, processing the information he was giving me. It wasn't clear to me why he was here. Did he want to talk about my grandfather? Did he want to tell me the whole story? "I also think that there were other factors to take into account. He was an influen-tial man, very well-regarded, respected. I don't think the news would have been taken lightly. I think that whoever covered this up did it to protect themselves."

He smiled at me and stood slowly, then made his way to the door. "If you want to ask more questions, you know where I live. I don't know if I'll have all the answers, but perhaps I can help you piece some things together. I loved him very much. He was a good man, and I think he would have been proud of what you've accomplished. Santiago has told me so much about you, I feel like I know you by now."

He let himself out and shut the door behind him, all while I sat, stunned, looking at the wall.

———

My mind was racing, and I was out of breath by the time I reached Santiago's clearing. It was still early afternoon; the town was sleepy and quiet, all activity stopped so townies could take their two-hour *siestas,* like every single day. No doubt, this town was quirky. I wondered if my grandfather really liked it or if he was just trying to pass the time until he could go back home and be with his family.

It was clear to me at this point that I needed to talk to Susana. I wanted to talk to Carlos a little bit more, and I wanted to do more research locally. Catalina was still looking into things back in the city and in constant conversation with her contact up here in Córdoba. So far, she hadn't been able to find much, but we were sure we weren't looking in the right place. I wasn't ready just yet to speak to my grandmother, but I did need to clear some things up with Pedro, my grandfather's business partner.

He answered on the third ring.

"*Hola*," I said. This man had been like a grandfather to us. When Susana's husband disappeared, he helped her out as much as he could. He was unmarried, had no kids, and devoted himself to our family. I specifically remembered him as the person that taught me how to ride a bike. Not only that, he also took over for my grandfather at their firm, and I worked closely with him early in my career.

"Hi, honey. Goodness, are you okay?" This was the first time someone from my family had asked me how I was. Cata didn't count. "Did something happen to you? Your grandmother is furious."

"Oh, I know. I'm fine. How are you?"

"Where are you? Do you need me to come get you?" He was in his late eighties, but it wasn't noticeable at all. He still had a full head of hair—albeit white—and didn't need reading glasses.

"I need to talk to you about something, and you need to tell me the truth," I said quickly. I knew that I needed to get him talking, otherwise I would lose my nerve. "What happened to my grandfather?"

A sigh. "Wha—where is this coming from, *mi amor?*"

"I've been realizing these past few weeks that I've never asked many questions. I've always accepted what was given to me. I'm lucky, I've never lacked anything in my life, but I'm slowly understanding that I never made choices *for* me. I've consistently made choices based on what was better for others."

"Is this about Manuel, Victoria? If you didn't want to marry him or weren't ready, I'm sure Susana would understand," he said, although I wasn't at all sure that he was convinced of what he was saying. "Marriage is a commitment that shouldn't be taken lightly."

"This has nothing to do with Manuel, Pedro, and you know it." I closed my eyes, willing all of this to disappear. "Please, tell me what happened."

"You need to talk to your *abuela*, Victoria. You disappeared on your wedding day. Do you have any idea what that caused?"

I could hear Pedro moving around, the door creaking in a familiar way. It was clear he was at my grandmother's house. His voice got lower, rushed. "Just call her, okay?"

"Why are you on her side, Pedro?" I had so many questions, but apparently, I wasn't going to get any answers to any of them. "*Por favor,* tell me."

I took a deep breath, eager to get answers, but the only thing I heard was the phone disconnecting on the other end.

So I stayed there, clearing my thoughts for a few hours. No answers yet. Maybe it was a sign I needed to go back to the beginning. Or to my old life, where none of this was even in question.

"What's going on here?" a voice said behind me. I could barely contain my smile, so instead I rolled my eyes. "Why are you in my spot?"

"Someone told me it's a really good place to clear your

thoughts," I replied, turning my head to see him standing behind the bench. His hands grabbed on to the back of the seat, and he leaned towards me. I had to crane my neck up to see him well. "How are you so stealthy? I never hear you come."

He shrugged. "Not my intention, by the way," he said, looking out into the distance. "I think you're so deep in thought that you block out the outside. What's on your mind?"

"Why are you being so nice?" I smiled at him, expectant of his reply. I knew he was going to laugh, but never in my wildest dream did the actual response match my expectations. He barked out a laugh so loud, it echoed through the valley. A few birds took flight at the exact moment, clearly ruffled by the sound.

"Are you always so uncompromisingly forthright?"

I grinned at his question. "I mean, you put it so eloquently." I preferred the term no-nonsense: simple and straightforward. It was the only way things got done. Maybe it was too Susana of me to assume that my candor got things done? I shrugged. "Some people call it being a bitch."

He smiled. "Who does?" His brow furrowed in confusion. His eyes were particularly dark today, a deep blue that reminded me of the sky at dusk. "And I'm not being nice to you. I'm nice in general, I think."

"You know how they say that when you're born in a burning house, you think the whole world is on fire?" I looked at him. He had taken a seat next to me, his hand reaching for mine and lacing our fingers together. Our hands rested on my thigh. I felt compelled to rest my head on his shoulder but stopped short of doing it because I wasn't sure I could handle his response. "It's not, obviously. It still feels this way most of the time for me. Like it's us—my family—against the world, always waiting for the next thing to happen, always counting down the next thing in a long, infinite series of steps that eventually, hopefully, leads you to a happily ever after."

"But it's not," he replied. He turned his body to me and looked into my eyes, searching. "It's not anyone against anyone, Vee."

"I know." I sighed. "It just feels like it. Like no one is on my side."

"I'm on your side." His lips turned up at the corners in a tiny, shy smile. He licked his lips, and then his eyes moved to my mouth in the exact moment as my lips parted. We sat there for a second, frozen, the anticipation burning between us. My core lit up like a fire on the coldest night of winter.

The sound of thunder broke the moment. I blinked.

"I broke up with Clara," he blurted. My eyes widened, and I turned to look at him, a question on my face.

"Okay?" I squeaked. It came out more as a question than anything else.

"Just wanted to put it out there," he said as he shrugged and stood to leave. He reached for my hand to help me up. "Let's go."

"No." I planted my feet, not wanting to move forward. I narrowed my eyes at him. "What happened?"

"It was overdue," he said, dragging his long fingers through his hair. "It wasn't working out anymore."

"But then why did you bring her here for your grandmother's birthday?" Was it me? Was this because of me? That couldn't be it, right? I wasn't that important. I was just in and out, just passing through this town while I found answers to questions that were riddling me.

"It was partially Lucía's fault," he said, scanning the surroundings. The sky was dark, and there was a flash of lightning in the distance. "I've been here for a few months and Lucía just… slipped up. Told her we were having a party. Oh wow, I sound like an asshole. I'm not an asshole, I promise. I needed space. From everything."

He was babbling. He wasn't a babbler. He was comfortable with his words. The sentences that came out of his mouth were thought out and thoughtful.

"Recently, I've been wondering if the choices I've made are the right ones and am really hoping they are. Let's go."

17

THE BLACKOUT

Maybe the storm rolled in fast, maybe it didn't. But it almost felt like one minute it was light gray clouds, the next it was thunder and lightning and heavy, heavy rain.

"No, no, no!" What *else* could possibly happen to me? "Whyyyyy?"

Santiago chuckled next to me, his hand guiding me through the dense trail. His eyes were fixed on the ground, either trying to avoid the water getting in his eyes or looking down to dodge anything that could cause an accident. Our steps were quick and clumsy, running away from the storm as fast as we could.

I didn't even have enough time to react. By the time I stood up, I was soaked, water dripping from my hair straight to my shoulders, down my face, and from the tips of my fingers.

"I can't believe this keeps happening to me," I said loudly to him. He looked back for a second and smiled wide.

"What keeps happening to you?" he yelled back. He was soaking wet in his running clothes. His long-sleeved T-shirt clung perfectly to his toned torso. The muscles on his back were defined, and I could practically count them out loud. I couldn't stop ogling.

Santiago cleared his throat, directing my eyes to his face. I felt myself blush and was thankful that my face was partially covered with my wet hair because I was sure it would have been tremendously evident to him. He laughed as he looked me up and down and smiled once his gaze reached my eyes. He stopped in his tracks, making me bump against his chest. His hands were on me immediately, holding me tight around the waist. He lingered there and took a step forward without breaking eye contact.

"Um. This…" I gestured at nothing in particular with my arms open wide. "It almost feels like I'm in one of those prank shows from the early 2000s and they just keep piling stuff on me to see how much I can take."

"You can take it." He winked. The moment dragged on, neither of us moving an inch. One of his hands let go of my waist, and his fingers grazed the back of my hands, running tingles up my arm. The rain was relentless, but everything stopped. It was just us. "Vee—"

A cell phone pinged twice, immediately followed by a loud ring.

"Who is it?" I said as Santiago took out his phone from

his shorts pocket. His biceps bunched with the movement, the T-shirt sleeves clinging to them. Water dripped from his fingers on to the screen.

"Hello?" he yelled over the sound of the rain.

There was a voice on the other side, but I couldn't distinguish who it was. He nodded his head a few times.

"We got caught in the rain," he said, looking at me. "We're heading back into town now. Okay, see you soon. Thank you."

"Who was that?" The rain was stopping. Large drops lingered on the leaves, slowly dripping to the ground around us. "What happened?"

"The director at the community center can see us today."

"Oh, okay. That was fast. I thought that lady was out of the office." Santiago had asked around, and it turned out that the woman who was currently the director at the center was the same one that had been there all those years ago.

"Yeah, she technically is, but she's going in to see us." He winked at me. "A little favor."

This was exactly who Santiago was. He was a charmer, and his intentions were pure. He loved helping people, and I was seeing it firsthand with how he was managing this whole situation with my grandfather.

"Right." I rolled my eyes. "I'll go change, and we can meet there in an hour?"

An hour later, we were standing in the courtyard inside the community center. It was the old railroad station, back when the town was inhabited by English railroad workers in the late nineteenth century. The building was small and quaint. It seemed that the courtyard had once been the railroad track, no longer operational. It divided the building in two sections. The closest one to the street housed all of the different rooms for events and classes, and the farthest one had a few offices, a kitchen, and the restrooms.

"Ready?" Santiago asked me, turning to face me with his whole body.

"As I'll ever be." I sighed dramatically.

"It'll be fine. We can just ask a few questions or maybe to see the town archives. My grandfather told me that the town used to keep very accurate records a few decades back, so they should have at least something for us to look at."

He turned, offering me his hand without hesitation. My body reacted automatically, extending mine to meet him halfway, like this motion was meant to be, like my hand belonged there.

We walked silently until we reached the office. The door was wide open, and a woman who must have been in her late sixties sat behind the desk, slowly humming a tune I didn't recognize and reading something on her computer screen.

Santiago knocked on the door frame with his free hand while simultaneously squeezing mine.

"Good afternoon," he said in a formal tone. I didn't remember hearing him ever use such a tone, but maybe this was his lawyer voice.

"Look what the cat dragged in! I haven't seen you in ages, Santi. You must be Victoria?" she said, standing up from her seat and taking a few steps to greet us. She looked at our joined hands and smiled. She immediately kissed Santiago's cheek, then turned to me. "Nice to meet you."

We walked forward and took a seat on the chairs across from her.

"How can I help you?" she asked, smiling softly. She took off her glasses and placed them by her computer mouse. "You sounded a little cryptic in your voicemail."

Santiago looked at me and squeezed my hand once again before he let go.

"We were wondering if you could help us find some information about a man that lived here in the eighties. If nothing else, maybe show us any data from that time and we'll see what we can find."

"Oh sure, that's easy," she said, grabbing her glasses and waking her computer up. "We actually just digitized all our records, so it'll take us no time to bring those up. What's the name?"

Santiago looked at me and lifted his eyebrows, encouraging me.

"Enrique Aguirre," I said quietly. The woman stiffened immediately and looked at me. "He was my grandfather."

"Oh, um. Sure, let's see here." She turned to her screen again, typing something on the keyboard. "Here we go."

I heard the printer fire up behind us. The office was dated but cozy, with wood paneling on the walls and unflattering overhead lighting. The director's desk was a mess of paperwork and folders stacked in overflowing piles. There was a plant in the corner behind the woman and a large bulletin board full of photos, event calendars, and copies of newspaper clippings.

The director stood up to go to the printer and grabbed the few pages that it spat out.

"Here we are. This is what we have for him." She handed me the two pieces of paper, the second one practically blank. The first one contained some of the things that I already knew: the address of his home, his date of birth and place of work. "He was here for a few months in 1988. This is everything under his name."

"And how did you collect this data?" Santiago asked, looking at the pages before lifting his head to stare at the woman. "Was it a formal process or was it anecdotal?"

"Mostly anecdotal, I would say," she replied confidently. "It was on a registration basis—people would become members at the center here, sign up for events or to volunteer. I will say, back in the eighties, we had a really engaged group of residents, so almost everyone around town is in the system."

She looked at me and smiled softly. Her eyes were fixed on my face, looking for something there. "I'm sorry I can't give you more information," she added. "He was a good man, you know? Such a tragedy, what happened to him."

I swallowed and turned to look at Santiago, his gaze

fixed on me. The few people I had spoken to already mentioned similar things—such a tragedy. Was there more?

"Oh, I didn't realize you knew him," I responded. My thoughts were going a mile a minute. Maybe this woman held the key to really understand him and what happened.

"Not too much, no. He mostly kept to himself, but he was very generous with his time. He told me once that he was a corporate lawyer. He helped us when we registered the community center as a nonprofit organization. It was when I first started here, so I didn't spend much time with him. He spent hours upon hours looking at all of our documentation and our books to make sure we had everything aligned."

This. This was the man I thought I knew growing up. My family had painted him as an honorable man, a man that was dedicated to his job, his family. A man that would invest hours of his free time giving back to the community. This was the grandfather I never knew but always wished I did.

"Yeah, that's what I heard from other people in town too." The woman stood up and turned to her bulletin board and unpinned a copy of one of the newspaper articles. "I never met him; he died before I was born."

"Is that why you're in town? Looking for information about him?" she said, extending her hand and offering me the paper. "Here, you can keep it."

I skimmed the article; in the middle, there was a blurry photo of the woman in front of me, three decades earlier in a ribbon cutting ceremony. It was the reopening of the community center, and my grandfather stood next to her, holding the giant scissors. The article mentioned him by name as instrumental in the new operations of the nonprofit, modernizing the way it was run and adding a few services that would benefit this sleepy tourist town. I felt Santiago's hand on my back, sliding up and down my spine in a soothing motion.

"Actually, no. I'm here on vacation and just stumbled upon this." Happenstance.

"I'm sorry I can't be of more assistance." She shrugged. "But if you have any questions, let me know. My door is always open, and this charming man right here knows where to find me." She winked at him and smiled.

I thanked her, and we walked out hand in hand into the street. The rain had all but stopped now, and the town smelled like a summer shower. The wind was still blowing on the tall trees, the leaves shiny with leftover water.

"Vee—"

"You know what's the weirdest thing in all of this? Your grandfather came to see me today, and he said almost the same thing as this woman," I said quickly. My day had been so emotionally charged, it felt like this had happened days ago instead of just a few hours ago. "He died in such a tragic manner, and he was so generous with his time and helped so many people. And in a way, that is the man that I thought I knew. That is exactly who has been carefully constructed in the narrative that my family built of him throughout the decades. Like, to the point that I became a fucking lawyer because of this man. To honor his legacy and his name."

The woman at the community center hadn't been able to provide any additional information relating to my grandfather—as a matter of fact, I learned absolutely nothing new—but it made it all an inch more final. I could feel closure coming. I felt like I'd exhausted all my resources, and this was as much as I would learn about him, get to know him.

"But at the same time, it's almost like he's a walking contradiction. Because if he was such an honorable man, why was he caught embezzling funds? Or mingling with loan sharks? I just don't get it."

"Why are you trying to find these answers?" He looked at me. We were now standing right in front of the community center, the evening falling upon us and a few stars blinking in the night sky. The streetlamps casted a shadow on Santiago's face, sharpening his features. "It's a genuine question. I'm not trying to be—"

"I don't know," I interrupted. "I obviously never expected any of this to happen to me, but this whole thing is making me realize so many other things and..."

Would things have been different if I'd grown up knowing the truth?

I took a deep breath and looked up at him, and the next thing I knew, I was enveloped by Santiago's warm arms, cocooned by his large body.

"I'm overwhelmed. I don't know what to do anymore,

Santiago," I said in between sobs. "What should I do?" I could feel the tension in my shoulders and Santiago's hand moving up and down my spine, this sudden level of intimacy that I wasn't prepared to accept just yet.

I took a step back and cleared my throat, looking at him with my eyes full of unshed tears. He looked back at me with such a sweet smile, and I could tell that he wanted to say more, tell me what to do and what to think. But he didn't. He kissed the top of my head and pulled me closer to him, our bodies flush, standing right outside the community center.

"I'm exhausted, really. Because up until this point, it felt like I had everything: the really great career, the perfect relationship, a really good family. I was content. Maybe not *happy* happy, but content, and that was pretty good considering the kinds of problems other people have," I added.

"Victoria, what you choose to do with what you inherit is just that, a choice. You can't expect that every single thing that has been handed to you, out of your control, is a mandate of some sort." He shifted his position so that he could look me better in the eyes. "Just because your grandfather was an attorney, it doesn't mean you have to be one, and just because your grandmother says you should marry doesn't mean you should. I understand responsibility, you know I do, because I'm doing a job every day that makes me miserable, only because it makes my family happy. But it's a choice that I make, every day. I choose." His shoulders sagged, and he grabbed my hand. "You should choose too.

You should write your own story." I blinked. "Obviously who your family is and what they've done forges a path, but it's a flexible journey, Vee, a journey where you choose your pace and the number of stops you take and which direction you go in."

I tilted my head in response. My eyes started to water again, the tears threatening to fall at any minute. I had done a very bad job of keeping them at bay where Santiago was concerned.

"Remember when I told you that I almost didn't show up that first day? I was alone *and* lonely too. I was so homesick, I was this close"—he gestured with his thumb and index finger and smiled wide—"to calling my mom to come pick me up."

"Yeah, but the difference between you and me is that your mom probably would have dropped everything and ran to pick you up, and I've been here what, two weeks, and I have yet to hear from my family. Cata doesn't count, for obvious reasons. Today was the first time that someone asked me if I was okay, and even that was immediately followed by the fact that my grandmother is furious."

I let that sink in. He huffed in frustration.

"What's that snort for? It's abundantly obvious that your family adores you—adores each other—and then there's Clara, and your sister and brothers are also wonderful and even this freaking town, everyone seems to love you, and then who do I have?" The tears were falling now, even with my eyes closed. "My grandmother? My ex-fiancé? My father is an alcoholic, and my brother is very much doing his own thing. Catalina is my only friend, and she's drifting away; her life is changing drastically right in front of my eyes. Pedro… I don't even know any more."

"We can work on that," he said. "Let's get you to bed. It's late."

He walked me to my room and waited patiently until I unlocked it. I felt his lips on my forehead, a small and familiar peck, like we'd been doing this for years, decades even. Casual yet charged with an unexplained energy. My breath caught in my throat, but I didn't react.

"*Hasta mañana*, Santiago," I murmured, walking in without looking back at him. Not allowing myself to fall deeper.

18

THE INVITATION

"WHAT ARE YOU DOING HERE?" I asked without even having to turn my head. I could feel him standing behind me, the hairs on the back of my neck alerting me to his presence. I could confidently bet my life savings that he was standing in the doorway, one of his big hands grabbing the frame, the other one tucked in the pocket of his jeans.

"I've been looking for you," he said, smiling. At this point I hadn't turned around yet, but my body had a way of telling me he was close. His footsteps were steady behind me, soft on the carpet of the hotel's sitting room. "You weren't up in your room."

I'd been holed up in the hotel's sitting room all morning, going through my work emails to keep me distracted. The entire journey I'd been on to finally discover that my grandfather was dead had drained me, both physically and emotionally. And being in close proximity with Santiago meant being vulnerable—even if that wasn't my intention at all. When I was close to him, all the walls I'd constructed year after year vanished.

I had managed to avoid him for a full day. It was a first, for sure, because he seemed to be everywhere in this town. Two nights ago, he had walked me to my room, kissed the top of my head, and left me there pondering what the hell I was doing.

He stood in front of me, taking me in. His gaze moved from my face to the computer on my lap, to the pages and pages of my legal documents on the coffee table, full of notes in the margins. "Why are you working?" he asked, immediately recognizing what I was doing.

"Just reviewing a few things. I have some cases that needed a little help in my absence," I said without even looking at him, my eyes glued to my screen to avoid him.

"Where did you even find a printer?" he said, taking a seat to my left. His smell followed him all the way down to where I sat. I bit the inside of my mouth to avoid smiling. He looked good, like always. He wore black jeans and a tight-fitting gray T-shirt. His tattoo peeked out of his shirt sleeve. He ran his fingers through his hair, and his bicep tightened. I sighed.

"Are you done?" he asked, smiling.

Ogling? Never.

"Working? No," I replied quickly. I felt my cheeks blush, so I turned to my right and pretended to straighten the documents that were on the wood side table next to the sofa. I could feel his eyes on me, following my movements. "I actually want to read a few things that Catalina sent me yesterday. Haven't gotten around to it just yet."

I cleared my throat and turned to him, shutting my laptop and placing it on the coffee table in front of us. I crossed my legs, then uncrossed them, unable to find a comfortable position under his intent gaze. I cocked my head and lifted my eyebrows in question.

He grinned. The silence stretched for minutes; our eyes locked together.

"Wanna go for a drink?" he asked suddenly.

"Santiago, it's eleven o'clock!" I wanted to smile so hard. It almost felt like our bodies kept finding each other, gravitating towards this. Like magnets. He lifted one of his hands and tucked a lock of hair behind my ear, his hand gently touching my neck. My breath caught with the intimacy of the action.

"Besides, I'm having lunch with your sister," I croaked, my voice much lower than normal. His hands lingered on my arm, making a slow and torturous way down to my hand. I wanted to touch his warm skin, tuck my head under his chin, and stay there for eternity. Safe. "I'm meeting her at noon at your parents' house, and then we're driving to who knows where for lunch. And I need to read those files too. Busy afternoon and all."

I shrugged and stood. He stared.

"Actually, I should go get ready," I said, looking at his handsome face. His stubble was back, and he looked delicious, his whole look put together but effortless at the same time. A lock of hair fell over his forehead, and he brushed it back with his fingers, the movement lifting the hem of his shirt and flashing me with a bit of tight abdomen. I swallowed hard. "Rain check?"

I needed to get out of there before he consumed me. This man was pure fire, setting me ablaze from the inside out. I grabbed my things in a haste, hurrying to leave his side.

"Vee?" he said from behind me. I was almost at the door and turned to face him, several meters of distance between us; there was too much nervous energy in the room. "Do you want to get a drink tonight?"

Like a date?

"Yes." My eyes bugged out as he uttered the words. "A date."

Did I say that out loud?

Santiago laughed, one of his carefree and happy laughs. He looked at me and smiled wide. "Yes."

"I don—"

"Not too soon," he interrupted, reading my mind. "And for the record, Vee, I don't give a shit what people say. Or think, for that matter."

I hesitated, running through every possible outcome in my head. The reality was that I wanted to be close to this man. For reasons unexplained, but we were gravitating around each other, our chemistry off the charts. *Say yes.*

He shifted his weight from one foot to the other and took a few steps forward, closing in on me and reducing the space between us by half. The sun was shining in through the window, directly onto his face. His eyes sparkled with anticipation, the color in his eyes a little lighter than normal, almost gray in the light.

"Say yes," he said softly. He licked his lips and took a step forward.

"Okay." I smiled and shrugged with one shoulder. "Sure."

The drive to the top was out of this world. The unpaved roads gave this town a mystical look, almost like it was stuck in time. Only a local would navigate the roads this way. The windows were down, and the wind was blowing in the car, my dark hair a tornado around my face. From this high up, it was very clear that everything was in transition. The colors of the leaves popped against the mountainous terrain.

Lucía drove us to a little lodge at the top of the mountain. It was only open on specific dates—mostly for big groups of hikers and to cater to the tourists that would venture up the mountain. It was a small wooden building, with a tiny front door and two windows on either side adorned with flower boxes exploding with seasonal plants. I could picture the black hellebores in the wintertime, maybe covered in snow.

"Oh, it doesn't really snow much here, not enough for it to stick anyway," Lucía said behind me.

I laughed and widened my eyes. "Did I say that out loud?" What was wrong with me?

We walked in and headed towards the back, where the wall had been replaced by floor-to-ceiling windows and the whole valley was visible.

"See right there?" Lucía said, pointing to the right and squinting her eyes. "It's barely visible, but you can see Santiago's bench from here."

I smiled and took in my surroundings: the creek was hardly discernible from this altitude, and we could see a few people bathing by the rocky shore. I couldn't directly see the bench, but the general area was obvious—it was clear of trees and the ledge was pronounced; the bench was probably tucked under the big branches. The sky was a bright blue, and there were a few wispy clouds slowly moving from one side to the other.

"He's such a weirdo." Lucía chuckled. With a smile on her face, she sat down and propped her big purse on the chair next to her. I took a seat across from her, repeating the same movement and setting my purse on the chair next to me. It was familiar, something we'd done the night we had dinner. A repeat action that created familiarity among us.

The view out the window was like nothing I'd seen before—even when I'd traveled to Europe with Susana when I was a teen. It truly was breathtaking.

"So," she said. "Santi has been very tight-lipped about

you, in contrast to his constant blabbermouth *about* you in the last few years."

"Yeah, I've heard," I said, trying to hide my amusement. "I think the last time I saw him was probably, what? Eight years ago? Maybe ten?" I shrugged.

Lucía pursed her lips. I wasn't sure if she was trying to conceal a smile or what. She looked out the window and narrowed her eyes, maybe in confusion. "Hmm."

That was that. Just a noncommittal hum.

I scanned the room. It was clad in wood, and it was definitely something that Susana would describe as "rustic," as to avoid calling it something else. "*Un espanto*," she would say. Disgusting, unpleasant. But it reminded me a little of a restaurant in the Swiss Alps I'd seen in a travel blog while doing research for my honeymoon. *Best Hidden Gems* or something like that. Manuel had been adamant we travel to Australia, despite my request to visit the South of France.

Should that have been the last realization that the man was a walking red flag? Probably. We'd never, not once that I could recall, done anything I had requested. I waited for him to be ready to get married, for him to suggest moving in together. I didn't even take the initiative to call him or text him early in our relationship, as to not appear clingy. *Needy,* he would call me behind my back when he thought I wasn't listening in on his conversations.

There was a big difference between having needs and being needy. But I was never needy. I kept mostly to myself, buried in work and curled up in a chair reading my books.

Occasionally, I would join him at a party or event, but over the years those were few and far between.

"This is really cute," I said, hoping to change the subject entirely. Although I was sure I would eventually endure one of her interrogations. The constant questioning was a family trait, apparently. "Never would have expected this to be here."

"Yeah, it's owned by my aunt and uncle, the same ones that own the hotel down in town." She quickly glanced at the menu, placed it on the table, and pushed it aside. "Do you want to share a charcuterie board to start?"

She looked at me. Her eyes were so similar to Santiago's, even in the way they crinkled when she smiled.

"Hey, Lucía," the waitress said as she approached us, her ponytail swaying with her body. "Are you ladies ready to order?"

"How do you guys get anything done in this town?" I asked Lucía as the waitress left our table after taking our order. It seemed like these people couldn't walk even a few meters without someone waving at them or calling out their names. Compared to my own experience, it was surprising. Because I was well known, my family was too, but I don't think I had many interactions unless someone wanted something of me—of us. "It's amazing."

"Bleh, small town." She rolled her eyes and gestured with her hand. "My family is the warden of all the town secrets." She snorted and immediately covered her mouth, embarrassed by the reaction to her own joke.

I smiled and chuckled, then looked out the window. How many secrets did my own family have? How many secrets did I keep?

"How so?" I said, curiosity getting the better of me.

"You know, my family runs the only law practice in town. We know who is getting divorced before they even know it," she said and grinned. "And I'm the town's doctor." She shrugged.

There was a moment's pause. It wasn't awkward. Despite us being acquaintances, the silence felt natural. Practiced.

"Are you going to tell me what brings you to town?" *Ah, the interrogation has started.* "Because by the sounds of it, it's probably not my handsome brother, huh?" she said with a smile.

I felt my skin flush, not with embarrassment, but with the thought of Santiago's body next to mine, his warm hands on my skin, the little touches here and there. I cleared my throat.

"I needed a break," I said, wringing my hands on my lap. "And believe it or not, it was pure coincidence that I ended up here."

"A break from what?" I didn't think she was asking to be nosy, per se. As a matter of fact, my cousins and I had been trained specifically for this—to know which people would approach us because it was convenient to them. Susana had always been adamant that our last name was so powerful, people would only want to be close to us because we could give them something. But wasn't that exactly the reason why Manuel and I would be marrying? Because it was a powerful union between two families? It sounded so Shakespearean it hurt.

"Life," I replied. Lucía's eyes were full of concern, and for the first time in a long time, I was inclined to open up. "I was supposed to get married." She nodded while I took a sip of my water. "But on the day of the wedding, I received a photo on my phone with him and another woman in our bed."

She gasped. "Who sent you the photo?" A logical question and something that until now, I had buried deep.

"I actually don't know yet. I've been preoccupied with other things lately." Manuel had been a coward; I had no doubts about that. And I couldn't think of anyone who would have bailed me out of that relationship. "I wouldn't be surprised if he sent it himself, like from a burner phone or something. He wanted an out but was too chicken shit to talk to me like an adult."

And I hadn't seen the signs, so why would someone else? I was too preoccupied with making my grandmother happy, and it cost me my happiness in the process.

"Ugh, what a jerk. I swear to god, men." She sighed dramatically. "What a waste of space." I looked out the window and heard her giggle to herself, the same reaction bubbling up in my throat. I started laughing because at this point, that was the only thing I could do.

"It's not funny," I said in between fits of laughter. "I wasted so much time with him... Ugh."

A sobering thought.

"What about you?" I tilted my head, trying to under-stand the sudden sadness in her eyes. "Santiago mentioned you just moved back."

"A little over a year ago," she said with a lingering smile. "Bad breakup during residency turned into this lingering need to come back home closer to family."

"Oh, I'm sorry to hear that." She looked sad, a contrast to the giggling woman she'd been seconds before. "What happened?"

"My career was too demanding for him, I think." She pursed her lips and looked out the window. "The hours are long, our free time is not ours, and he just couldn't take it. It's fine, I get it. He's married now and has the cutest son. It's what he wanted, and I'm happy for him that that's what he got."

"Do you want kids?" I was surprised at my question. I didn't get close to people. "Sorry, you don't need to answer."

"No, it's fine. I do, but I'm still young, and I need to be established in my career first."

"I totally get that," I said, fully identifying with her. She smiled in return.

"Victoria, you'll be fine." She wiggled her eyebrows. "My brother is a good man."

"Don't know what you are talking about." I felt my skin flush beet red. I wasn't a blusher, but thoughts of that man were wreaking havoc in my brain and on my body. "I think we're just friends. We didn't like each other before, but I think it's getting better."

"Are you guys enemies turned to friends that now go on dates?" She smiled wide, her eyes shining conspiratorially.

"How do you ev—"

"Small town, Victoria. Small, small town."

19

THE DISCOVERY

My nerves were frayed.

Such a Susana thing to say.

Ever since getting back from lunch with Lucía, I couldn't stop my brain from wondering.

Was he really a good man? So far, he had been the *best* man I knew, going above and beyond to be there for me despite our complicated past. He was the same way with his family and his community. He was solid. I didn't want to keep comparing him to Manuel, but it was automatic, inevitable. He was the complete opposite, and for some reason I couldn't understand, he wanted me. *Me.*

But also, who sent me that photo? I would probably need to talk to Catalina about this, see if she could help me figure it out.

Almost like I had conjured it by magic, my phone pinged

with an incoming text from Catalina. I didn't even read the text before clicking on her name and calling her directly.

"Hey," she said, her mouth full of who knows what. She was very into baking and was probably having one of her famous (to me, at least) sugar cookies. "What are you up to? I'm bored." She rolled her eyes and pouted like a small child.

"How are you feeling?" She looked tired. "You look tired."

"Yeah, no shit," she said and laughed. "Your brother is making me crazy with all the hovering. He stopped going to work."

I smiled at the thought of my brother taking care of her. They were so good for each other, and it was so disgusting I grimaced. "Why?"

"He says he's on maternity leave," she huffed. "I want to be left alone and be allowed to binge watch shows and obsess over unsolved mysteries by myself. But he's around all the time."

"*Ay, amiga.*" She sounded annoyed, but I was sure she was enjoying it. It was a matter of weeks until their lives changed forever, and I'm sure she was soaking it up. "He went to see your dad the other day," she said nonchalantly.

I closed my eyes and took a deep breath. "And?"

"He's fine, same as always." My father's alcoholism had gotten worse throughout the years. It wasn't terribly bad now, but Catalina had seen how it progressed, first as a friend and later, as family. It wasn't bad, really, only mildly inconveniencing, especially because Susana had done a lot of crisis management around him. A few years back, he stopped being the lead attorney at the firm, and between Pedro, my brother, and me, we were able to take over and manage just fine. "Have you decided when you're coming home?"

Home.

"I've been thinking—"

"Oh boy." She laughed, and I saw her moving about on the other end of the call. She placed the phone on the kitchen countertop and shuffled over somewhere in close proximity. The sound of a cabinet opening and closing was clear over her voice. "It's always dangerous when you do that because you're already too smart for the rest of the world when you are *not* purposely thinking. I can't imagine what you're up to now."

I smiled. She was, possibly, my biggest fan. "*Ay, callate.*" I took a big breath, afraid of what would be coming out of my mouth, but I wanted to run it by her nonetheless. "Do you think that it was Manuel who actually sent me that stupid photo?"

She stopped moving. The silence on the other end had me looking at my phone to check if the call had dropped. "Um, why?"

"I don't know. I had lunch with Santiago's sister today, and she asked me who sent the photo, and obviously I didn't have an answer because with everything going on, it never even registered to check, but she's kinda right. Maybe I should be checking?"

"Have you been on social media recently?"

If I was good at googling, Cata was a master sleuth. If she couldn't find any information, she knew someone who would help her. Exactly like she was doing with my grandfather's information.

"What?" I sighed. "Just tell me."

"He moved to Australia. Allegedly"—such a lawyer—"he accepted a promotion within his company three months ago and starts a new role next week."

"What?" I narrowed my eyes, trying to map everything out in my head. "He never said anything." I shook my head. "Wait, what? I…"

That didn't make any sense. Because if he had accepted a job offer, he would have said so. But also, he knew I would never move, so he just went ahead and did it behind my back? I tried thinking of conversations we'd had, about his insistence on going to Australia for our honeymoon. Was he going to try to convince me to move there once I visited?

"I'm confused."

"You and everyone else, buddy," she added, her tone chirpy and clear.

"Oh my god," I whispered, the realization tight and heavy in my chest. "Oh my god."

I heard Catalina's deep sigh on the other end. I could picture her shaking her head in disappointment and closing her eyes in slow motion, like she did many, many times when someone had fucked up.

"Yep," she said, popping the *p*. "It's fucked up."

"Why didn't he tell me?"

"I don't know," she whispered. "I'm sorry."

"What do I do?" There was nothing to do, of course. "The little shit. How did I not see this coming, Cata? Ugh. I'm an idiot."

I ran to the door after noting the time on the phone screen and absentmindedly grabbing my purse. I took one last look in the mirror by the closet in the entry.

"Hey, I-I have to go," I said quickly. I wasn't ready for my best friend to listen to this just yet, especially if the man in question was standing right there. "I'll call you later, *beso.*"

Oomph.

"Shit, sorry, I didn't see you there." I lifted my head and Santiago was standing there outside my door, looking as delicious as that morning, when he'd shown up with the purpose of asking me out on a date. I smiled. "Hey, I thought we were meeting downstairs."

"I don't mind coming up here to pick you up." He was wearing those dark jeans that looked so good on him, a light blue button-down that did wonderful things for his arms, with the sleeves rolled up to his elbows and a cardigan draped around his shoulders. "Are you ready?"

"Where are we going?" I asked. He was being a little mysterious about this whole thing. I mean, the whole town knew what was happening except for me. "And also, how is this any different from what we've done since I got here? Because if I recall correctly, we've had dinner together a bunch of times already."

He laughed, his eyes crinkling at the corners like always. Pure joy. "You look good," he said, looking me up and down while we walked out of the hotel. I was wearing a tight pair of jeans and a loose dark gray sweater, a repeat outfit since I'd only packed a few options that were appropriate for this weather. The night was a little chilly, nothing out of the ordinary for this time of year, according to Lucía. "I like when you wear your hair down."

He noticed that I started wearing my hair down. I had, up until this point, religiously worn my hair up. I never learned how to manage my hair—maybe because Susana always wore it up. "It's a sign of elegance," she would say. Or maybe because I had more important things than to figure out what to do.

We walked in uncomfortable silence for a few minutes, crossing the town square in the direction of his parents' house, past the restaurant and the small dive bar that was mostly for tourists. My mind was still reeling with the fact that Manuel had hidden all that from me. It was clear it had been deliberate.

"Manuel moved to Australia," I blurted. I was angry at that idiot of a man who had messed up my plans, but somehow relieved because it had led me to *this. This is what you want. A man that looks at you this way.* "He moved to Australia."

"What?" There was confusion in his voice. "When?"

I narrowed my eyes and took a deep breath. "I don't want to talk about it because I'm still fuming. Cata told me just now." I stopped abruptly. "Fuck, sorry."

He reached over to me and pulled me to him, kissing my head before saying, "I'm so sorry, Vee. That sucks."

I blinked. "Like…" I sighed. "This was deliberate. He took a job there and never told me. The fucking coward. *Un cagón.* He made me waste so much time." I rested my head on his chest—his smell there, everywhere—and I yelled into him. I could feel his body shaking with laughter at my frustration. I didn't need to look up to know that his eyes were crinkling at the corners and his head was tilted back. "Don't laugh at me!" I swatted at his chest but smiled nonetheless. "Sorry, didn't mean to be such a downer. I'm just so angry, Santiago. Because, ugh, so fucking inconsiderate."

He grabbed my hand and pulled me down the block. "Forget about him."

You're better, I wanted to say. *You make me feel wanted.* I hoped I wasn't reading things wrong.

"What is this?" I said as I inspected the small one-level house tucked in one of the side streets of the town's square. The walk from the hotel was short, and we had chitchatted and discussed trivial things, like the weather. *Eye roll.* The house was dark except for a faint warm light visible from the entryway. It smelled like fresh paint and newly refinished hardwood floors.

"It's my house," Santiago replied, opening the door

wider to let me in. He followed me and took off his shoes. I mimicked his movement while keeping my eyes on the bare walls and the empty space.

"Wait, you have a house?" He took a step further into the room, where there was a large living area with a fireplace in the center and a blanket and pillows just a few meters from it, on the floor. "I thought you were staying with your parents."

"I am staying with my parents." He smirked. "I also have a house." His eyes were shining with amusement, something I'd come to notice was a very Santiago thing to do when he was trying to tease me. As we got closer to the center of the room, I could hear the fire crackle.

I halted and turned to face him. "Not funny," I said with a small smile on my lips. "What is this place?"

"I told you," he replied, reaching for my face. He tucked a strand of hair behind my ear and moved a half step closer. "It's my house. Would you like a tour?"

The kitchen was tucked to the side, and it had a large sliding door that opened to a large back patio. It looked like there was still work being done. Pavers were lined up against one of the sides of the house, and a few bags of sand were piled neatly next to them. The lot backed up to a section of brush with large, mature trees that towered over the neighborhood. It was so quiet; the stars were almost like fireflies in the dark sky. I could hear my breath and the insects around me. The motions of the town were faint over the sounds of nature.

"If you sit still and really, really quiet, you can hear the creek." He stood behind me, his shoulders relaxed, and the corner of his mouth ticked up. I felt his warm breath on the back of my neck. "I got the keys a few weeks ago, and we've been doing some work on it."

I cocked my head and turned to look at him. "Is this like an investment property?" I asked, trying to grasp what he was telling me. "Or, like, are you keeping it for when you visit?"

He smiled and took a step forward. "Something like that." He extended his left arm and pointed back to the sliding door. "Wine? I stole a few bottles from my grandparents' house because I wasn't sure what you wanted to drink, so I have a few options inside for you to pick."

I wanted to scream at him. This was more attention to detail in a few short weeks than I managed to get from my ex in seven years. He would come home from the store with six-packs of beer and say that he got the kind I liked, even though I hated beer and preferred wine, always. "This is fine, thanks."

"Also, I have some appetizers inside, or we can bring them outside and sit here?"

"Can I ask you something?" I whispered, taken aback by the sudden urge to ask him a million questions, starting with *what in the actual hell are we doing?* I took a moment to look at him, then cleared my throat. "I don't mean to be nosy, but why did you buy this house?"

He smiled and grabbed my hand, dragging me inside

into the kitchen, where he had set up a spread on the countertop I hadn't seen on my way in. The wine bottles were lined up neatly on the other side of the island. He grabbed the appetizers and started walking to the living room. "Pick some wine," he called over his shoulder.

I grabbed the first bottle I saw, not wanting to miss out on a second of being next to him, then walked to the living room, bottle in hand.

"Sit," he commanded. And I obeyed.

"Well, you are being nosy, but I'll tell you anyway," he said as he sat right next to me, his long legs stretched out in front of him, his thighs touching mine. He took the bottle from my hands and then grabbed the opener by my knee. "I'm getting ready to move back home, but the timeline for that is still uncertain. I got an in with the previous owners of the house, so I just went for it. I think I'll move in a few months, so in the meantime I'll probably let Lucía stay here until she figures out what she wants because she's been staying with my parents, and it's definitely getting on her nerves." He shrugged.

"Ah, gotcha," I said, narrowing my eyes at him.

"What's that look for?"

"I can't figure you out, is all." He smiled, and I shook my head in response. "Whatever."

He moved a little to the left and crossed his legs, then placed the tray of food in between us. The Santiago I was getting to know now was definitely not the same one that I thought I knew those many years ago, with his calculated pauses and his well-thought-out arguments. This version of him was abysmally different. Looser. Still thoughtful, but less stiff.

"How was your day?" he asked as he opened the bottle of wine. I tucked my legs to the side and under me and balanced my weight on my left hand, angling my body closer to him. He filled two small glasses, then nudged mine towards me while he fixed his gaze on my face. His smoldering look made me squirm in my seat, and a flash of heat went through my body. "Did you have fun with my sister?"

"Yes, she's the best." I smiled, remembering the drive up and down the mountain we'd taken just hours earlier. "We went up to the Grand House. God, it's gorgeous up there."

I took a small sip of my wine, and when I lifted my head up, Santiago was looking at me with his bewildering blue eyes. He glanced down at my lips and his gaze lingered there, a sweet smile on his lips.

"Good," he finally said, the tension palpable.

"What was it like growing up here?" I said, smiling awkwardly. He took a long pause, never breaking eye contact. "So?"

"Small." He laughed. "But quiet and calm most of the time."

His family was almost like royalty here, in the complete opposite sense to mine. My family was the sort of family that people aspired to be, with the money and the properties and the material things. The influence we exerted over others. His family, on the other hand, was kind and loving.

Everyone wanted to be with them, near them, because they opened their hearts to others and couldn't care less about who they were.

"Yeah, I can see it," I replied quietly. My world was also small but never quiet and calm. "Sometimes I wish I were a little bit more invisible."

"I would have never noticed you if you were invisible," he said, his eyes searching my face for a reaction. "That's the most attractive thing about you, how you command a room without even trying."

My nose tingled, and my eyes started watering with panic at all the feelings for him, for Manuel, for my family. I felt safe here with him. Wanted, desired, loved. I swallowed a hard knot stuck in my throat and directed my gaze to the fireplace. The kindling was still glowing, the deep orange comparable to the brightest sun on the hottest day of the summer. I scoffed, trying to push the tears away. He angled his body closer to me and cupped my face with one hand.

"I'm serious," he said carefully. "Like a moth to a blinding, irresistible flame."

He looked at my lips, lingering there for longer than acceptable. I licked my lips in response, the movement completely instinctual.

This man was pure fire. This man, who was all smiles and sunshine, was here with me. Genuinely. Not because someone said so, not because of what it meant for either family, but because he was genuinely interested in me and what I had to offer.

Because he likes you.

My mouth went dry at his confession. I had been in denial up until now, but this made it clear. Clearer than water, actually.

And I... I was elated.

Because you like him.

20

THE MOMENT

TIME WAS FROZEN, and the only thing I felt was my heart thumping inside my chest. Santiago's thumb swept across my bottom lip, and my lips parted in response. His strong body leaned into me, and a small gasp escaped my mouth. I took a deep breath, preparing myself for whatever was to come. I was not stopping this man; I would let him do whatever he wanted with me. To me.

In a quick succession of movements, he grabbed my hips and pulled me onto him, so now I was sitting on his lap, my legs straddling him. His eyes went dark, feral.

Impulsivity in its purest form.

His hands rested at my waist, one of his thumbs sneaking inside my shirt, and both my hands were on his forearms, holding me steady. The butterflies in my stomach were ready to take flight, waiting for the signal. I pushed myself closer, forcing everything of mine against everything of his, until our bodies were flush with each other and the only thing I could feel was our hearts beating against one another.

I could hear his breath in my ear, erratic and out of control. His tongue darted out and he licked my neck, a hum making my whole body vibrate. I tilted my head to give him better access, and I felt a smile forming on his lips.

"Vee?" he rasped, his voice gravelly with want.

"Yeah." It was not a question, but an affirmation. An affirmation of what could happen if I were to allow it. We were both silent. The only thing I could hear was our panting. "*Si.*"

And then his mouth met mine. I let him kiss me because in that moment, there wasn't a better feeling than that of melting away. As soon as his lips touched mine, everything inside me caught fire. I deepened our kiss, getting even closer to him. My hands wrapped around his neck at the same time as his arms tightened around my back, pushing us impossibly closer. There was virtually no space between our bodies, both of us holding on to the other and moving in tandem as if we'd done this hundreds of times before. The familiarity was exhilarating.

His tongue searched mine hungrily, desperately, like the time we had was not enough and we needed to use up every single second. I bit his lower lip and heard him grunt in approval. I smiled against his mouth. His hands lowered to my ass and held me there, rocking me into his hard body. He stood slowly, taking me with him. My legs wrapped around his waist, holding on to his strong body, closer.

"What are you doing? Where are we going?" I squeaked, stunned by the sudden movement, and he chuckled in response. His lips met mine, and he kept kissing me, our lips moving in an elegant choreography. He took two, three, four long steps and then set me on the kitchen counter, standing in front of me and searching my face.

His features were somehow highlighted in the shadows, his strong jaw sharp and blunt in the soft light of the fire glowing in the next room. He lowered his head and peppered kisses down my throat and stopped at the crook of my neck. I shifted my body to get closer to him, closer to the edge. My hands searched for his hair, and my nails gently scraped his scalp, eliciting a satisfied sound that I felt against my chest.

One of his large hands drifted up my side, from my waist to my ribs to right next to my breast, where he stopped, either in hesitation or as if he was asking for silent permission. This was, most definitely, the best kiss I'd ever had in my life, soft and needy, calm and greedy, a slow fire burning through me and straight to my core.

"Yes," I whispered.

He dragged his hand to my breast, my nipple hardening under his thumb and finger. Goosebumps sprinkled across my body, making me aware of the sudden chill in the air.

"Fuck," he said. He took half a step back, his hands dropping to his side. "Sorry," he rasped, running fingers through his hair, trying to tame his wild locks.

"For what?" I cocked my head, a silent question in my eyes. *Do you regret this?*

"I got carried away," he said with an exhale.

"Okay," I replied, nodding my head. "Should I leave?"

He rested his forehead on mine, and a deep sound sighed from his lips. I could smell his scent, all clean and crisp and very much his.

"Okay," he said, his eyes closed. But neither of us moved an inch. A smile formed on my lips, and my arms wrapped around his neck again.

"Okay, I'll leave."

"Okay." He moved closer to me and kissed my shoulder, both of his hands slowly moving up my arms. Once his hands reached my shoulders, he moved them back down my side, placing them on my waist and squeezing. He kissed my temple, my cheek, the corner of my mouth, my lips.

"Okay." I smiled against his lips. "Okay."

Best kiss ever.

———

The smell of coffee and freshly baked *facturas* permeated the air. I was either very vividly dreaming of delicious pastries or my powers of manifestation suddenly had become increasingly strong. I slowly blinked the sleep away from my eyes. My whole body hurt, and my neck and back were stiff as I flipped on to my back.

"Hey," I said to a very relaxed Santiago. He was looking out the window, still wearing last night's outfit. I sat up, admiring his striking face. The morning light highlighted his day-old stubble, and his hair was mussed, like he'd been running his fingers through it. "You got us food?"

The night before was intense. After that kiss, and me asking him if I should leave, we had more wine and more food and sat chatting by the fire until it went out. By then, it was so late that we decided it was better if we slept on the floor like teenagers. *I was making out with my college rival on the floor like a teenager.*

"Yeah." He smiled and turned to look at me. "I went over to the *panadería* by the hotel and got one of everything."

He stared at me, a sweet smile on his face.

"What? What's wrong?" I said quickly, trying to fix my hair and rubbing my fingers under my eyes. "Oh my god."

He laughed and walked over to me, still smiling. "Hi." He bent down and kissed my jaw, somehow making that move-ment hotter than if it had actually been my lips. "How are you feeling?"

I couldn't help but smile at this delightful man. "Sore. I don't think I've ever slept on the floor before."

I giggled. Like a swoony teenager. *What is wrong with you?* I touched my lips, stinging and swollen from the night before. I could still feel his skin on mine, igniting every cell he touched. I had a tender spot on my neck where Santiago had bitten down, then blown on, giving me goosebumps. The memory sent a shiver down my spine.

He reached for my hand and pulled me up, steadying me with his big hands. He interlaced his fingers with mine, and we walked to the kitchen island.

"Hop on," he said. "I'll grab you a coffee."

He grabbed my waist and lifted me on to the counter. He dragged a bag and left it right next to me before turning to the stove. He started moving, and his muscles followed. He poured coffee from a pot, immediately adding two sugars to one of the cups and walking it back to me on the other side of the kitchen. The world melted away, and all I could see was him. For years, I had ignored this man, paid no attention to him whatsoever. My feelings for him bordered on jealousy, but now, now he was slowly becoming the center of my universe.

"Have you been up for a while?" I asked, trying to clear the awkwardness in the air. At least, that was how I felt at that moment. Awkward because I was giving myself to him, no intentions and no strings attached.

"A few hours. I couldn't sleep." He smiled at me. His eyes held my gaze so intensely. He pushed a lock of hair behind my ear, and I looked at him, his handsome face completely relaxed and happy. My eyes followed his messy hair, the stubble on his face. Carefree. He tilted his head and cleared his throat, interrupting the moment.

"Why?" I rasped, my voice cracking with anticipation.

"The floor is very uncomfortable." He laughed. "A lot on my mind too."

"Tell me."

He gave me a sad smile and then grabbed my waist with his two hands, one on either side. He shook his head and turned, looking behind my shoulder. From this angle, I could only see his strong profile, but he looked cloudy, confused, like he was trying to solve all the world's problems from this very kitchen.

"You want to know something?" I asked, interrupting his seemingly murky thoughts. I didn't wait for an answer because I knew he was going to say yes. "What the worst thing about all of this is? It's that I'm starting to doubt myself and the choices I've made. I've always been so fucking sure of myself, of everything that—in my grown-up life—I've decided to do. I've never, not one single day, doubted what I want and what I go after."

He made a surprised face and turned to me. His eyes were glued to my face, paying total and complete attention to what I was saying.

"But all of this," I said, gesturing towards the house and him with my left hand, "is making me doubt my instincts. I mean, now I can see all of the red flags, but hindsight, right?"

He was quiet, his eyes fixed on me, and his breathing was slow and even. He was listening to me. Paying attention.

"It feels like I've been reduced to a small child, like the

decisions I make now need to be run by someone because my life is suddenly completely out of my control." It felt like I could see where I needed to go, except that when I took a step forward or reached out my hand to grasp it, that thing kept sliding backwards. "So now, I'm paralyzed. I don't know what to do. I'm in limbo, in a town that doesn't belong to me but every day that goes by feels like it should, *and* I'm unable to go back home, because that doesn't feel right either."

Tears streamed down my face. I couldn't remember ever crying this much, let alone in front of basically a stranger. "Sorry," I said, my voice wet with the tears stuck in my throat. "It's so much. I don't know how to move forward."

I took a deep breath, trying to organize my thoughts. This happened to me sometimes when I was in court—I had so many things to say that things would just come out, unfiltered. I could feel the tension in my shoulders. At some point Santiago had moved one of his hands to my thigh and had it stretched across possessively.

"I still can't figure out how my grandfather ended up here, which, to be honest, is the least of my worries but really changes everything, you know?" Santiago's thumb moved in a soothing motion on my inner thigh. "Everything I've built to get where I am today is almost a sham. And pushed by Susana. Hard. She pushed and pushed, and the only thing I did was give. And how is that rewarded? Like this." I swept my hand from the top of my head to my torso in a showing motion. "A fucking mess."

He smiled. He looked at me, unblinking. His eyes went to my lips, and I instinctively licked them. I set my mug down on the countertop, trying to calm my beating heart, a traitor of an organ that was trying to leave my body through my throat. I felt his forehead on mine. "Sorry," I said.

"Hey," he replied. "Why would you apologize?"

"I don't want to burden you with my baggage, Santiago."

"Burden? Never, sweet girl." He took a step back and tilted his head, his blue eyes holding mine. "You are not a burden."

My laugh came out wet, more like a yelp than what I intended. "You are too sweet," I said, not even recognizing the words that were coming out of my mouth. *I like you so much,* I wanted to scream.

Santiago leaned in close, so close that my vision went blurry, and whispered, "I like you so much too." I was stunned, too stunned to speak. So I closed my eyes and sighed. He waited, watching me intently with those deep, expressive eyes, until I opened my eyes and looked at him. The moment was charged, and I was immediately covered in flames, my body burning from head to toe as soon as his lips found mine.

I was melting from the inside out. And it felt so good. Too good.

"I should leave," I said, smiling into his mouth. Instead, he pushed deeper, opening my legs wider and standing closer to me, between them. He moved his hands from my waist to the countertop. The small movement gave me a moment to pause. "We need to stop kissing on kitchen counters."

He barked out a laugh and pressed his lips to mine urgently. Our tongues danced, searching for each other like they were two lost souls, finally finding the other one after years apart. I savored him and the movements that felt so natural to me. My hands found his hair again, and I pulled on it softly. He groaned and took a step back, looking at my mouth like it was his most prized possession. His gaze flickered between my eyes and my mouth, and a small smile formed on his lips.

"I'll walk you back," he said, kissing down my neck, burning a path to my shoulder through my collarbone. "In a minute."

21

SUSANA (1988)

I KNEW BACK THEN that the life that I had would never be the same again. Forget about traveling and the latest fashion and the events—those I could cover. But the pity. The sad eyes, the whispering when I walked into a room.

I vowed to never be humiliated again. Was it petty? Maybe. But I was also protecting myself and my family. I needed to take matters into my own hands, to finally have a semblance of control.

"*Señora,* what should we make for dinner tonight?" one of the staff asked. She had consistently been one of the best ones we had. I had never been able to retain the good ones; they always left to pursue other opportunities. Maybe to go to a house with less work. "I was thinking a lentil stew, but it might be too hot for that."

"Nothing too elaborate. I will be out tonight." It wasn't uncommon for us to dine outside of the house on weekends.

But since my husband walked out, the invitations had stopped. The woman raised one of her brows in question. "My daughter can have whatever she wants. Maybe make her a *tarta*. That's fine."

I drove all day, left right after breakfast. Pedro was preoccupied with a few business affairs and was out of town. He wouldn't return until the end of the week, so this really was the only moment I could attempt to do what I was going to do.

The town looked charming but was a little rundown. Some of the roads were still rustic, but I could see a few large houses in the distance. There was a particular one on the edge of town that called my attention—the large structure loomed over the other, more basic ones.

The car was parked a few streets ahead, in a spot where no one could trace it back to me. I still had to kill time, so I headed to a small café in the center of town. I ordered a cup of tea and a few pastries and looked through a few outdated magazines. Was it because I was from the city that I kept up with the gossip? Or did it have to do with my social standing? In any case, everything I read was old news to me, but it was refreshing to know that my name was still out there, even after the chaotic past few months.

A few minutes past seven, I made my way to the address I had memorized all those weeks ago. The stack of letters kept growing as the days turned to nights and the nights turned to weeks, all of them addressed to my son, the return name a familiar one. This behavior needed to stop, for my well-being and that of my family.

I started moving through the streets, strolling slowly under the shade of the large trees. The street was tucked by the corner of the town square. All of the houses were one level and painted white with similar styles. It looked very much like a pocket of a city where the working class lived, all coming back to their small homes after a long day of manual labor.

The large structure that I had admired earlier inched closer to me as I moved towards my destination. The front door was visible from the end of the block, either side of the house adorned with barely blooming hydrangeas in different shades of blue and purple.

I knocked and waited. If he was the same man I thought I knew, it would take him no less than three minutes to get to the door, and he would greet whomever was standing outside with a scowl and those serious eyes.

"Can I he—" he said, stopping mid-sentence in surprise. He opened the door wider and signaled for me to enter the house with his hand. "*¿Qué pasó?* Is everything alright?"

"*Nada,*" I said quickly. Even though I was furious with this man, I knew he cared deeply about his family. The last thing I wanted right now was for him to be concerned and decide to return to the city. "Everyone is quite well."

Roberto closed the door behind us and walked ahead of me. I stood in the hallway, taking in the simple home, the spaces furnished with modest, cheap furniture. The complete opposite of the home we had created for our children.

"Is this your home?" I asked, my tone neutral. "It is rather... austere."

"It is a summer home. They will be remodeling it soon, so all of the remaining furniture is in storage. It serves its function."

This man had always been unassuming, unimpressed with material possessions.

"Why did you do it?" I asked, straight to the point. There was no need to ease into conversation with this man. He had always been blunt and honest, sometimes brutally so. "I don't fully understand your reasoning."

I walked further into the room, searching my purse for the stack of still unopened letters burning a hole inside it. "Here," I said as I extended my hand and offered them to him. "We don't need these."

"These are not yours, Susana," he said. He was calm, standing in front of me in his work clothes. The top button of his shirt was open, his sleeves rolled up. From my vantage point, I could see the kitchen table, a large glass of club soda, and the bottle right next to it. The table was set, and a few lit candles were peppered on the tablecloth.

"Are you expecting someone?" I asked. In the many years since I'd known him, he never cared for much. He was a serious man, kept his head down and provided us with what we needed. I didn't think he ever cared what our home looked like, so the candles were a surprise.

"No," he said seriously. "Why do you have those letters?"

"I need you to back off."

"That is not what we agreed on," he said. His eyes were on fire. His exterior was cool, like ice. But his eyes spoke a different language, sang a different tune.

"I didn't agree to anything," I said, recalling the night he had left. He walked into our home in silence and left it in silence too. Didn't care to utter a word to me. "In fact, I don't think we ever spoke a word on this matter."

"Didn't Pedro tell you the plan?"

"What plan, Roberto? Please, enlighten me with your wise words."

"Susana, *por favor*, don't be crass. It is beneath you," he said as he moved to the table and took a seat at the head. I trailed him with my eyes, sure that my emotions were written on my face and that they would easily betray me. "This is absurd."

"We are finally in agreement," I replied. "You're being absurd."

He sat in silence, looking firmly in my direction. I knew what he was doing. It was most likely his favorite power move: intimidate them with silence.

I held out the letters again. "You need to leave us alone, Roberto."

"Or what, Susana?" I blinked and swallowed hard. *Or what?* "I was always going to come back. Did you think I would just disappear and leave? How little you know me."

I scoffed. Anger was rising inside me; my heart thumped inside my chest, and the only thing I could hear was my heavy breathing. "Why are you like this?" He tilted his head to the side and arched one of his brows. His expression was still serious, but there was a small hint of confusion. "You ruined my family and my reputation. The least you can do is stay away."

"I did it exactly for that reason, Susana. For my family, my children."

"You stole! You stole money, to what? To keep up the charade?" I moved a step closer, my hands shaking. I fisted them and clenched my jaw, trying to compose myself. "You ruined me."

He stood abruptly. The table shook, and his water glass sloshed with the intensity of the movement.

"Ay, Susana, *no seas ilusa*." Don't be naïve. His voice rose in volume, his face stern and unrelenting. "Did you ever think that what we built together was organic? It was never enough with you. So I had to do more. It clearly did not work as a wakeup call because you're here—me being away is still not enough for you."

"Don't you dare put this on me, Roberto." I took another step, ready to meet him where he was. I held on to the table for purchase. "This is all on you."

"What are you going to do about it?" He knew I was stuck between a rock and a hard place. There was nothing I could do. Not now, not in the future. Because it was either my ruin as an influential member of society because I was associated with a criminal, or my ruin as an influential member of society because I was a liar. Neither of those options worked for me. *"Estás entre la espada y la pared, Susana."*

"Why are you being so cruel? What did I ever do to you to deserve this?" I was pleading now. All my cards were on the table, my vulnerability showing. "Just agree to back off. Don't come back."

"The pot calling the kettle black." He smiled. "Cruelty is a different thing, dear."

He was infuriating. He was transformed. This was not the man I thought I knew.

"You are a coward, you know that?"

"Now I'm a coward? Susana, make up your mind." He took a step forward, the tips of his shined shoes touching my heels. I had to crane my neck to look into his eyes. His breathing was slow and even, but there was some sweat beading around his shirt collar. He was nervous. "It's not fair to me that you decided to be selfish. The plan all along was to lie low for a while, then return when everything calmed down. Pedro is actively taking care of things, and I'm working here to figure out how to fix this."

I took a deep breath. "I don't want you to fix anything, I just want you to stay away from us. Stop contacting your children, stop sending letters. Stop it." This man would never back off. He was extremely loyal to his family. If his past actions weren't evidence enough, he had consistently written letters to our son. I never delivered them; the lies ran too deep. "I never asked you to take money that didn't belong to you. You cheated me and the system."

He closed his eyes and shook his head. "Susana, are you blind? We couldn't keep up with the lifestyle you forced on us! This was never meant to happen, but you wanted more, more, more. More traveling, more jewels, more things. Why do you even care about that? You don't come from money; your parents were middle class at best. You were never used to the luxuries you demanded of me. You are a nobody."

"How dare you?" I moved closer to him and used both of my hands to push on his chest. I kept pushing him until the backs of his thighs slammed against the table, toppling over the lit candles onto the tablecloth. "How dare you!"

The cheap cloth caught fire quickly. We both stood there, looking at it, unable to move. Neither of us reacted. The flames grew tall in front of us, the dark yellow turning to orange and the temperature in the room rising to impossible levels.

It felt like hours had passed, when in reality it had only been a few seconds. I blinked the angry stupor away. *What did you do?*

"*¡Mirá lo que hiciste!*" I yelled in panic. *Que desastre. Que desastre.* How was I going to get out of this mess?

I slowly backed away, then turned to face the hallway. When I looked back, the flames were engulfing the kitchen and Roberto was moving swiftly in the room. He didn't turn to look at me, but I could see the panic in his gaze as he picked up a few papers and grabbed the briefcase that was perched by the doorway.

"Susana," he said without even looking my way. He was still moving around hurriedly. *"Salí de acá, rápido."*

Leave, fast.

I ran out the door, closing it behind me. I took a moment to center myself and took a deep breath. He was going to be fine. He was going to grab his things and leave, maybe even call the fire department. He was resourceful, a grown man who was capable of taking care of himself and others.

I looked around, paid attention to the sounds of the scene. No one had been made aware. The street was quiet; there was a gentle breeze that made the branches of the trees dance against the muted sky. The sun was setting, and the horizon was turning a bright orange, the clouds a shade of gray in the dusk of the evening; two completely different scenes inside and out. I heard a door close and that snapped me out of my reverie, making me move my feet, one in front of the other.

My car was parked a few blocks away, so I hurried, looking around and trying to catch a glimpse of what just happened. Apparently, nothing, because there was hardly any movement.

I drove through the night—praying and asking for my efforts to not be in vain—and straight to my house, where I didn't find any comfort at all.

22

THE CASE

"Hi, baby," Cata said into the screen.

"Ugh, you know I hate that word." A shiver ran through my body at the mere memory of Manuel calling me that. "What's wrong? Why are you so happy?"

"I feel great," she said. "I'm moving around; I can breathe. It's great."

I narrowed my eyes at her, doubting this was the only thing that was happening. "Is it like the calm before the storm?"

"I have no fucking clue, but I love it."

"What did the doctor say?" She had been on official bed rest for two weeks now, waiting for her baby to arrive. It was the longest I'd ever seen Catalina sit still. Even on their honeymoon, she and my brother didn't allow themselves to take a minute to stop. They went on a luxurious trip to the Caribbean and didn't sleep in a single day. There wasn't one single photo of them lounging on the beach, enjoying themselves. "Are you still on bed rest?"

"Yes, until the baby comes." She rolled her eyes. "I need you to entertain me."

I was lying on my bed, still high on giggles and butterflies from whatever had happened the night before. I turned to my side and rested my head on my arm, holding my phone with my free hand.

"Cata," I warned. "What's wrong?"

She grabbed a notebook from somewhere in front of her and took a deep breath. Her eyes were a little sad, like she was getting ready to deliver the worst of news.

"Nothing that you tell me right now is going to make this worse," I said, hoping to encourage her. "It's already as bad as it can get. And I read everything you sent me, so I have *some* pieces of the puzzle, I think."

"Okay." She took another deep breath and started talking, using her fingers as a visual aid. "First"—she brought up her index finger—"we have the embezzlement, but you know that already. Second"—two fingers—"there's the cover-up. There was definitely more than one person involved in all of this. And I think that this was the reason behind everything. Most likely this is why he had to lay low. So anyway, in everything I've been able to find, there isn't a lot of proof behind the embezzlement."

She then went on to explain that the embezzlement was in the form of services provided, so Roberto and the firm were billing at a higher rate than normal, and at a much higher rate than what other firms had presented during the discovery phase. "There was an alleged kickback to one of the people involved in the project—I'm assuming for guaranteeing that the firm was actually hired. It's not clear if other consultants applied, but you know, it's literally chasing a paper trail, and I haven't found much."

"Okay." I scrunched my nose. My eyes were sore from all the reading I'd done to try and follow the paper trail. "But why is the kickback alleged? I read what you sent me, but it doesn't really make a ton of sense. I also couldn't find which other firms had initially presented their proposals for the project."

"Yeah, so here is where it gets a little bit more complicated. The bank was a private entity, so the laws that protect those assets are a little different. But the services your grandfather's firm was providing—essentially consulting on legal matters—were for a project that was publicly funded. I don't understand the details yet and exactly how the laws apply, but the kickback he paid? It was to a public official who was part of the committee that decided on who to hire out."

"Fuck."

"Yes, exactly." She was rambling, getting excited at her discovery. "So then it's not clear to me how or who found out about this kickback and the fact that Roberto and the firm were pocketing these extra funds, but the case was taken in front of a judge who was looking into it pretty intensely. And then, suddenly, everything stopped."

"How can you tell?" I knew that historically, the records kept in the eighties were a mess. It was almost impossible to find any information, especially because the judiciary system had been overloaded with cases during those years. The courts began digitizing their records starting in the early nineties, and that information was easily accessible.

"Well, there are no digital records obviously because of the times, but my clerk has been looking into this pretty much every single free hour he's had, and the paper trail stops very abruptly in the fall of 1988. I mean, to the point where there are bank records for like six or seven years prior to that and then nothing else. So I think that either the judge or one of his clerks or adjuncts was paid off. I'm leaning towards the judge, because like I said, suddenly everything stopped. I don't know of a judge that has such influential clerks to convince them to stop investigating just because of a hunch, especially when they were pretty advanced in discovery."

"So we're talking about two different things?"

"Yes, and I also looked into the public official that was given the kickback for that project, and he was also going to be prosecuted for corruption, but that also stopped."

I took a deep breath. "I don't understand."

"Yeah, no shit. It's super complicated and honestly, I want to say it was almost like a mastermind planned this. But I can't figure out where it went wrong, like, who is the snitch."

I didn't understand. Because Santiago's grandfather,

Carlos, had mentioned that he had gotten in over his head with some creditors, and this didn't sound even remotely close to that.

"So on top of the embezzlement, there's the corruption charge? Maybe conspiracy?"

She was standing up now and walking around, her belly round and popping in front of the screen. "No, no conspiracy. Although I would have charged the public official for that, but not your grandfather, no."

"What is the sentencing generally for that?" I wasn't well versed in sentencing because my career was mostly around private contracts and deals. Catalina knew the criminal code by heart, but things had changed a lot since the eighties.

"Well, embezzlement is really hard to prove, especially if it's for services provided. And I think Roberto knew this very, very well, because he overcharged by a few million dollars, or its equivalent. But—and this is a big but—his firm was always a top firm, so he was able to overcharge in some instances, because they were—still are—experts. So again, impossible to prove. And the bank statements that I see here show a regular salary, normal, and then a few additional deposits, every three months or so, of identical, large amounts that can be easily disguised as bonuses. Easy."

"So, like, a slap on the wrist, and then you're on your merry way?"

"Yeah, essentially. Especially since we are talking about

exchange of money, and if the money can be paid back, done. Case closed."

"But there's corruption and intent."

"Exactly. Especially a public official." She was out of breath, pacing her living room right in front of the screen. "And then add to that the potential of paying off this judge or his clerk. And then that's massive."

"And what is the punishment for that?"

"Hmm, back in 1988? Probably thirty-six months or something like that, maybe out sooner for good conduct. It's a classic white-collar crime. But again, it has to be proven."

"Is there a money trail?"

"Not for the judge. The only indication I have at this point is the abrupt interruption during discovery—literally no more bank statements, no more inquiries, no more nothing. Just, *poof*." She motioned with her hands. "Gone."

This started to make a little more sense to me now. What Catalina was saying made sense in more of an abstract way: someone committed a crime and then tried to cover it up by committing another crime, so the only solution was to lie low and wait until everything blew over. And was that the reason that my grandfather ended up in this town? Leaving his family behind? Carlos had also said that he deeply regretted it. But was that the case?

"And so why would he leave then, if the judge was paid off?"

"Well, I think that he followed the advice of someone that told him to lie low, especially if they were tapping into his financial movements. I would say that it was a decision that was made until it died down, especially if the judge was being public about it. So they all let it die down, judge included, as to not generate any suspicion. It went away quietly."

I looked into the screen, hoping she would stop pacing the living room and sit down instead. "Sit down. You are supposed to be on bed rest."

She rolled her eyes at me and said, "I can't help it. This is super exciting."

"Exciting?" But I couldn't help smiling at her enthusiasm. This was exactly how she lived her life.

"Your brother needs to go into the archives and see if he can find the proposal and any invoices for the services. Or, for example, the paychecks with your grandfather's bonuses to see how they were coded into the system. I mean, as the head attorney for the firm, he could bill whatever he wanted, and I think that's why this particular case is impossible to prove—the embezzlement at least."

"And Pedro?" They were partners, although the firm was only named after my grandfather, and Pedro's existence was a mere "and associates." "Was he involved in any way?"

"Couldn't find a single thing on him. But I'm sure he was at least aware. I mean, there are no bank statements for him, but I assume he was also getting these quarterly bonuses. His name wasn't attached to the original proposal either."

"So what's next? Statute of limitations on this?" I shrugged with one shoulder, then flipped onto my back.

"Definitely past that, so no one can be charged. Not even as accessory after the fact."

"A classic he said, he said."

"Yep," she huffed and finally sat down in front of the screen. I could see her face, her eyes wild with anticipation. "That was a lot."

"I agree." Although I still couldn't understand it. I stood up from the bed, my body still sore from having slept on the floor the previous night. I moved slowly into the living area, stopping by the small kitchenette to grab a glass of water. "Who could have been the snitch?"

"Oh, anyone, really. I mean, if the public official suddenly came into money somehow and bought a new car or, I don't know, a new house, and the wife mentioned it to someone, then that someone to someone else? It's impossible to prove. My theory is that's how it happened. They suddenly got noticed because of a change of habits, and that was all it took. For someone to flag it."

"Was it ever in the news? You said that the judge might have gone public with it, and Roberto was a high-profile attorney," I said. I sat on the couch and left my glass on the coffee table. The water was cold, and condensation was quickly forming on the outside, drops moving slowly downwards towards the tabletop. "How was that handled?"

"I couldn't find it anywhere. I sent my clerk to the National Archives, and we couldn't find anything. So it was definitely buried. No chance of leaking, obviously."

"My mind is blown." It almost felt like my brain had

been fried. It was a lot to take in, because this was more than just getting involved with creditors and borrowing more money than could be paid back. This involved planning and intention. "This is way more than what I bargained for."

Catalina laughed a sad smile. "I mean, I guess? I don't even know how this never made it out, with Roberto being so visible and all."

"Was the project ever finalized?"

"Oh yeah, definitely. I think it had to do with some sort of loan? The details escape me."

"These details escape you? You basically just explained corruption to me in four minutes without taking a breath, and suddenly you don't remember?" I smiled. "You are such a nerd."

"You know it," she responded and finger-gunned me through the screen. "How does this change things for you?"

"It's a lot to take in, for sure," I said. "But the fact remains that I won't be able to do anything except maybe try to understand why. Maybe talk to Susana and Pedro? I don't even know anymore."

She sighed.

"I know the feeling." Defeat. Impotence.

"There's not much we can do now," she said.

"Yeah." I sighed. "I guess."

"I'm so sorry."

"It's actually fine, surprisingly." My bubble was bursting, maybe in slow motion. I could see the place it popped around me, but the actual residue still lingered around. Just like the consequences of the actions we took.

"What are you thinking?" She cocked her head and looked at me, breathing rapidly and absentmindedly rubbing her belly. "Sorry I spit that out too fast."

"I don't know. I think I need to sit on this for a while." We sat there in silence for a few minutes, Cata on her living room couch, me on my room's loveseat, just staring into nothing. "Tell my brother, then call me, okay?"

"Yeah," she replied quickly, still looking behind her phone screen and lost in thought. "I'll call you later."

23

THE RUN-IN

MY FIRST INSTINCT was to run. It was what I'd done every single time things got difficult around me. It was primal at this point, second nature. I naïvely told Catalina that I was fine, that everything was okay, but the only thing I could think about was how much deceit I'd grown up around. Evidently, my grandfather was not the man he was said to be, not by him and not by Susana. I wanted to run, but I wanted to run to him. Run to Santiago and tell him everything I'd just heard.

The man had the ability to read my mind, because within minutes, there was a knock on my door. I heard it once, twice, so patient on the other side of the door, but I was numb. Numb with uncertainty, with not being able to take a step—both literally and figuratively.

Knock knock. Pause. *Knock knock.*

I took a small step, then another, and walked to the

door. I opened it wide, turning immediately towards the living room. He followed in my footsteps, walking faster to catch up to me. I felt him hovering behind me, unsure if he should touch me or not.

"What's going on?" He grabbed my elbow and pulled me to him, his long arms wrapping around my body. I rested my cheek on his chest, his breathing steady and calming. "Are you okay?"

I smiled at this generous, kind man, who had been consistently concerned about me since I arrived in this town, even when I'd been aloof and annoyed by him. "Shit just keeps piling on, and I don't think I can take it anymore. I need to talk to my grandmother, and I'm avoiding it," I said matter-of-factly. "Cata just—" I took one more deep breath. "Cata just walked me through a bunch of things that happened with my grandfather, and I'm so, so confused."

But no tears came, just a heavy realization that my life had imploded on me, and that this was the moment where it finally turned. Was the fire extinguished? Or was it merely steadying, still burning in the background?

"Hey," he said, his voice muffled by my hair. "I'm here."

"Why?" I blurted, not even thinking about where this would go next. "Why are you here? We never got along back then."

I felt him chuckle, his hands slowly trailing up and down my back and his body moving slowly to a silent song. His breathing was still even, grounding me to the moment. He took a deep breath, then let me go and took a step back.

"What are you talking about, Vee?"

"Back then," I said. "It was awkward between us, tense. I don't know." I breathed in deeply. "It's like from the moment we met, we couldn't stand each other."

He smiled sweetly then shoved his hands in his pockets. "You have it all wrong."

I frowned, confused at his response. "No, I don't," I said in a childish way.

"Yep, you do."

"I'm not tracking."

"Are you sure you want to have this conversation now?" he said calmly. His voice was firm, realistic with a hint of amusement. "It seems to me that you just received a lot more bad news. Perhaps it's not the right time."

"What conversation is there to have?"

He grinned at me and took a step forward, cradling my face with his big hands. "I've always had a thing for you. Isn't that obvious? But you never let me in. You were always so exasperated, annoyed by every single word I used to say."

I smiled and rolled my eyes at him because that had once been true. But not anymore. I was now enthralled by him.

"Like a moth to a flame," he whispered. He lowered his mouth to mine and kissed me softly. "You were always so focused, so confident in what you were doing and what you knew. You never let anyone in, but at the same time you *belonged*. It always felt like you were there for a purpose, and then you were out."

"I was," I said. "I thought then that was what mattered. I was told that was what mattered." But I was realizing it wasn't that way. Nothing really mattered if you were alone. "I don't feel that way anymore."

"Maybe not right now," he said softly. "Maybe right now you feel defeated. But you used to walk into a room and heads would turn. When you spoke, everyone paid attention to what you said." He placed his hand on my chest, and my heart started pounding inside. "I always admired that, how confident you are, comfortable."

"I don't know," I replied. "It's like all my life I've been this person that was ruled by my family's expectations of me. And that Victoria that you're describing doesn't exist anymore because I'm now realizing that I need to live for me, for my expectations and my desires, you know?"

He smiled, his forehead now resting on mine. "That's my girl."

———

We walked hand in hand across the square and to his parents' home. The town was quiet; a few people were on the streets walking to lunch. It was a unique thing, watching this town transform in front of my very eyes every day. It went from bustling and happy to lazy and quiet in a matter of hours. Every single resident took their lunch break seriously, the town paralyzed by it every single day of the year.

"It's so weird how everything stops for lunch compared

to the city," I said, looking around as the pharmacist flipped the open sign and locked the door behind her. She looked up and waved at Santiago, giving us both a big smile before she went in the opposite direction to us. "It's not something I'm used to at all."

"Yep," he said, popping the *p*. "But it can get annoying if you are used to things moving quickly."

"I think it's charming."

It took us only a few minutes to arrive at his family home, and he walked in like he belonged. There were noises coming from the kitchen, and the faint laughter got louder as we walked to the back. Santiago's parents were sitting at the kitchen table, looking casual and relaxed.

"What?" I whispered to Santiago. "Everyone is here." I felt my cheeks heat just as Santiago tightened his hold on my hand.

"Yeah, it's fine," he said and dragged me inside. His mother smiled wide and stood.

"You made it." Her comment was completely nonchalant and friendly, like this happened every day, showing up with no notice. "Grab a plate. We just started eating."

If it hadn't been obvious before, it was obvious now, the contrast between my family and his. Not in a million years would I be welcomed this way if I showed up unannounced to my grandmother's house, not even for a casual lunch. I wasn't sure exactly what Susana did every day for lunch, but I doubt she ever sat at the kitchen table, close to the help. Susana also wouldn't be caught dead standing up for a guest—if you arrived at *her* home, you were responsible for greeting her. But this family was the exact opposite. Not even flinching at our presence here.

His mom approached us, and I let go of Santiago's hand. "Victoria, it's so nice to see you again." She smiled and closed the gap between the two of us, moving close enough to give me a kiss on the cheek. It was so genuine, so relaxed. Like she greeted everyone this way.

"*Hola, ma,*" he said. She repeated the motion with her son, squeezing his bicep a little before letting go. Santiago smiled and then walked over to the kitchen island to get some food. He grabbed a plate from the stack next to the food and held it out to me, his expectant gaze prompting me out of my stupor.

"Vee," he said as he cocked his head, inviting me over to his side.

"*¡Mamá!*" There was a loud bang of a door closing, followed by hurried steps towards the back of the house. "Sorry I'm late, a patien—" Lucía stopped and beamed at me. She followed that up with a light jog towards me and a sound that could only be described as a squeal. "You're here! I didn't know you were coming for lunch today."

"That makes two of us," I mumbled. But her smile and her genuine joy at seeing me were contagious. She hugged me like she hadn't seen me in months, and even for only having met a few days ago, it was a welcome gesture. "Hi," I added as she released me and grabbed a plate.

She started talking nonstop about her day in the most

casual of ways. Lucía moved naturally in her parents' kitchen; there wasn't a sign of discomfort in her movements. I had lived in my grandmother's house until I was out of college, but I couldn't remember ever feeling like that house belonged to me. Like it was a home. This, this was a home. To anyone, it seemed, because they welcomed me with open arms.

The lunch was lazy and slow, much like the town at this time. The family members shared their days, their weekend plans, and talked about how they could support some of the neighbors who were going through a rough patch. I was mesmerized by the moment.

"Victoria," Santiago's mother asked. "How are you enjoying your visit here?" She smiled, and her eyes crinkled, just like her son's.

"It's so nice here," I responded. "I love how quiet it is."

I looked at Santiago sitting right next to me. His eyes were fixed on my lips, and I instinctively licked them. He moved his hand, slowly raising it, his body following the movement. The next thing I knew, his thumb was tugging at my lower lip and his lips were on my ear. "You have a little something here," he rasped. His low voice made me shiver.

I blinked and from the corner of my eye saw Lucía bite her lip as if to contain her smile—maybe another squeal. My heart was beating fast. When did this man looking at me make me nervous like this?

I cleared my throat and looked at his mom, who was smiling widely at us, a glint in her eye. "Dessert, anyone?"

She stood and started clearing the table, stacking the plates by the sink. She moved slowly to the fridge and explored the contents, pulling out a few bowls of fresh fruit. She set everything down on the kitchen island and then grabbed a few strawberries and placed them in a bowl. "The fruit is really good this time of year," she said, smiling at me.

I took a deep breath. The whole situation confused me.

Santiago stood to clear his plate, and Lucía used the opportunity to sit right next to me, immediately looking at me and smiling mischievously, like she was hiding a secret. "What's up?" she said. "I haven't seen you in forever."

I laughed out loud. "We had lunch yesterday," I said in between giggles.

"Was it? Gosh, it feels like it's been forever." She rolled her eyes. "I'm still not used to how slow this town is. Some days stretch out so much. That is something I forgot about living here."

I smiled because I thought it was charming. How time seemed to pass by at the exact speed I needed it. Neither slow nor fast. Just perfectly. I was perfectly in the moment, enjoying every single thing this place had to offer me for the time being.

"We were just talking about that," I added. "I think it's charming. It's almost like it makes you stop and enjoy instead of going full force ahead."

"Yeah, well, whatever." She rolled her eyes and laughed. "You should spend more time here and then let me know how you feel." She winked and started talking about someone that I didn't know, her voice loud and directed to her mother, who was standing by the sink, rinsing the dishes. The image was so domestic, so casual, that I couldn't help but smile.

The conversation shifted a few times. I answered questions, asked questions in return. Spoke to both of Santiago's parents and to Lucía. I stole some glances and caught Santiago looking at me. His body relaxed at the kitchen table, his arm resting on the back of his mother's chair. He smiled at me, and my insides turned, sending heat right to my core. This had never happened to me with Manuel. It was natural, instinctual. My body craved his, and by the smolder in his eyes, I could tell he also wanted me.

He stood abruptly and walked to me, hugging me from behind and lowering his face to mine. "Ready to go?" he asked gravelly. "We're leaving," he announced to the group and held out his hand to mine.

I looked at Lucía and smiled. "Thank you for lunch," I said. "It was lovely."

"Bye," he said and tugged on my hand to get me moving. His steps were hurried, urgent.

"Where are we going?" I whispered, trying to catch up to him.

"We're going home," he said without even turning to look at me.

Home.

24

THE ACT

WE WALKED FAST and blended with the crowds of people moving about town. The lazy hour was over, and townsfolk were returning to their jobs and running their normal errands. The late afternoon was crisp, and Santiago's hand was hot on mine. My heart thrashed inside my chest.

We walked into the hotel, flying past the reception desk, and he only acknowledged the woman there with a small nod of his head. He took the stairs two at a time, never letting go of my hand.

"Hey," I said quietly. "Give me a chance to catch up."

He slowed down his pace, looked at me over his shoulder, and smiled. He paused for a moment and then continued with his hurried steps towards my room.

"What's gotten into you?" I asked quietly. He was moving at lightning speed, like he was running late to something. I fished the key out of my purse and handed it to him, my hand shaking. The door was opened in a second, and he pulled me inside, kicking it closed behind us.

I was burning from the inside out. He took a step forward, immediately invading the space I'd so protectively guarded for years. It felt natural, like this was the logical next step into whatever this whole thing between us was. His scent, despite the long day, was overpowering, reminding me of a younger self, of those many hours we put in with our study groups ten years before.

He lifted one of his big hands and caressed my cheek, dragging it back under my ear and parking it there, his fingers on the back of my neck and his thumb under my jaw. His eyes searched me, asking for a silent permission that would inevitably be given to him. My lips parted, and a small sound escaped me. I couldn't remember where I was standing, the energy sizzling in my hotel room.

His lips brushed mine in a delicate way, almost like if he moved too fast, he would scare me out of this. Like a scared little animal—and he was right. I had my moments of feeling fragile and weak. This was not one though.

I moaned, and Santiago picked up his pace. He eased his tongue in between my parted lips, searching for my own, pulling me deeper into him. His other hand went down to my lower back, pushing me into his rock-hard body.

"I—" I said into his lips, stopping myself before I could even continue with whatever train of thought was ravaging my head, because there was none. I had no idea where that sentence would go. I shook my head and Santiago took two steps back, immediately dropping his arms to his sides. My eyes widened in surprise or regret—who even knew at that point. My heart thumped loudly in my chest, the tips of my fingers tingling with the anticipation of touching this man before me.

"Sorry, I got carried away," he said, like this had been strictly on him. "I'm going to leave," he said as he sighed, not moving an inch from where he was, right by the door.

"No, no. That's not what I meant. Stay." I swallowed. "Please?"

I took a step forward, and he responded by mimicking my action. He lifted one of his hands and placed it at my hip, pulling my body. My hands instinctively went to the back of his neck, and the space between us closed, leaving us flush against each other.

Santiago's lips found mine once again, and my breath caught. I felt a small smile form on his lips, and that moment alone made me feel wanted, like maybe I was everything he ever expected, and he was happy he was getting such a response from me. I couldn't know for sure, but it gave me a good feeling, certainty that I was doing the right thing. That we were both exactly where we wanted to be.

I couldn't remember if I'd ever been kissed like that before. Up until this point, I'd had a handful of kisses from different men in my life, the most recent, Manuel, but Santiago kissed like he was ten steps ahead and knew exactly where he was going at all times. Just like his pauses in conversation, his pauses here were intentional and controlled. He was patient and dedicated, his full attention on my lips.

There was fire pooling in between my thighs. My hands found a way under his shirt, feeling his soft skin below it. He let out a groan and took me deeper into the room, walking us both to the bed. It felt as if his hands were everywhere, but at the same time like we were moving in slow motion, his fingertips memorizing every cell of my body.

His hands found the hem of my dress, lifting it to remove it. The momentary pause in our kissing gave me a second to look at him, his brows furrowed in concentration with every movement, his eyes ping-ponging all over my body. He dropped my dress by his side and turned back to me, kissing my jaw, my neck, my shoulder, one of his hands trailing down my exposed body.

"You." *Kiss.*

"Are." *Kiss.*

"Spectacular." *Kiss.*

My body responded with a shiver, immediately followed by a sense of urgency. Urgency to take his clothes off, to feel him, to see him, to hear him. I dragged my hands up his chest, and the movement made him lift his arms. He bent his elbows towards the back of his neck and grabbed his shirt, removing it in one swift movement and immediately dropping it on the floor beside us.

I gawked. That was exactly what I did, because it was the only thing I could do in front of such a specimen.

Manuel had a great, lean body, but it paled in comparison to Santiago's strong build. The bright tattoo on his bicep was now fully visible, the intricate flowers wrapping around his sculpted muscle all the way up to his shoulder. I knew he had a tattoo—it was faintly visible the day we got caught in the rain—but now I could see it in all its glory. It was, at the same time, so different from what I had imagined of him, but also exactly what I would expect of him, matching his sunshine personality entirely.

We stood there, watching and devouring each other with our eyes. Santiago took a step forward and wrapped his arms around me, pressing hard against me. He placed his knee on the edge of the mattress and laid me down on the bed. He took a step back and without taking his eyes off me, he undid the button on his jeans and pushed them down.

"Vee," he rasped. "Is this okay?"

I hummed in response, my eyes falling closed with anticipation.

"Look at me," he said slowly. "I need to hear you say it, sweet girl."

"Yes, *yes*," I responded. "*Please.*"

His eyes swept me from top to bottom, assessing my form on the bed. I leaned on my elbows, tipping my head back. Our mouths collided in response, faster, stronger, and growing more frantic by the second. Santiago's hands slid up my legs, leaving behind a trail of goosebumps. He found the elastic of my underwear and began to pull, slipping it down my legs.

The entirety of my body was shaking and begging for more, my heart hammering so wildly inside my chest I was sure even the people in the room next door could hear it through the walls. He nipped his way down my torso, stopping for a moment to swirl his warm tongue on my nipple, and then continued down my stomach, leaving a trail of small kisses on his way.

"Santiago..." I rasped, my voice foreign to my ears. "You don't—"

"I want to," he interrupted, his breath hot in between my thighs. "Let me."

A gasp escaped me because I couldn't remember the last time my body had reacted this way to anyone. My breaths came in faster, my vision cloudy and my hips rolling on their own as the pressure increased.

And then. *Then*.

My hands were in his hair, pushing down slightly while at the same time angling my body to show him where to go and what to do. I didn't recognize myself, as if my body were outside looking in at these two people enjoying themselves. My body arched on its own, and his name escaped my lips in a wild cry. And I saw stars.

Santiago's mouth was back on mine immediately, kissing my lips with a sense of gravity, like time was running out and he needed to finish what he started. I moved quickly too, my shaking hands dragging down his back, reaching for his boxer briefs, ready to push them down his strong legs. He took a step back and stepped out of his underwear, the movement so intimate and confident that my belly flipped.

Breathtaking. He was breathtaking.

I found his gaze, his eyes locked into mine like he was ready to swallow me whole. His lips turned up to a smile, the corner of his eyes crinkling. "Right back at ya." Wink.

My eyes closed and a flush ran through my body, my cheeks heating up instantly. *Fuck.* When I opened them back up, Santiago was hovering above me, a minuscule smile on his mouth. He licked his lips, and I mimicked his movement, our need growing as the minutes passed until we were both desperate for each other.

He rocked against me, moving in a way that felt like he knew exactly what and how I needed it. My legs were shaking—either from the intensity of what had happened minutes earlier or because of the nervous anticipation. If him going down on me made me like this, I couldn't imagine what would happen next.

"Is this okay?" he asked, his voice gravelly.

"Yeah," I murmured. *It's incredible.* The way he was moving had me writhing under him, and my legs wrapped around his trim waist, pushing him down to me, closer. He kissed my neck, the electricity making me gasp.

"Protection?" I asked, not sure what had possessed me.

"Yep, yes. Yes." He stood immediately, searching around for his wallet inside his jeans pocket. The air was suddenly cold, having lost the warmth of his body over me. "I got it."

He looked straight at me, waiting for a response while

slowly sheathing himself with the condom. He moved towards me, placing all his exquisite weight over me once again. "I've been thinking about this for a really fucking long time," he said, his voice teasing.

"What?!" A laugh escaped me, making me giggle with incredulity. It helped ease my nerves and directed my attention to his gorgeous face.

His eyes crinkled in response, a big grin taking over his mouth, like he was proud of what he finally, after so many years, accomplished. "Really, I have."

I hid my face in the crook of his neck, my tongue making wet circles on his hot skin. He groaned in response and then, *finally*, he pushed into me. I could feel his pulse racing, my heart matching his in excitement. My body was aching, trembling.

The Victoria from before would have hated this. He was so attentive, so in tune with his body and mine. She would have rolled her eyes and sighed in exasperation because it usually came with a request. Because people didn't engage me without wanting something in return. But somehow, somewhere along the last few days, this town and this man had transformed me. Transformed me into a person I barely recognized but who I was starting to like.

"Oh my god," I hissed. His movements were electric inside me. My hips matched his pace, and our hearts met up conspiratorially, our rhythms aligned and beating to the same secret tune.

His face lit up with a blinding smile and then returned to

my body, working hard to explore every nook and cranny. My jaw, my throat, my shoulders. The middle of my chest. By god, this man.

He knew exactly what to do with his hands, molding my body into the perfect position, moving together in tandem. It felt so natural, like we were meant to be all along. This was effortless, for me at least, so easy and fun and sensational. So much so that I was close to the edge. Again. And then the fire burst inside of me and Santiago's body went stiff, and the world around us stopped moving, frozen.

"Shit," he said, his face hiding in my hair. I could hear the smile in his voice. I could picture his delighted, contented face. He rolled over to his side, taking me with him and hugging me close. My forehead tucked under his chin. Our breaths were synced up, slowly returning to normal. "That was…"

My eyes widened because the only thing I wanted to say was "perfect." But I didn't. I just moved closer to him, smiling softly against his warm, damp skin. We lay there for a long time, or maybe not that long, just enjoying the silence and the stillness around us. His fingers roamed my body, and mine held him tight against me. I didn't want to let go.

"What's on your mind?" His voice was husky. I smiled against his chest again, taking a moment to clear my thoughts. Weren't we the ones supposed to ask men what they were thinking? The roles were reversed here, for sure.

"Nothing," I said as I tipped my head back to look into his eyes. I smiled wider and moved my hand to his forehead, slightly pushing the hair that had fallen over and was partially covering his eyes. "Just…" Sigh. "This is nice."

It was a moment of vulnerability for me. A moment when I finally accepted the things that were happening around me that were out of my control. And I was enjoying them. I was letting life take me in the direction it should, without thinking so much about consequences. Without thinking much about what people—Susana—would say or if this fit into my plans at all. Because I didn't have any plans anymore. And that was nice.

He huffed a small laugh. "Yeah, nice."

And then we lay there in silence, slowly drifting to sleep, the evening sky darkening around us, the town growing quieter as the hours went by. His hands never left my body, his warmth cocooning me to sleep. I wasn't this type of woman, but maybe for him, I could be.

Maybe.

25

THE CONVERSATION

"Why are you awake?" I asked her, not understanding how I ended up on a video call with my best friend so early in the morning. The events of the previous night were a blur, and to be quite honest, I was still high on the adrenaline of it all. It had been a whirlwind of a few days, my body running on the high of being so close to Santiago it felt I could almost burn to the touch.

"Because this baby is kicking the living daylights out of me, and I can't sleep. Duh." Catalina rolled her eyes so hard I could basically hear her do it. "And my stupidly coherent husband reminded me that I wanted this, so now I feel guilty and..." She shrugged. This was a common thread between my brother and her. Catalina was the most passionate of them both, and my brother was logical, more rational. They both were a bundle of energy, unable to sit still, and I thought that was what made them incredibly successful in their professional lives.

"What's up?" she asked, settling her body on the couch. She was whispering, maybe because my brother was still asleep in the next room in their small apartment.

"I need to tell you something," I said while removing my makeup. *Santiago and I had a moment*, I wanted to scream at her. *It was amazing, and I can't get it out of my head. And why did you never tell me it could be this good?*

I was only going to let myself call it a moment. It was a blip in time, an escape from my normal self. An outlier. A lapse in judgment, maybe. Obviously, I willingly agreed to go on a "date" with him, or whatever that was. And whatever happened the night before had also been entirely consensual. But things were getting blurry. "Don't freak out."

"Oh my god! I knew it!" she squealed. "I fucking knew it, Victoria!" She grinned, her smile covering more than half her face, her eyes shining with mirth.

"You knew nothing," I scoffed. I ran the cotton pad over my cheeks more times than necessary, hiding my rapidly heating skin. The memory of the previous night made me blush, then sent a shiver down my spine.

"Of course I knew. I could feel it in my bones. Call it... mother's intuition," she added with a laugh.

"You're not even a mother yet," I huffed, but a smile started to form on my lips. "And besides, you're not my mother. I think that only works with your own children."

"Nonsense. And by the way, I take offense." She was moving in her kitchen, reaching a tall cabinet where her glasses were. Her belly had grown considerably since I last saw her, but she was as gorgeous as ever. She really did have that pregnancy glow. "And also, everyone knows he's been pining for you for years," she added while filling up her glass with water. She took a long sip and walked back to where her phone was, her eyes dreamy and ecstatic. "How was it?"

"Ugh." I rolled my eyes, annoyed at myself. "Disgustingly perfect. He's so... good to me. I don't understand."

My body was tender from the activity of the previous night. He had slept over but crept away an hour earlier to avoid running into any of his family members in the lobby or on their way to work. My lips still stung from his kisses, swollen from rubbing against his stubble.

"I am legit swooning," she said dramatically. She loved eavesdropping, and she would make up unbelievable stories while overhearing things, especially when she was in court waiting to see a judge or clerk. Her tales were always so entertaining, I always wondered why it never crossed her mind to be an actress or even a writer. Her imagination was wild, and it ran rampant often. And this was exactly what made her good at her job; she always knew where to look. "I'm going to live vicariously through you."

"What are you talking about?" I said, smiling. Catalina and my brother had a fast and furious love story, and it was sickening to watch. In the time I dated Manuel, they dated, moved in together, got married, and were now days away from having a baby. Meanwhile, I was single once again. "You are about to have a baby with the love of your life."

"Yeah, whatever," she replied, then started rubbing her hands together in a cartoonish motion. "Tell me more. Tell me everything."

Where to start? What about with the way he looked at me, like I was the most scrumptious dessert ready to be devoured? Or how his hands moved, like he was trying to commit my body to memory, to later carve me out of stone? Or maybe the sounds he made, grunting in awe of what was happening?

"I don't know." *I'm confused.* "Maybe it's too soon?" *It's definitely too soon. And what would your grandmother say? This is unbecoming for someone like me.*

"Please, you deserve it. And who says it's too soon? It's not like you're marrying the man. Just enjoy yourself."

I sighed. "I don't know, Cata, it just feels so different."

"So? Different is good."

Another sigh, this time more dramatic. Everything was easy here. Everyone was happy. "Everyone is so happy here. It's a little intoxicating at times, almost *un*believable, you know?" I tilted my head and looked straight to the screen, where Catalina was scrunching her nose in response. I blinked. "What?"

"That's how it's supposed to feel," she said. "When people have your back, when someone loves you. It's easy. Yes, life is hard and all that, but honestly..." She winced.

"You need closure. Close that terrible chapter and then move the fuck on. You deserve this."

I looked at her intently through the screen. Maybe she had a point.

"Stop," she said abruptly. "I can hear you thinking all the way from here. Don't think too much, Victoria. You think too much, all the time. And look where that got you? Speak to Manuel and be done with him. Move. The. Fuck. On."

"Fine, but don't be so curt about it." I smiled. "Jesus, you are relentless."

"I already told you, I'm living vicariously through you. I'm so excited about this that I have butterflies in my stomach." She sighed theatrically. "I love this."

"Have you heard from Susana?" She'd been on my mind since Catalina told me all the details of the case. I was avoiding her at all costs, now more than ever, but I was stalling because I knew that the conversation I needed to have with her was bigger than what I could offer right now. "She's been radio silent."

"I haven't actually, which is weird because she was all over us right after you left." She looked behind the screen, her eyes fixed on something above my head. "Are you going to talk to her?"

"I know I have to, but it's making me anxious. It'll dampen the mood for sure."

"Yeah, sorry, friend." She squirmed in her seat, her eyes still fixed somewhere else. "Anyway, gotta run, I'll talk to you soon. Call Manuel. *Beso.*"

She was right. I did need closure. Because I couldn't make a new plan—if I ever did need one—if I didn't close the chapters that came before this one. Ticking the boxes off my to-do list, if you will. But I was so over it all. I was ready to move on. Go back to the city and get back to my life. Because for sure this wasn't what I wanted long term, was it? I didn't even know what Santiago wanted. What he was looking for.

I sat down on the table in my room and opened up my computer. My mind was gravitating towards work, my distraction when I needed moments of clarity. Instead, I propped my phone on the screen and called Manuel, setting the call on speakerphone. It rang a few times and when I was about to give up, he picked up. He was out of breath, but he answered with what sounded like a smile on his face.

"You are a little shit, you know that?" I said as soon as I heard him speak. I was glad about the fact that this was, in fact, a regular call and he couldn't see my face. Because I couldn't explain the anger that was radiating from every pore. "How much of a fucking coward do you have to be that you send a picture to me instead of talking it out like a normal person?"

He was speechless. I could hear music in the background and a few inaudible voices around him. "I don't even know what's wrong with me. I'm smarter than this," I continued. "It never occurred to me to check your work phone number. Why would I? I trusted you entirely. So much so that I was going to fucking marry you."

"Why are you being like this?" he said finally. I kept silent, waiting for him to explain himself instead of blaming this on me. "I don't even recognize you anymore."

"Anymore? Manuel, you hardly know me." I was enraged. I had wasted so much time with him, thinking he was my future, my all. "You're starting to sound like Susana. And I would say the same to you. I don't recognize this. Why did you do this to me? The least you could have done is respected me a little to tell me what was going on."

Would I have pleaded? Begged? Probably. Begged him to stay with me and marry me, for the sake of what? Of appearances? Of Susana's wishes?

"Yeah? And what would you have done, Victoria? Would you have said 'oh, okay, that's fine, let's not get married then?'" He was mocking me. This was something he did when we fought. "Please, you have been obsessed with the idea of marriage since the day I met you. That grandmother of yours really filled your brain up."

"What the fuck, Manuel? At least own up to your mistake. Don't put this on me."

"Okay, you want to hear the truth? I'll tell you the truth." He took a deep breath and released it. "I was never interested in this. I wanted to travel the world; you know that. But my parents, much like your grandmother, had a different idea. They pushed, and I pushed back until I couldn't anymore. You were my out. But you are so fucking obsessed with your grandmother and doing right by her and being close to them that you wouldn't even entertain the idea of going on adventures. And guess what? It was exhausting. Living with you and trying to be something I'm not. I got tired, and this was my way out.

"What would you have said if I told you that I got the job in Australia? Would you have moved with me? Of course not! You wouldn't even consider the idea of going on an extended honeymoo—"

"I have a job! You have a job too!"

"You work for your fucking family, Victoria! Of course Pedro would say yes to you. He has been saying yes to the women in your family for decades. Do you think he would have cared? You just said it; you are smarter than this. And to be honest, you're too smart for me."

"I agree," I said out of spite. The things he was saying were not foreign to me. Yes, I had wanted to be close to my family because they were my all. But maybe, maybe? Maybe if he had given me a reason, I would have taken it. "Manuel." I sighed. "Whatever. I called you because I needed the closure, but I realize this was a mistake. Everything was a mistake, and although this was not the way I would have done it, I'm glad I dodged this bullet. Tell your parents what you did. Susana already knows, so it better come from you."

I blinked a few times. "Have a good life. I hope you are happy."

Because I was working hard to be happy too.

26

THE CONFRONTATION

I STOPPED PACING my hotel room and sat down on the loveseat, where I had a view of the town square right out the window. The town was barely waking up, and the vibrant colors from the late sunrise shined past the square and behind the mountains. I could see the bus stop brimming with people, their suitcases and their hopes and dreams, possibly embarking into their future in the city.

The line rang on the other end, my knee bouncing up and down in nervousness. I knew I could do this easily. My whole professional career relied on me having difficult conversations with difficult clients.

"Pick up, pick up," I murmured, biting on my right thumbnail.

"Victoria, *¿dónde estás? Dios mío,* do you have any idea what you've done?" Where are you? Really?

"Really, *abuela*, that's your first question?" The nick-name came out with a snarl, but I tried to hold my smile, because I was infinitely aware of how much she hated that. "Never a 'how are you,' huh?"

I immediately regretted those words. This wasn't the right time for that conversation.

"Where are you? Are you planning to ever come back to your life or are you going to continue to act like a child and run away from your problems?" she asked, contempt in her voice. "Do you realize the magnitude of this situation, Victo-ria? You've humiliated me to no end, running away like this, like a child would do. It's the only thing people talk about."

I was stunned. It didn't come as a surprise to me, the way she was describing this as if the impact of my actions was solely on her. For the first time in my thirty-something years of age, I was realizing that this woman, who, by the way, I revered ever since she took us in, was nothing but a selfish, self-centered woman who cared only about her appearance and what people thought of her. And I was no different. I was her blood through and through.

All I could offer her at this point was silence. Because I had nothing left to say to anyone about my failed marriage. I had my closure. I knew that I needed to move on. And I was trying, damn it!

"Where are you?" she asked. "We'll come get you, and you and I will have a conversation and figure out how to fix this."

"I'm not coming back, Susana." At least not yet. I needed to figure out my shit. "I need time and space to figure out some things."

"Victoria." She sighed. "What has gotten into you? Why are you like this? Manuel is heartbroken."

"Oh yeah, so heartbroken that he went on our honeymoon with another woman?" Silence. "Did you know that? He never wanted to get married. But you pushed me on to him, and vice versa. Made me believe he was in love with me, that I was in love with him. And you know what? I dodged a motherfucking bullet."

I let that sink in for a minute. I wasn't supposed to curse around her, but the words were liberating.

"Do you think it would have been worse if I was divorced within the year?" She would have been appalled. "Who would ever look at me again after I'd been divorced, right, Susana?"

I heard her take a breath, but I cut her off. "There were so many signs I ignored, so many, over and over again, like the fool I am. And why? Because he had a good last name? Because he would make *you* look good? I'm done living my life because of you, Susana."

"Where the hell is this coming from, you ungrateful child," she said. She was rolling out the big guns now, using minor curse words and insulting me. She would only ever do that if anyone hit a nerve or told a semblance of truth that contradicted what she said. "Let's not forget that you ran away on the day of your wedding, Victoria. You left your groom at the altar, with no explanation or warning. Tell me how that is a mature response. To anything."

"This isn't why I called. We need to have a conversation but not this one right now." I stood up again and planted my feet by the window. Maybe if I found a place for me to look into, the words would come out calmer. I took a deep breath and rolled my shoulders. "Did you know that my grandfather wasn't kidnapped?"

Silence. On both ends. Intentional on my end, of course.

I could picture her closing her eyes in slow motion, keeping them closed for a few seconds and then opening them up again, an answer on the tip of her tongue. She would hold the bridge of her nose with her index finger and thumb and take a deep breath.

"Victoria, your grandfather was kidnapped in 1988. You know this. You've known this all your life." She was moving now. I could hear her shuffling in the background. It was still early, and there wouldn't be any movement in her house except for her. Her steps were even, and it sounded like she was going down the stairs. "We paid the ransom, and he was never released. End of story."

"I beg to differ, Susana," I snarled. "Tell me the truth. I have evidence to explain the contrary."

She gasped. Gasped! An audible gasp. I hadn't expected this response from her.

"What are you talking about? Are you delirious? Is this

why you ran away?" She was changing the subject. This was easily one of Susana's most used resources when the conversation wasn't going her way. Sometimes it was subtle, but other times it was rampantly obvious. "Do we need to come find you with a doctor?"

I laughed out loud and could feel Susana getting angrier by the second.

"I already know everything, Susana, so might as well tell me the truth. It doesn't really matter, right? You've sold your story, and people have pitied you for years, decades."

"No one has ever pitied me, Victoria. People respect me. Don't you ever forget who you are. People respect the likes of us."

"Ay, Susana, stop. You don't need to sell that bullshit to me anymore. I don't give a fuck who we are, what our last name is, how much money is in your bank account." I was agitated now, words coming out fast and uncontrolled. I took a deep breath and continued. "Let me fill you in, in case you aren't aware of the truth.

"My grandfather was a thief. I don't know his reasons, and honestly, I don't care. Actually, you know what? I do care. I think it was because of you. Because you were so demanding of more and more and more that he had no other option but to take what didn't belong to him. So to cover it all up, he ran away from you and your family in 1988 because he was most likely going to get charged with embezzlement. He had been doing it for years under everyone's noses. I'm guessing you never knew. Tell me if I'm getting close to the truth or if this is a lie."

I waited for her response, but all I could hear was her uneven breathing.

"He showed up at a small town in Córdoba and begged a friend of his for a job, making a comfortable and respectable life for himself there. Didn't bother anyone, kept his head down. In the meantime, you told everyone that would even look at you that your husband had been kidnapped, the ransom paid, but he was never released. Am I getting closer now?"

Silence. I paced my room, walking from the door to the window and back, trying to get my thoughts in order. Presenting my case.

"For decades, you've let your family, your friends, believe that your husband had been killed. You've victimized yourself for what? Honor? Respect? Control? Of what? Of the illusion of being superi—"

"Shut up!" She was screaming now. "You have no idea what you're talking about. *Mocosa insolente, ¿quién te da el derecho de hablarme así?*"

"Oh, so you're going to tell me that you had absolutely no idea that your husband walked out of your life, never to be seen again?" I said a little mockingly. "I doubt that's true, Susana. You are a smart, smart woman. You pay attention. I'll bet my inheritance that you knew exactly what you were doing."

I swallowed, hoping that stroking her ego would get me the results I was looking for. If nothing else, Susana loved the attention, the compliments. She never fished for them, of course not, but she not-so-secretly reveled when she was on the receiving end of one.

I sat down on the bed, still looking out the window, hoping that my silence would get her talking. The sun was slowly inching up from behind the mountains. The sky was clear and a deep blue that I could hardly remember ever seeing in the city.

"So what? So what if I did that?" My eyes went wide, my mouth completely dry. "I made a choice, and I lived with it for decades. I had to do what was best to protect myself and my family."

"Protect us from what, exactly? Who was going to hurt you?"

"Ay, Victoria, *no seas ilusa.* Don't be so naïve. Use your brain a little. What did you expect me to do? Sulk and let everyone call your grandfather a thief? I had a reputation to protect, a name to stand for. You have to understand, I..."

My skin started itching, like my body was getting too big for it. I was dumbfounded. Completely at a loss for words. I was suddenly furious, my blood boiling inside my body.

Furious at Susana for lying to us, her family, for lying to her friends, for keeping up with this narrative that my grandfather was a larger-than-life man who was taken from us too soon for unknown reasons. Furious at my father for never looking into this and accepting Susana's version as the absolute truth. Furious at Manuel for just existing. And furious at myself for taking everything at face value.

"The decisions that we make have an impact on much more than the immediate future, Susana," I said, thinking back on how this narrative had shaped my life, my career, my being.

"Oh, don't fucking defend him, he was a thief!"

"I'm not defending him *at all*, but what you did was wrong, Susana, on so many counts. You let your *children* believe their father was dead! You built your whole existence on lies. You are no innocent bystander either, Susana, and stop playing the fucking victim."

"Language." That was all she had to say to me. We were possibly having the most honest conversation of our *lives*, and this woman only cared about what I was saying that could hinder my impeccable (or maybe not so much anymore) reputation.

"I don't fucking care anymore, Susana. You are a liar, and what you did was wrong. You broke a family. You made us believe— made *your children*—believe that their father was dead?" Did she not know that he was, in fact, dead? Or was she playing me like a fiddle?

"He *is* dead!" she screamed, her voice broken. Ah, there it was. "He's been dead for years! Why do you care anyways? You were born with a silver spoon in your mouth. Your life never changed because of this. *No te metas que no tiene nada que ver con vos.*"

This has nothing to do with you, she said. She was

pacing now. I could hear her shuffling her feet on the marble floors of her house.

"Susana," I said, matching her tone. I knew he was dead, but the sudden confession surprised me nonetheless. I opened my mouth to say more, but she spoke first.

"No, *escuchame bien*." Her tone was firm, and her voice was deeper than normal. "*Te lo voy a decir una sola vez,* so you better pay close attention, Victoria."

I took a deep breath and closed my eyes, expecting the worst. Because anything could come out of Susana's mouth at this point, or at any point. She wasn't known for having a filter. She was blatantly and brutally honest unless she wanted something, and in that case, she was as fake as a mannequin.

"I'm not the one on trial here," she said. She was seething. I could almost hear her jaw clenching while she spoke. "This has nothing to do with me, and you know it."

"Do I know it, Susana? Because the only story that has ever been told to me—by you, by the way—is how he was an honorable man. You made him sound like a hero, and that left you as a victim. Is that what you wanted? Because that's not respect, Susana. That is pity. People felt—feel—sorry for you."

She scoffed into the phone. "I did my best," she whispered.

"Did you do your best? Because your best would have been to stand next to your husband and support him while he was being prosecuted. That's what a person who loves someone does. For better or for worse and all that bullshit, right?"

"Victoria, be careful what you say. Don't say anything you'll regret because you are going to come crawling back to me eventually, and then what? Huh? Who is going to give you back the life you had?"

I shrugged, aware that she couldn't see me. I wasn't interested in going back, in having the life I had before. But what did I want?

"What do you want from me, Victoria? What do you want me to say to you? Do you want me to ask for forgiveness? Because I won't. I don't regret it one second. We—*you*—have the life you have because of the choices I made, so don't you dare say that the decisions *I* made for *my* family had an impact on anything else. Would you be saying the same if you hadn't had such a comfortable life? No vacations, no trips abroad, no top schools, and no career prospects? You have the life you have because *I* forged your path. Don't you dare forget that."

The line went dead.

She wouldn't ever get it, right? She wouldn't ever understand how the narrative that she created gave us all illusions of grandness. She carved a path for herself, a path where there was no potential for humiliation, where she was seen as a victim and adored by her peers for her strength and composure.

She made my grandfather a larger-than-life man when all he was was a thief. He must have had his reasons, but I wouldn't defend him. But was she right, though? Was she correct in her narrative that she built everything we had from the ground up? That everything I'd become was because of her?

27

"*¿MAMÁ?*" The sound of one of my daughters calling me snapped me from my daydream. The images of Roberto's kitchen swallowed up by flames ran in a loop inside my head. For six nights, I hadn't been able to sleep, the nightmares coming immediately once I closed my eyes—the memory of Roberto's hurried movements inside the house, the heat of the flames, his words. The staff was starting to notice. My disheveled look was completely out of the ordinary, and my temper was shorter than normal.

Monica, maybe? Or Cristina. I heard the footsteps down the stairs, and then her gaze immediately landed on the massive display of samples at my feet. From napkins to chair covers to tablecloths, everything in every single shade of white was splayed in front of me. "What is this?"

"Cristin—"

"*Mamá*, I already told you." She sighed. "We should

cancel." Her voice sounded sad, but her eyes looked hopeful. "He'll come back. I feel it."

Always so hopeful, this girl. She was in her mid-twenties and late to the game where marriage was concerned. She wasn't a late bloomer, per se, but she always believed in fairy tale romances, obsessed with love, marriage, and children. In the past years, she had resisted every attempt I'd made at setting her up with the sons of the people we knew. Thankfully, she met and fell in love with a wonderful boy who carried an even more wonderful last name. I was anticipating a grandchild within the next year.

"Cristina, we've been over this a million times," I replied sternly. "The wedding is happening."

She looked around the room. All the samples were on the floor, and there were at least ten binders on the small loveseat by the window filled with photos of floral arrangements, place settings, and many other wedding-related things that I hadn't had a chance to look at yet. She frowned.

"*Mamá, por favor. ¿Qué va a pensar la gente?*"

"Exactly, what are people going to think?" I couldn't afford another scandal. It was still a few months out, so I was hoping that everything would die down by then. "What is your fiancé going to think?"

She walked over to the loveseat and sat, grabbing one of the binders and putting it on her lap. She started looking through it, running through the pages quickly, barely paying any attention. Of all my children, she was probably the most hopeful that he would be freed and that he would return to us.

"I'm not getting married without *Papá*," she said without looking at me. Her voice trembled. "I don't understand why you are being so nonchalant about this."

"*Basta*, Cristina. That's the end of this conversation," I barked. The topic was getting too repetitive at this point. He wasn't allowed to return. End of story. "We need to make dinner plans with Mariano's parents to discuss some outstanding details."

"Why are you like this?"

"I'm not discussing this further," I said. "What did you want?"

"Nothing," she huffed and crossed her arms across her chest. She stood and stomped out of the room, pouting like a spoiled child.

"Susana!" Pedro yelled from the front entry. The sound of a door closing startled me, even though I knew it was coming. "Susana!"

He sounded agitated, and his steps grew louder as he approached me. I was in the library, only a few steps away from the entry. It was a matter of seconds until he found me, especially now that Cristina had left the room with a scowl on her face.

"What did you do?" Pedro said when he entered the room. I turned to face the door as he got near, his gray eyes ablaze with anger. "*¿Qué mierda hiciste?*"

"Pardon? Do not take that tone with me." I was taken

aback. Pedro never raised his voice, let alone addressed me that way. "Not in my house, not anywhere. And for the love of god, lower your voice."

"Tell me, Susana, what did you expect was going to happen?" he asked me. I had a vague idea of exactly what he was talking about, although I was mostly certain that my story was airtight. "Please, enlighten me."

I blinked up at him, looking straight to his eyes.

He was being condescending, something that I'd never seen him do. He was never like this, a contrasting image to the kind man that had been by my side all these years. Growing up together had been something almost out of a book, a classic childhood friends turned something else. Except that our story ended the moment Roberto entered my life, and there was no turning back.

"I don't know what you are talking about," I replied, my tone cool and even. I wasn't trying to give anything away, and although I was good at pretending, I always thought that Pedro could read me well. His eyes were trained on me, and his jaw was clenched. He fisted his hands by his side, the knuckles turning white with the intensity of the grip. "I've had enough today with Cristina acting like a brat. I don't need any more drama."

"*Cortala.* Enough with the snark, Susana," he said. I took a seat on the desk chair, trying to give myself time to think. "I know you were out of town last week."

I took a deep breath. "Yes, I went to visit my frie—"

"Bullshit! *¡No me mientas más!*" he yelled. "What did you expect was going to happen, Susana, huh?"

"Pedro, please do not cause a scene." He needed to leave immediately. I ran the risk that one of my daughters, or god forbid, one of the staff, would hear what he was spewing about. "Sit down."

He obeyed, taking a seat where Cristina had been minutes earlier. He looked around, focusing his gaze on the large pile of cloth samples on the floor. "You're not canceling the wedding?"

"Why would I?" I cocked my head. "He's not coming back."

He scoffed, then crossed his arms across his chest and took a deep breath. "Is that really how you feel?" he asked. "How are you so certain he won't be returning?"

Pedro leaned back on the loveseat, uncrossing his arms and placing his hands on his lap. He arched one of his brows in question, waiting patiently for my answer. I blinked and swallowed a few times, my mouth immediately dry at his charged question.

"I just know."

"You just know," he said a little mockingly. He tilted his head and stretched his fingers on his lap. "Hmm."

"Listen, he made a mistake, and this is how he is going to repay me," I said. I had no expectation of him ever returning, despite his children, despite the family we had created together. "I think I was very clear, and it's the least he could do."

Pedro swallowed and turned his face to the door. For a split second, I thought someone was just outside the doorway, listening in on this conversation.

"So you just went there and had a conversation, and then that's it?" he asked. "The conclusion was that he would stay there and leave you and your children alone?"

"Why are you asking me this?" I replied, taking a deep breath to calm myself. The image of the kitchen on fire was burned into my eyes. "I asked him to back off. Period."

"I can assume, then, that you haven't heard?"

"What did he say to you?" I asked, starting to panic at his tone. "Do you think he's coming back?"

"Susana, what did you do?"

A beat.

"Nothing." Except it came out as a question.

"What did you do?"

"Nothing! I did nothing!" My hands were shaking at the double meaning of what I had just uttered. It was an accident, a slip in my control, and the tablecloth caught fire. And then I didn't react, the flames engulfing every single space around us both. But I also did nothing to stop it or to help him, although he never needed much helping. And I didn't react. "Nothing." I sighed.

"He's dead."

My world stopped. Ended.

Pedro looked at me, unfazed. "What did you do?" he whispered.

"I don't know. Nothing. I..." How could he be dead if I

saw him moving around, gathering his work documents? He was fast, his briefcase in one hand. I was paralyzed, but he was moving around, alive. "How?"

"There was a fire."

"No." No, no. No, this had to be another one of his ploys, a decoy to make me believe he wouldn't come back, and then when I least expected it, he would return, triumphant and like a hero. And then everyone would know for a fact that I was a liar. That I manipulated everyone around me. That I was unreliable and shouldn't be trusted.

"Susana, do you really think that?" he asked. I must have said something out loud. "They found his body outside of the house. Smoke inhalation. Ruled accidental."

"*¿Mamá?*" I heard my daughter call from the top of the stairs. "Can you come here for a second, please?"

"*Ya va.*" I turned to look at him. He wasn't angry, he just looked like he was about to give up. "This can't be happening."

"I don't know what you mean by that, but it's already been happening. For months now."

I looked down and scratched my forehead. I needed a minute to think. At this point it was clear to me there was nothing else to do. I couldn't tell the truth. No, that was not possible. That was my biggest fear, being caught in a lie, humiliated. But I could always say he was confirmed dead. Request the death certificate. Bury him. Something.

"*¿Qué hago, Pedro?*" What should I do? What *could* I do? I closed my eyes and took a big breath, willing everything to go away.

"*Susana, yo te lo dije,*" he said. I told you so. He had warned me. But I didn't listen. My stomach was in knots. And the only way out of this was straight ahead.

"Fine, I'll figure it out." I turned around, headed toward the door and up the stairs. He followed behind me, his steps quick, trying to catch up with me before I took the first step up. "Leave," I said, without even looking at him.

I heard him sigh and stop right behind me. As I reached the top of the stairs, I heard the door close. And the last card that was still standing at the top of my brittle house of cards flew away in the wind.

28

THE FIGHT

THEY SAY that time flies when you're having fun. But what happens when you were stuck in a rut, in a life that didn't belong to you, in a town that is the exact opposite of what you always knew and a place that was making you doubt everything you ever thought you wanted?

That was how I found myself. Holding my phone a few inches away from my face, frantically grabbing all my clothes while I spewed incoherent sentences at my brother.

"How is it possible? She's not due for another three weeks!" I said as I walked into the bathroom to collect all the items that littered the countertop. I left my phone on the granite facing up while I quickly zipped my toiletry bag, then headed out the door into the room.

"Victoria," I heard my brother say. He was oddly calm, given the circumstances. I walked back in the bathroom to grab my phone and saw him laughing a little at the screen.

"What?" I barked but didn't look at him while packing everything in my suitcase. There was strategy, and this was not it. This was pure chaos.

"It's been four weeks. She's actually overdue." He laughed out loud, and a snort escaped him.

Four weeks? "How?" I whispered. "Already?"

I could see him moving inside his apartment, Cata sitting still on the couch. "What are you doing?" she said loudly over my brother's shoulder. "Don't you dare come home, Victoria."

"Of course I'm coming home. Do you think I would miss this?" Not for the world. Not for my best friend and my only brother. She needed me there. I needed to be there for them. "I'll be there as soon as I can, end of day. I love you."

I kept pacing around my hotel room, my thoughts running wild in my head, my heart thumping in anticipation. I couldn't focus on what needed to be done. I just wanted to transport myself to another time and place, somewhere that would take me immediately to them.

Everything came crashing back down on me: Susana, Manuel, this baby. I needed to be back there with them, fixing my life. This, this was a mere fantasy. Something I had constructed out of thin air. It wasn't foundational, and it would never be, because this wasn't me.

This is you, the little voice in my head said. *This is much more you than the old Victoria.*

Maybe that voice was right. But maybe Susana and

Manuel were also right. I was no one without my family. I was nothing without my name, my profession. So making the choice to go back for the first time in—apparently—four weeks was the right one. It felt right.

"What are you doing?" a voice said behind me. My back went ramrod straight, my chest heavy with guilt. "Where are you going?"

His gaze was soft, almost like someone had hurt him. Me? I turned around to look at him. He was looking all over my room, to my half-packed suitcase and then back to me. His voice was rough, and his hair was wilder than ever, like he'd run his fingers through it almost obsessively. He took a step towards me, and the heat from his body almost made me melt.

"I need to go," I said. I turned back, unable to look at him, and continued folding my clothes and putting them inside my suitcase. He was silent and motionless behind me. The only hint he was still there was the faint sound of his even breathing. "I spoke to my grandmother," I added as I watched the breeze hit the tree branches outside the window delicately, almost teasing. In the time since I had arrived in this town, the colors had begun to shift from green to yellow to deep, rich oranges and reds. A telltale sign of change.

"What did she say?" he asked. I turned to face him, searching his face for anything that would clue me in on his feelings. "What did you say to her?"

I smiled softly at his interrogation, one of his many quirks, one that made him the man he was: caring and detailed and interested. He did this thing where he would lean, just so, into a person when he was talking to them. It was probably a natural reaction to his curiosity and his interest. Something that in the past was annoying to me, but now it was charming. And knowing his family and this town and how he shined, it was everything.

"You know, Susana is the only mother I really ever knew. My mom died when I was three years old in a freak accident —she was taking some boxes up to the attic and fell backwards and broke her neck—and I would give anything to be able to hug her again, even just for a few minutes." A new realization, definitely. I missed her so much. And it had gotten to the point where I didn't know if the memories I had of her now were actual memories or if it was a narrative I had constructed throughout the years, of things I imagined my mom could be, of the ways she would treat me and the relationship I would have had with her. "But I just want my mom."

Santiago moved closer to me until I could feel his breath on my face. He reached one of his hands towards me and laced our fingers together. I sighed.

"Where is this coming from?" he asked softly. His eyes were still moving around, searching my face, maybe in confusion at the scene in front of him.

My time in this town was coming to an end, my body itching to go back and figure out the rest of my life, to go back to how things were. Back to my friend and her baby, to my family—as flawed as they were—and to life as I knew it. I wanted to go back to my old self, the one who hated this man for being such a natural fit, the one who didn't know he was so caring, loving. The one who didn't know him, who was sure they would never be a good fit.

And it was completely overwhelming because being there in that town with him made it abundantly clear that I could never go back to how things were before.

Before what?

It made me sad for everything I never had and never knew I needed.

Like him.

"I think she's right." To a certain extent, what Susana said was true. I had the life I had because of her choices. She forged the path and made way for everything I had. So I guess I could understand her. "I am who I am today because of her."

"I disagree," he huffed. He wasn't looking at me, but instead his gaze was fixed somewhere behind my shoulder. His thumb was still moving in a soothing way, his hand burning hot on mine. I shivered. "You are incredibly driven, ambitious. I don't think I've ever met anyone like you, Vee. You are one hundred percent you."

My cheeks were burning. When did this man begin to read me the way he did? I rolled my eyes, and he smiled, his eyes fixed on my lips.

"Just let your grandmother go, Victoria," he said quietly

as he moved closer to me and reached up to tuck a lock of hair behind my ear. His thumb grazed my earlobe, and goosebumps erupted on my skin. "You have to stop letting her rule your life."

"What do you mean? She's the only one I have. She's the only one that has consistently cared for me."

"What about Cata? Your brother?" he asked. He tilted his head to the side, looking straight at me. "I care. You have me. You'll always have me, Vee."

I had no idea what to do with that; my heart was hammering so loudly in my chest that the only thing I could hear was my blood rushing to my brain, all thoughts over-taken by the noise.

"Santiago, you and I are an illusion. You know that. We don't exist outside of this town." I cringed as soon as those words came out of my mouth. What we had was good, but it was a bubble. A fling. It was fun. It was perfect, but temporary.

"Are you hallucinating, Vee? I've been waiting for you for ten fucking years. Since that first day I saw you. Haven't you realized by now?" My breath caught. He took a step back from me, dropping my hand as he grabbed his head, pulling at his hair with both hands. I averted his eyes, instead focusing on the suitcase on the bed and the clothes strewn about the room. "Look at me."

He looked defeated, exhausted. He was looking at me intently, like he was trying to communicate so much more. His eyes softened as he sighed.

"What are we doing, Victoria?"

"*We* are not doing anything. *We* don't exist." We were in this bubble, the forced proximity playing with our brains. We were just getting to know each other in this awful, constructed context. "You don't even know me, Santiago! We lead very different lives. We are very different people."

"Then what are you still doing here, Vee?" he asked. "Because if this—us—doesn't exist, then you should have run by now, no?" His tone was filled with anger. He took a deep breath and ran his fingers through his hair once more, then dropped his hands to his side and curled them into fists.

"What are you talking about?" I stood tall and faced him, my arms crossed over my chest, guarding my heart. The cold air was suffocating, the silence following my question deafening.

"Stop running away," he said in a rush. I took a step forward, and he moved back, allowing more distance between us.

"I'm not running away. I'm choosing to go."

His face crumpled. "Why? Why are you choosing to go? Why are you so scared of things—good things, even—out of your control that you don't even give them a chance?" He took a deep breath and swallowed. I blinked at him, wanting to tell him everything but also nothing at all. Because Susana was right. Because my life was moving on without me, and I didn't recognize the woman I suddenly saw in the mirror. The woman that Santiago saw in front of him.

"You are such a hypocrite, you know?" he added, his voice raised and agitated. The Santiago I got to know during my stay in this town was nowhere to be seen. In his place was an emotional man, reactive instead of constructive with his words.

"Look who's talking! You preach about how I should be making my own decisions, but you're stuck in your ways too. At least I recognize that I'm not capable of making decisions without having the approval of my family, but you are stuck in the wrong one and refuse to make a change, evolve."

I hit the nail on the head. He retreated a few steps back, his breath fast and erratic.

"I can't do this, Santiago. I'm tired of feeling like this." Like no one was on my side, like this was not my life. Maybe going back home was exactly what I needed. I gained perspective here. Maybe it'd happen again if I was *there*. "I'm not like you, okay?"

"Like what?"

"Like this! All free and giving with your feelings. And so comfortable anywhere. Happy with things not turning out how you want them to. Able to make your own decisions without anyone caring what they mean."

"Victoria." He swallowed audibly. "What do you think life is? It's not a master plan where we can control every step of the way. It doesn't work that way." His shoulders slumped, and he fisted his hands. He was rarely frustrated, but today it was very visible. His eyes were a dark, deep blue, darker than I'd seen them before. He clenched his jaw and flexed his fingers, then took a deep breath.

"No, don't you dare."

"You have no idea what I'm going to say," he said quietly. He looked broken, his eyes barely meeting mine. We were still facing each other, my hands still crossed over my chest defensively.

"Yes, you were going to say what everyone else thinks about me. That I was born into this easy life, given every-thing served to me on a silver platter." I raised my voice, the volume completely unnecessary for the conversation we were having. I turned my body and faced the bed again, trying to do something with my hands, trying to avoid this conversation at all costs. "I know how you feel about me. I get it."

"Why do you keep trying to put words into my mouth? That's not what I think at all," he said. I turned back to look at him, and he shook his head. He wiped his hand down his face and opened his mouth to talk but quickly closed it.

"I know you feel sorry for me, Santiago." What could I even say at this point? This wasn't going anywhere. I had my life back in the city, and I needed to go back to my best friend and meet my niece. Life moved on, and I needed to move on with it.

"Damn it." He was flustered, both his hands in his hair. He scratched his scalp, the sound taking me back to the one and only night we shared. "I'm in love with you. Do you need me to spell it out too?"

I gasped. "What are you talking about?" I whispered. *Love? Who ever talked about love?*

"I refuse to love you in the dark, Victoria. You've been on my mind every single day since that first day in college, and fuck if I'm letting you go again."

"Santiago." He moved one step closer to me. The back of my knees were already touching the bed. Everything was on fire. His gaze, set on me. My body, yelling at me to take him, make him own it. "I can't."

"I'm done." His palms slapped his thighs, and he took a step back. "I'm not doing this anymore." He shook his head, the pain in his eyes real and rawer than I'd ever seen because I put it there.

"Do what?" I spat out. "What is it you aren't willing to do anymore?"

"Victoria." He took a deep breath and then released it. The tension was palpable. I knew I was pushing him away, but it was exactly what I needed at that moment. Because I didn't recognize myself there in that town with him. "Okay. Well, if you ever decide to come back to me, you know where I am," Santiago said and turned towards the door.

If I hadn't been paying close enough attention, I wouldn't have noticed his microsecond of hesitation. Just a tiny glitch in time where maybe he stopped to give me a chance to say something, to take it all back. But then he kept going, all the way to the door, closing it behind him, his back tense and his muscles bunched. Defeated.

He walked away.

From us, Victoria.

29

THE REALIZATION

The air in the city was still humid, despite the signs of an early fall. I stood outside the airport doors waiting for a car to pick me up, to take me straight to Catalina's side. Her baby had been born while I was flying, and my phone was flooded with messages as soon as I landed. Mostly messages from my brother, but the majority of them were messages from Susana. Because she knew I could never say no to my best friend, and I would come running back to her the moment she needed me. In that sense, my brother and I were similar—we were controlled by Catalina. She had us wrapped around her finger. And Susana hated that but knew exactly how to use it to her advantage.

Susana was waiting for me back at her house, she told me, and I was preparing myself to get castigated for what had happened. She would never let this go, even if I was already on my way to closing that chapter. I felt a strong pang of guilt running through my body. I wanted to talk to her, to my father and his sisters, to my brother. I knew what I had to do for my sake.

The drive to the hospital was short but so different than my past four weeks in that small town. The sounds of the city were overwhelming, the silence so rare that you would have to actively seek it out. People moved at a different pace on the sidewalks, something uniquely missing from Tres Fuegos. I rested my head on the car window and closed my eyes, willing time to go by faster. By the time I got to the hospital, it was getting dark, and the streetlights were slowly turning on. The sidewalks were filling up , people leaving work and going about their night.

"Hi," I whispered, tears already forming in my eyes as I walked into the room. I had taken the elevator up from the lobby, my suitcase trailing behind me. "How are you feeling?"

Catalina looked exhausted, but her eyes were exploding with love, a true depiction of heart eyes. My brother was sitting at the foot of the bed, cradling their little baby girl in his arms, unable to look away from her.

"Oh my god, what are you doing here?" she squealed, flinching as soon as she realized it was probably a little too loud for the brand-new tiny ears in their proximity. "I told you to not come back," she said, staring daggers into my eyes. "When did you get back?"

"I landed a couple of hours ago. Came straight here," I said, walking fully into the room. Catalina scooted to the side and patted the spot right next to her on the bed. "I hope it's okay?"

The room was large, with the typical hospital bed to one side and a full sitting area to the left, where there were already a few white-and-pink flower arrangements and a gift basket, maybe sent to her by her work colleagues or her small but close family members. The view out the window was incredible. The sun was slowly setting in the horizon, and the golden light reflected on the rooftops all around.

I walked closer to her, taking a moment to admire the small little family in front of me. She was beaming.

"How are you feeling?" I asked her again as I sat next to her. I kissed her cheek and slid my arm around her shoulder, squeezing tightly and pulling her closer to me. "You look good."

"Please, you can't lie to save your life," she said, huffing but smiling softly at the same time. "I feel exactly the way I look. Like shit. Do you want to hold her?"

I stood and washed my hands in the small sink by the bathroom door, then turned to them, ready to hold that precious baby in my arms. Sink into her, admire her, smell her. Relish her. Agustín placed her in my arms in a swift but delicate motion, then told us that he was going to grab a coffee and let us catch up.

The baby was adorable and looked like a perfect combination of both of her parents' best features. Her skin was perfectly pink, and her eyelashes were dark and long, just like her hair.

"Why are you here?" Catalina asked, getting straight to the point. "No one wants you here, you know?" I pointed my gaze at her, narrowing my eyes until she laughed loudly.

"My time there came to an end, and I need to get back to work." Bullshit.

"Bullshit. You are running away again." How did she do it? She knew me even better than I knew myself. I sighed and sat at the foot of the bed, facing Cata, who was still resting against the headboard, her hair matted and stuck to her neck, her skin a little shiny with sweat. "What happened?"

"I..." I didn't know. I took out all my anger on him, and in the hours since it all fell apart, I realized that maybe... "Susana is expecting me for dinner tonight. She's going to berate me until the end of time. Fucking destroy me."

"Yeah, okay, but you can hold your own." And she was right. "Why are you trying to defend yourself if you did nothing wrong?"

"She has a hold on me. It's the only way I can explain it." Catalina knew exactly what I was talking about. She had witnessed years' worth of interactions between Susana and me. My grandmother never liked her, said she was a bad influence on me, but the real reason was because her parents were "the help." Her mother was a housekeeper, and her father was a mechanic. "You know that she owns me."

"Vicky." Her eyes were soft now, but her face was serious. She sat up and put her hands on her lap. "I think it's enough, don't you?"

Maybe.

"Maybe," I replied quickly. "But there isn't much I can do. What are my options, really, at this point?" Susana was my family.

"Just because she's family doesn't mean you have to keep her." She cocked her head. "You have to be honest with yourself. There's a thick line between loyalty and respect. Just because you are her family and expected to be loyal, doesn't mean that she shouldn't respect you—or anyone, for that matter."

"I disrespected her, my whole family. I disrespected you guys too." I shrugged. "My actions have consequences."

"Why do you think that? You didn't do anything wrong. And please get it out of your thick head that you disrespected your brother and me," she said, confused. "Correct me if I'm wrong, but that fucking dumbass you called your boyfriend has moved on, couldn't care less about what people say. He is the one that disrespected everyone." She took a deep breath and rolled her shoulders. "And one last thing: no one gives a shit about what happened. Susana is going to make you believe that she's been humiliated, that she can't be seen in public. But guess what? You're old news." She shrugged and looked at me, almost apologetic in her words.

I blinked at her several times, trying to control my emotions. She was so bold, so brave, getting what she wanted and needed. She had a thriving career, an incredible new family. She and my brother couldn't care less what my grandmother thought of them, still loving each other and getting married despite her very vocal objections. Why couldn't I be the same way?

"What really happened with Santiago?"

"He basically said the same thing you just said to me," I told her, tears in my eyes. The baby started squirming in my arms. She scrunched her little nose and opened her eyes. My eyes welled with the sudden realization that the things I wanted so desperately and could have with him were just out of reach and drifting away by the second. "Except that I seem to be stuck to you, and now you go have a fucking cute baby, and how am I supposed to leave you like this? I'm only friends with you for your baby, so we're clear."

I was full on crying, the tears streaming down my face and out of control. Catalina had only seen me cry once, the one and only time I failed a test. It was early on in law school when everything was new and overwhelming.

"What? I'm confused."

"Same," I huffed. "I don't know where I went wrong. One day it was all perfect—*perfect*—and then the next, I'm picking a fight because he dared to tell me something we all know is true. Did I mess it up?" I studied her face, hoping she could give me the answer. "What do I do?"

She looked down at her baby and then back up at me, her eyes shining with unshed tears. We were so close, our relationship so intimate, like we were sisters that found each other in their early twenties and never lost each other again. "You need to allow yourself to want things, Victoria," she said. "You have gone your whole life living it according to what others think is best for you, and you've been unable to take any single step without approval. Which is fine for some. But that isn't you."

Tears were falling down my cheeks, and my mouth was dry. She was right, of course. And she'd seen it firsthand with Manuel. How everything I had wanted had to be approved first.

"You are the only thing that's stopping you. Not your grandmother or your job or whatever the fuck is back in this city. It's you," she said. "You need to go to him. He's right for you."

"I don't even know if he'll want me back, Cata. I pushed him away, and maybe I deserve it."

"My god, stop being so dramatic." She rolled her eyes and reached for her baby. "You know how to find him, Vicky."

I laughed, the sound coming out wet with the tears I'd been shedding. My brother chose that moment to come back, two large cups of coffee in one hand and a bag of pastries in the other.

"Not exactly Susana-level but will do for an impromptu five o'clock tea," he said, a big smile on his lips. He had been defying Susana ever since we were teenagers. Missing curfew, hanging out with the wrong crowds, doing every-thing in his power to make her angry.

"I don't know how you did it." I turned to face him as he sat on the couch in the sitting area and put what he had brought with him on the coffee table. "Survived so many years of her torment."

He smiled wide and looked at his wife right next to me, and she replied with a grin to match his. "Easy," he said, taking a sip of his coffee and wincing, either at the taste or at the temperature. "You learn to tune it out, ¿no, Cata?"

I could feel her nod right next to me, the smile still wide on her face. "After a while, you actually start to enjoy it. She gets tripped over the tiniest things." She laughed, the sound startling the baby and making her wail in surprise. "Shhh, baby, it's okay. You'll learn in time too."

They made it look so easy. My brother sitting there, sipping on his coffee and completely enamored with his girls. Cata, a powerhouse and taking the court system by storm, but totally natural in this new role as a mother.

"Victoria." My brother interrupted my thoughts. "I don't know why you think you owe her anything, but you don't. She has proven time and again that she's not the person she pretends to be, and she only cares about herself. Fine, she helped raise us, I'll give her that, and she did a fucking tremendous job when it comes to you, but that's it."

"Why does everyone keep saying that to me?"

"Because it's the truth," Catalina chimed in. "There's nothing wrong with making informed decisions." She rolled her eyes because of course she would say that, and everyone in the room knew that too. "But living your life like this? No, Victoria, that's no way to live."

"Easy for you to say," I added, but it sounded childish

coming out of my mouth. Which was not my intention at all. I wanted to scream, wanted to tell them that I didn't know what the fuck I was doing.

"No, not easy for me to say at all, actually." She was serious, her brows furrowed. "Don't you think I question my actions all the time? I have a tough job, the hardest job, really. And there's nothing wrong with asking for guidance. But Victoria, our actions have consequences. Every. Single. Time. No matter if it's the correct one or not. We just can't all make decisions because they please others."

I looked up at her with tears in my eyes. My brother looked at me, some confusion in his face, probably because Cata hadn't filled him in on the Santiago shenanigans.

"Okay."

"Okay," she replied and turned to look at her daughter, who was silently sleeping in her arms.

30

THE FIRE

I sat on the bed in my childhood bedroom for what seemed like hours, completely numb. Susana wasn't home yet, so I snuck into my bedroom to gather my thoughts. It looked just like it did the day I fled. My dress was still hanging from the door to the ensuite bathroom, the garment bag half open and only the lace bodice peeking out. My shoes were lined up neatly to the side, exactly the way I'd left them.

There was a soft knock on the door, and it took all of my energy to stand up and open it. Half of me hoped it would be Santiago, either ready for round two or ready to grovel and apologize. The other half was being a realist and knew that the ball was in my court and there wasn't a chance that he would have come find me. Not this time.

"Pedro? What are you doing here?" I said, dumbfounded. He looked tired, the bags under his eyes more prominent now. He had gotten a haircut the week before the wedding, but his hair was looking untamed, and his whole appearance was disheveled. One of the buttons of his shirt was in the wrong buttonhole, making his collar askew around his neck.

"I wanted to check on you." He smiled. "Agustín told me you had seen the baby earlier today, so I assumed you would be here," he said matter-of-factly.

"She's cute," I said, smiling as I remembered the tiny baby I had just met. "I think she's the perfect combination of both of them."

He smiled and walked inside, his movements slow and uneven. So much had changed in four weeks. He looked much older, much more tired.

"Can we talk?"

"You made it pretty clear that you had nothing to say to me, that I should talk to Susana instead, so I'm here to do just that."

He looked resigned. He also looked like he wanted to say more but something was stopping him.

"Did you like that town?" he asked. My eyes widened in surprise at his question.

"How did you know where I was?" I asked. I'd spoken to him weeks ago at this point. Everything was a blur, but that conversation had happened pretty early on. I never mentioned where I was because of the risk of someone coming to find me and dragging me back to the city.

"Carlos," he said softly. "I knew immediately where you

were as soon as you started asking questions, honey. Carlos confirmed it for me."

He sat down on the other side of the bed, his legs at an angle and his torso facing me.

"Why are you on her side?" I blurted out. It was definitely not my intention, but my temper was flaring. The whole conversation with Susana, the fight with Santiago, everything had my blood at its boiling point, ready to burst. I closed my eyes, waiting for his words.

"It's not about sides, honey," Pedro replied. His eyes fixed on whatever was happening outside my window. It was already dark out. There were few stars to be seen, covered by wispy evening clouds.

"You know what I mean." I sighed. "It feels like you've protected her and covered for her all this time. Did you ever stop to think what that could cause?"

He froze for a moment and slowly turned to look at me. "Because I love her."

"Yeah, but love isn't enough." My mind immediately went back to Santiago. *Does he really love me like he said? Does love mean that you let people walk away?*

"Sometimes it is. Sometimes it's the thing that moves us forward, keeps us going."

"What really happened to him?"

He was still looking at me, but at the question, he darted his face around the room, examining its contents. "Are you staying here tonight?"

"Pedro, *por favor*. I've had enough lies. Just tell me." I

closed my eyes and stayed silent. After a few seconds, I heard him sigh. His mouth opened and closed a few times, as if words were hard to come by.

"Were you able to speak to Carlos?" he asked. The question was genuine, like he was prepared to tell me everything.

"Yes, I talked to him," I replied, annoyed at his stalling. "You can fill in the blanks."

So he told me.

He told me that they were both involved in the multi-million-dollar scam, that Susana never knew nor suspected anything. And that he and my grandfather, together, decided that it was better to lay low for a while until the waters calmed down. The plan all along was for my grandfather to retreat to that small town, work for a while to pay for his life there, and then as soon as he was able to, he would go back to his family. The judge had been paid, so it was only a matter of time until things cooled, until people high up forgot about what they had done. Everything lined up exactly like what Catalina had explained to me. Except Susana.

"But Susana did not take it well," he said. "We were prepared to say that he had a sick relative in Europe that he needed to take care of, something along the lines of your grandfather being the only heir and whatnot. But she was adamant that people would sniff it out, and she wasn't going to be subjected to any type of humiliation in front of her peers. And that's how the story was born. She wouldn't even listen to anything I had to say."

"I don't understand why you kept going with it," I said, confused at the role Pedro played in all of this. "Why didn't you just come out and tell the truth?"

"I don't know, honey. We were in too deep, I guess." He took a deep breath. "By the time I had time to process it, your grandparents' friends had rallied around Susana, and it was too late to take it back."

I looked at him, studying his face to see if I could figure out his thoughts. I was never good at reading him, but I did know he had a weakness for Susana.

"But you had to know the impact that would have on everyone. I mean, it's three decades later, and we are still living with the lie. It's a bit too extreme, don't you think?"

"Honey." He intertwined his fingers on his lap and looked at his hands. "We did what we could."

"What you could? You literally destroyed a whole family, decades' worth of people. Multiple generations. For what?"

"Victoria," he said. His tone was firm. "You don't understand."

"Of course I don't understand! This is crazy." I stood, my hands fisted by my thighs, my breathing coming in faster and faster. "Do you realize what you did?"

"Victoria, you are being too sensitive about it," he said. But his eyes betrayed him. He seemed lost, sad, maybe guilty. "We did what we could with what we had."

"*Andate a la puta que te parió*," I spat. "Fuck you for thinking that the consequences of your actions would go unnoticed and wouldn't have any impact. Do Dad and his sisters know?"

Probably not.

"That's up to Susana," he said. *What does she have on him?* Why was this man so loyal to a woman who only cared about herself? "It's not my secret to share."

"What are you even saying right now? Seriously? Listen to what you're saying. You wrecked a family because what, Susana was too frail and too selfish to even care about her own children? And you were too blinded by unrequited love that you did anything you thought would make her yours? You are a fucking coward."

"Victoria—"

"Did you know he died in a fire? Did you also consciously decide to keep up with the charade? To make Susana look like the victim in all of this?"

His shoulders sagged, and he looked decades older than the last time I'd seen him. "Victoria, honey—"

"Leave. Now."

"Sometimes good, decent people do bad things. And sometimes they actually believe they're doing what is right."

I stood and walked to the door, yanking it open and tapping my foot on the hardwood to get him moving. His eyes were sad, but he stood and left, walking slowly up the hallway and down the giant marble staircase of Susana's house. It baffled me that this man still thought that what they did was good, the best they could have done. When the best thing, always, was to tell the truth. Maybe I was too polarizing, maybe, but for me, there were no in betweens. You were either good or bad.

A few minutes later, I heard my grandmother's cadence of steps, followed by a few barked instructions to the maid.

"Victoria?" I heard her voice coming up the stairwell, her tone even, like always. She didn't seem flustered like the last time I had heard her, but I knew she was putting on a front. "Come downstairs."

I took my time, and as soon as I came down the steps, I saw her standing in the foyer with Pedro by her side. He looked crushed, his shoulders slumping and his eyes soft. He looked tiny compared to the woman right next to him. Not in stature, but in power. Powerless. Had I been too harsh on him? And was he right to protect her at all costs?

As soon as she saw me, she turned to the living room and Pedro followed, a sign that I should do the same. It was always like this with her in this house, a silent command, only allowed to be broken if Susana approved.

"What did you do?" she said immediately. She stood in the middle of her living room, the place as immaculate as always. It had no signs of life, like no one actually lived here. This house was Susana's most valuable possession, her *in* as a respected member of society. Appearances, starting with the way she looked, followed by her home.

"I'm not here to talk about this, Susana," I said. "Especially without my father and brother here to listen to what I have to say."

"Of course you are," she replied. Her hair was perfect, not a single strand out of place. She must have recently gone to the salon because it was shinier and darker than normal. "You are in my home, and you will do as I say."

"*¿Por qué siempre temenos que hacer lo que decís?*" Why do we always have to do as you say? I was sure she was going to reply with her usual: *because I'm your elder and you should respect me,* or *because without me, you are nothing.* More of her superior crap.

"Do not disrespect me in my home, Victoria, or I swear to go—"

"*Mamá,*" I heard my father say, followed by the front door closing. My brother had agreed to bring my father over so that we could sit down and discuss things together, neither of us trusting him behind the wheel of a car. Especially because Catalina had said that he had been holed up in his house, probably in a drunken stupor. This way, our dad would also have the closure he deserved.

"*Acá!*" I yelled. He walked into the living room, my brother trailing him. My father's eyes widened when he saw me standing across from Susana and Pedro in the middle of the room. He stopped for a second when he saw me, then walked straight to the small bar cart Susana had set up in the corner of the room.

"What's going on?" he asked, his hand shaking as he

reached for one of the crystal glasses. "When did you get back?"

"Nothing," Susana replied quickly and with a little shock, like she had just been caught red-handed.

"Susana has to tell you something," I said at the same time. Confusion marred his face at the mere scene, and Susana shot me a menacing glance.

"Why don't we all take a seat," Pedro said, trying to appease us both.

"Roberto, *no la escuches a esta chiquita que no sabe de lo que habla*," she said immediately. It sounded desperate, pleading, almost. Like what I was about to say would destroy her. Because it would.

"*Papá*," I said as I sat on one of the living room couches. I could count with the fingers on one hand the times I had actually sat on the white sofas. They were mostly reserved for company, and unless I was invited, they were completely off limits. "Sit."

He complied, my brother sitting right next to him, across from me. Susana remained standing, Pedro right behind her in the center of it all. She looked uncomfortable, out of place in her own home.

"Did you know that our grandfather wasn't kidnapped?" I went straight to the point, because there was no reason in the moment to deal with small talk. I heard Susana gasp, followed by a few steps towards me. I kept my gaze intent on my father, trying to decode his face.

"*No digas estupideces, Victoria,*" she said to the group. "Be careful what you are about to say, little girl."

"Susana, stop! Enough with the lies. They deserve to know the truth."

Between my brother and I, we filled my father in on all the details, starting with the crime and ending with his death. Our father was speechless, trying to make sense of the information we were giving him. He opened his mouth a few times to speak, but then kept quiet and took it all in.

"So many things make sense now," he whispered, turning to look at Susana. She was fuming, shaking her head, her stiff hair following the movement. Her jaw was clamped, arms crossed, fists clenched. "She refused to cancel Cristina's wedding. She moved on with her life as if he had never existed. She banished him."

I nodded in agreement, but I said nothing, waiting for Susana's reaction. It didn't come; she just stood her ground, Pedro still backing her up.

"You are toxic, Susana," I said. A weight lifted off my chest immediately. The words Santiago and Catalina had uttered earlier kept running a loop in my head. Just because they were family didn't mean we had to keep them. "This is the price you pay for the things you do. Because our actions have consequences."

"Stop it with the consequences, Victoria," she snapped. "This has nothing to do with you and everything to do with your grandfather."

"Maybe not with me but definitely with my father and

his sisters. You ruined their lives." I stood from the couch and walked to the front of the house, my brother following behind me. I turned one last time to look at her. My father was staring intently at her, ready for a fight. She looked tiny, standing in the middle of her lies. "I'm not letting you ruin my life."

I opened the front door, the muggy air bringing respite despite the humidity. I took a deep breath and turned to my brother, who smiled and nodded. He shut the door behind him, and we walked to his car. And I heard the sounds of my father's screaming and Susana whimpering in response.

EPILOGUE

FIVE MONTHS LATER

I sᴀᴛ at the same table I was at the day I saw him again and he reentered my life. Except that this time, I was on fire. Not literally. But I was heated with everything I wanted to tell him. It was like my heart ignited like a rocket ship and was ready for takeoff.

The months that followed my departure from Santiago's town and presence were a jumbled mess of events. I quit my job at my family's firm but gave plenty of notice so that my brother could take over and hire someone—probably two different people who had different responsibilities. Pedro decided to fully back off and retire, making my brother the head of the firm. My father was recovering, mostly, and the answers he got were healing in their own way. He was enjoying spending a lot of his time with his granddaughter.

"Victoria?"

I beamed. And for the first time in a long, long time, I felt happy.

"You aren't my sister." He blinked a few times, almost like he was trying to focus his eyesight.

"Is that how she lured you here?" I asked. I had been in constant contact with Lucía. She never outright said it, but she heavily implied that Santiago was a mess. And I could relate.

"What are you doing here?" he asked, his brow furrowed in confusion.

"Um, I came to find you." I tilted my head, trying to decipher Santiago's expression. Was he not happy to see me? Had I understood wrong? "You told me that if I ever decided to come back to you, I knew where to find you. I owe you an explanation." I took a deep breath. "Quite a few, actually."

He was frozen in place, his hands opening and closing into tight fists on either side of his body, right there in the middle of the sidewalk.

"Do you want to sit down?" I asked, motioning with my arm to the chair in front of me. In my periphery I could see the waitress—the same one from those many months ago—approach us, a smile already plastered on her face at the sight of Santiago. He swallowed and nodded, then took a few steps and sat across from me. There was so much silence, it was deafening.

I cleared my throat. "I owe you an apology."

"You do," he replied. He was serious, not a single smile

in sight. His eyes looked tired, like he hadn't slept in weeks. And again, I could relate.

"I realized that you are one of the only people who know me for me, and you don't want to change me. Just like Cata and my brother, I can be myself around you, and that's rare, especially for me. You know that. I don't have friends. I'm—I was, rather, too attached to my grandmother."

He nodded, acknowledging my statement.

"Catalina was having her baby, and I freaked out. Because my life had changed so much in just a few weeks, and then the whole thing with my grandfather and…" I sighed. "You deserved better, but honestly, I didn't know how to react."

"Victoria." He sighed and crossed his arms, relaxing a little bit in his chair.

"I know," I replied quickly. "I'm not going to make excuses for myself. I fucked up, didn't talk to you, and then fled. I'm sorry."

"What happened with your grandfather?" he asked. His eyes were softening a little now, curiosity back to his face.

"Catalina figured it out. We think he ran away to cover his ass before he was charged for embezzlement, and your grandfather helped him settle here until things fizzled out in the city. But then the fire happened."

"I'm sorry."

"Yes, a series of unfortunate events." Whatever. I was trying to get over it, get both my grandparents off the pedestal Susana had placed them on. Because when you place someone on a pedestal, you had to look up to them. "It'll be fine. My family is healing, and that's what's important. I think we are all learning to let go."

He smiled.

"How did you know I was here?" he said as his smile grew bigger. The corner of his eyes crinkled with the movement. It was probably his most genuine smile.

"I have my spies." I smiled wide. "It's a small town, after all."

We were frozen in place, smiling at each other. We didn't break eye contact, but I could feel his nervous anticipation.

"What are you really doing here, Vee?"

"Can you believe your dad has a job for me? What are the odds, huh?"

He laughed one of his hearty laughs, tilting his head back. His whole body vibrated with mirth—a good sign. My eyes filled with happy tears at hearing that sound again.

Lucía had been a godsend during the months we were apart. After confronting Susana and everything that went down with my father, I made the decision to finally do something for myself. I wasn't exactly sure that Santiago would take me back, but at least this was a step in the right direction. We could try it, and if it didn't work out, I could go back to the city and work with my brother. Lucía managed to schedule a few interviews with Santiago's father, and he gave me a job at his firm. Turned out, Santiago decided to quit his career as an attorney and bought out his aunt and uncle's hotel. He was managing the property, and it was thriving, obviously, because everything that this man touched was painted with intention and passion, and he put his whole self into it. That meant there was a role available at the family firm, and although it wasn't my specialty, Santiago's dad decided I would be a good fit.

"You were right," I said. "I run away. That's my M.O. And I'm so sorry I hurt you."

He stood up and took a step closer to me, his hands shaking at his sides, his smile still blinding me. I stood and closed the distance between the two of us. I lifted my arms and draped them around his neck, then craned my head to look up at him. I ran my fingers through his disheveled hair, lightly scraping his scalp, a movement that helped me control my happiness. "I'm done running, Santi."

"Okay," he said with a big smile on his face. He rested his forehead on mine and took a deep breath.

"Okay." I sighed. Everything in the past got erased.

"*Te amo*," he said, closing his eyes and smiling into my mouth. "And I'll love you for as long as you let me." He kissed me, and his taste lingered on my lips. The mere feel of his warmth on my skin shot shivers up and down my spine.

"I love you too," I said into his mouth. It felt so right, for the first time, to say it like that. To let myself go and trust that the choice I was making was the right one.

If we think, for even a minute, that the decisions we make will not have an impact on the lives of others, either today or in decades to come, we are being naïve. What remains after the fire is more than a life; it's a legacy. A series of opportunities, a future. What remains after the fire is the ability to learn from our mistakes.

FIN

———

Did you enjoy Victoria and Santiago's story? Scan the QR Code below for some bonus content!

If you liked this book, please consider leaving a review. Support from readers like you really help indie authors like me get our work out in front of more readers, and it would mean the world.

AFTERWORD

Learning and Liberation
by Mabel Iam

I began my journey, following the dictates of my
heart.
My conscience told me: "You owe it all to them."
My body asks: "My ancestors?"
"Sure, who else?"
My heart sends an order to my brain: "Listen to your
truth; don't stop."

Then my whole being reflects:
My ancestors have given me life.
I feel honored and grateful for that.
Their legacy vibrates in my DNA.
Their emotions go through my cells, I perceive them
trapped in my body, but I can register them:
Sadness, joy, chaos, compassion.

And then I say to myself: "My lineage has given me
this intense throbbing."
Its thoughts and messages were: "Daughter, existence is not easy. You can choose, but it all depends
on the others
and your circumstance."
"No, I identify with that statement. I was born to be
free, even from myself."

My higher self begins to whisper to me: "Free your
thoughts, beliefs and feelings. You are peace, power,
love and happiness.
Now you are connected with me to infinity."
"Your true origin is divine"
"You are the universe."
"Thank your parents for their inheritance. It is now
grown to your true stature."
"You don't need them anymore"

My BEING embraces me and I don't doubt anymore,
I follow the only path, the one that my soul chose,
from and to eternity.

—Mabel Iam, dedicated to my True Self

ACKNOWLEDGMENTS

The whole idea of writing a book came from a night out with friends, while our kids were running rampant, and we were talking about ways to make a passive income. Someone said that writing a book was a great side hustle, and I accepted the challenge.I have no idea when I wrote this book, but it happened and now it's out. And it was everything but passive. Apologies if I drove anyone insane in the process. It was long, but I think it was worth it.

Thank you to my husband for giving me pockets of time and space to sit down and create these characters and the small, dreamy town of Tres Fuegos. Olivia and Rosario: I hope this book shows you that we can do anything.

Kari, Lau, Mini, Nati, Paula — you know who you are and what you did to encourage me to write this story. Thank you for reading my early work, when this was just an idea and a bunch of words strung together.

Thank you to my friends for just being there, whether it was through kind words of encouragement or simply as a sounding board for my ideas.

To the many people who helped me along the way, including my editors, beta readers, coaches and illustrator.

Your expertise and guidance have been instrumental in making this book the best it can be.

To my readers: thank you for taking the time to read and share my work. I loved creating this universe, and I hope you end up loving (and maybe hating) these characters as much as I do.

I think that this book is the ultimate proof that if you set your mind and your heart into doing something, you can do it.

And most importantly, if this novel were a song, it would be "Delicate" by Taylor Swift. Go listen to it.

ABOUT THE AUTHOR

Maria Rigou is a Latina writer living in the US. Her debut novel *After the Fire* is a story about our past, our present, and our future, and how the actions of those who preceded us have much more pull than we think. However, no matter the expectations others have of us, we are masters of our own future and of our own choices.

She lives in South Florida with her husband and two daughters and loves to read.

———

CONNECT ONLINE
www.mariarigou.com
@mariarigouauthor